The camera panned, showing the side of the genie's face as his mouth moved down the taut slope of a curvaceous breast. Darrel stared at the profile of the man in shocked recognition: it was Zal! Somehow it seemed worse to be watching someone he knew, but he had no option. Embarrassed, he saw his friend clutch at a pair of the nicest tits he'd seen in a long time and as the camera widened its view he saw that the woman had an attractive face, too. She was blonde and green-eyed, with full sensual lips. Darrel couldn't help wondering why she had to resort to the Plezure Plaza for her gratification. Maybe she got off on the idea of impersonal sex with a paid gigolo. He'd known women like that.

Suddenly his attention was drawn to the cranial map where a string of connections had lit up in red, just like the route-finder on the dashboard of an autocab. Darrel realized that the highlighted pathways were constantly changing as Zal responded to the woman's arousal.

The camera moved down, showing Zal's lips at the bud-like navel of his client, who was writhing and moaning with accelerating passion. Now her mound was visible, covered with a curly mesh of fine golden hair that proclaimed her a natural blonde . . .

Also by Nadine Wilder in New English
Library paperback

Rock Hard

Satisfaction Guaranteed

Nadine Wilder

NEW ENGLISH LIBRARY
Hodder and Stoughton

Copyright © 1997 by Nadine Wilder

First published in 1997
by Hodder and Stoughton
A division of Hodder Headline PLC

A New English Library paperback

The right of Nadine Wilder to be identified as the Author of
the Work has been asserted by her in accordance with the
Copyright, Designs and Patents Act 1988.

10 9 8 7 6 5 4 3 2 1

British Library Cataloguing in Publication Data
A CIP catalogue record for this title is available from the
British Library.

ISBN 0 340 66057 0

Typeset by Avon Dataset Ltd, Bidford-on-Avon, Warks
Printed and bound in Great Britain by
Mackays of Chatham plc

Hodder and Stoughton
A division of Hodder Headline PLC
338 Euston Road
London NW1 3BH

Chapter One

Room 301 in the Plezure Plaza was probably identical to every other room in the complex, but to Darrel Nunn it was home. Rescued from a hostel at the tender age of fourteen, Darrel had been delighted to find that he no longer had to share a dormitory with nine other abandoned kids, most of whom were already embarked on a career in crime.

The man and woman who had come to The Glades on that fateful morning ten years ago had told him he was special, and would be taken out of the only environment he had ever known and be placed in a new and far more luxurious one. The original Cinderfella story.

'You are the product of a unique genetic experiment,' the woman had told him, her golden irises gleaming at him. 'Your genetic parents were both sensualists. Do you know what that means, Darrel?' He hadn't. 'It means they were chosen for their sexual prowess.'

Like any healthy teenager, Darrel's ears pricked up. She had gone on to explain that he was one of that rare breed of 'genies', children spawned in the lab to have certain characteristics. It was new technology, of course, and not all the experiments had been successful. But they had high hopes in his case. That little incident at Fernlea had alerted them to his potential. Of course, Darrel could not possibly have known that he was acting true to form, simply following the blueprint of his chromosomes.

Now, ten years on to the day, Darrel smiled at the memory. He had expected punishment. Or expulsion into the harsh netherworld of the alleys where no one survived longer than a few years. Instead they had rewarded him with a life of pleasure and luxury. All because he had breached the defences that protected the girls' hostel and had made frequent nocturnal visits to the girls' dormitory. Oh, those sweet nights of unlimited passion! If they had executed him for the crime he would have died happy. Like a cock among chickens he had mated with them ecstatically – sometimes several at once, hands and lips also pressed into service to satisfy their insatiable lust – until one night he was caught by the stern housemother, whipped and humiliated, then reported to the authorities.

Darrel sank into the comforting embrace of his relaxer and surveyed his domain. Although he was allowed no personal possessions the familiarity of his surroundings was enough to evoke an ersatz sense of ownership. Dominating the room was the huge four-poster bed, the only concession to a bygone age and one that his clientele really appreciated. Beneath all the drapes and frills, however, the touch-sensitive mattress was alive with wires and air sacs, cunningly engineered to provide whatever was needed in the way of angles and inclines, softness or firmness, vibration or undulation.

Each wall bore an ever-changing screen, designed to appeal to a different erotic taste. On one, a succession of Afro-Caribbean or Eurasian girls were subjugated by slave-masters and taken from behind. On another, lesbians pleasured each other continually. A third screen showed perfect examples of pale or bronzed beauties – men with large penises and sculpted bodies, girls with gorgeous faces and perfect figures – acting out seduction scenarios. The fourth wall displayed images of Amazonian women, forcing men to do their bidding.

After years of research, the Controllers had decided that the ultimate in women's sexual satisfaction was best attained through a combination of fantasizing and expert physical stimulation. Women needed a flesh-and-blood man, but they also wanted to be free to explore the full range of erotic possibilities, and so often fantasies acted out fell short of expectations. With their imaginations stimulated by the screens and their bodies aroused by supersensitive lovers like Darrel, every woman could achieve her orgasmic potential. The Controllers of the Plezure Zone offered a money-back guarantee, and boasted that they'd never yet had to issue a refund.

The ambience of all the rooms was centrally controlled, and Darrel had become so accustomed to the range of musky, aromatic perfumes that he breathed in night and day, so inured to the mood-enhancing music that issued in subtly-changing patterns of rhythm and melody from the concealed speakers, that he was only aware of it when the constant stimulation ceased.

While he was reminiscing about a particularly exciting experience at Fernlea, the background music stopped. Alerted by the sudden silence, Darrel looked directly at the opposite screen where an image of his next client appeared. In addition the speaker buzzed, informing him that she was on her way.

His heart dropped as he saw the grotesque figure

waddling down the walkway towards Room 301. Why didn't he get any honey these days? He was tired of skin injected with so much silicone it tasted more like wax.

Darrel's new client was wearing a figure-hugging turquoise outfit that revealed every bulge in her body, but there was a 'Fat is Fun' campaign on at the moment designed to make people eat more. Food sales had been slumping since the market had shrunk and people had been faced with the same boring options day after day. All the genies were privileged, of course, and their special high-protein, vitamin-rich diet was way above what most of the population could afford.

The hatch slid open and the woman entered, rather nervously, sweat beads on her pink forehead. Darrel held out his hand and smiled a welcome in his usual manner.

'Come in, my dear. I've been expecting you. How good of you to drop by.'

The fiction that they were honoured guests was one that most clients responded to at once. This woman, however, seemed a little confused.

'Are you the . . . er . . . I mean . . .'

'My name is Darrel, and I am here at your service, Madam. Would you care for a cocktail?' He pressed a button on the wall and a trolley slid out on silent wheels. 'We have all the usuals, and a few specials too. I can recommend the Sweetly Passionate Subliminal. Fermented passion fruit, sugar cane and lime with a secret ingredient, guaranteed to put you in just the right kind of relaxing mood.'

'That sounds nice.'

She was twisting in her fingers a silk handkerchief

that she occasionally used to mop her brow. 'So warm in this place!' she commented, as she took her drink.

'I can reduce it a couple of degrees. No problem.' Darrel pressed the temp-reg and the room grew perceptibly cooler. 'I'm sure we'll both be warm soon,' he added, with a hint of complicity.

'Oh!' she giggled girlishly and sipped her drink. 'That's nice.'

'I can see you need some relaxation therapy, my dear.' Darrel went behind her chair and began to knead her fat shoulders. 'We'll soon have you feeling good, don't you worry.'

'Yes.' She downed the rest of the aphrodisiac then leaned back against his fingers with a sigh. 'This is my first visit, you see. I wasn't sure . . . well, I didn't quite know what to expect.'

'You can expect the best. Everyone at Plezure Plaza is treated like a princess. And you deserve it, my dear. You especially. I can tell you're a woman who has worked hard all her life and is seldom appreciated. But now you will have your reward. Soon you will feel like a pampered pussy cat.'

As Darrel slowly pressed into her abundant flesh he could sense that she was starting to unwind. She was craving direct contact now. He slipped open the strip that held her garment together and revealed the pink skin of her shoulders. His palms spread out, his fingers stroking her more firmly, and somewhere beneath the blubber he could feel her nerves tingling, awakening, anticipating.

'Oh, that's so good!' she breathed.

'It will get even better!' he murmured in her ear. 'Better and better, until you'll forget about everything except how wonderful it feels. Trust me. I know exactly what I'm doing.'

Gradually he was stripping the elasticated cloth from her body, exposing more and more of her rotund form. The blue folds gathered around her waist, exposing her huge, pendulous breasts, and his hands worked their way around her sides until he was stroking her fat stomach from behind. She gave a few excited wriggles and he knew it was time to move her onto the four-poster.

'I think you might be more comfortable on the bed,' he whispered, stepping round to help her to her feet.

She was a bit wobbly, as he'd expected. The cocktail was starting to kick in with its potent blend of sedatives and aphrodisiacs. Her eyes looked hooded, sensual. She laughed throatily as she stumbled towards the bed with her clothes falling about her knees, and then landed, face down. 'Oh, I think I'm a tot high. Just a tot!'

Darrel removed the last of her clothes revealing her huge, pale buttocks. He guessed she'd respond to being bitten there, and as he sampled a mouthful of the marsh-mallow flesh he deftly stripped off his own suit, then knelt on the mattress between her spread legs. She squealed in delight as one hand delved straight into her arse crack and the other tickled the smooth skin of her inner thigh. Then he bit her other buttock.

'Yes, yes, give it to me hard!' he heard her mumble into the lacy counterpane.

After some more biting and stroking Darrel sensed that she was ready to roll over. His hands moved up her sides to the squashed breasts and he began to work on them, inducing her to wriggle round until she was on her back. The stiff red nipples were craving his touch but he knew they must be saved till later. What she needed now was to have that great whirlpool of energy in her solar plexus dispersed to her sex organs. He began to stroke the bloated stomach in a circular motion, making her tremble and moan.

So far his tool had remained flaccid, but Darrel wasn't in the least worried. He knew that the thing would spring into action at a moment's notice, as soon as it was required. Presumably that was all part of his genetic inheritance, but he didn't speculate about it. The main thing was, it had never once let him down in ten very sexually active years.

His hand lightly brushed against her sparse pubic hair and she began to shake. Too soon. He moved his face up to her neck, where his tongue insinuated itself between the fleshy rolls, making her quiver with delight as his teeth grazed her softly. It was time to stroke her breasts. Darrel seized handfuls of each soft bosom, keeping clear of the nipples, and gently squeezed.

'Mm, oh yes!'

Her tone was urgent, verging on the desperate. Darrel could tell that the old cycle was beginning, the see-sawing between arousal and restraint, between optimism and despair. She was probably one of those drone-clones, bred for dumb obedience and little else. They had no self-esteem, no inkling of what their own potential was. He felt almost sorry for her.

'Lovely firm breasts,' he told her. 'Nice big nipples. Big is beautiful. Fat is fabulous. I just adore large ladies.'

She giggled at the absurdity of his flattery but it had the desired effect. Her system was speeding up, heart beating, adrenalin pumping, tissues swelling and engorging. Time to pay her some attention down below. His right hand slid over her mountainous stomach and felt the slack, wrinkled cunny lips. She gave a long, guttural moan as his fingers slipped into her wet chasm and found the opening of her sex. While his forefinger dipped and probed, his thumb circled over her jutting clitoris and felt it stiffen and throb.

Now was the time for his lips to enclose her nipple, sucking her strongly like a hungry infant. Her moan drifted up an octave, squealed with excitement. Darrel could feel the juices running from her now like hot fruit, making her all soft and squelchy. He took the other nipple between his lips and rasped it with his teeth. She thrust her hips upwards, her mons banging against his wrist, and he judged that she would soon be ready. For the moment her desire was overriding her fear of failure, buoying her up on a wave of optimism. It was his job to keep her afloat.

His erection grew swiftly, as it always did, pumping up his prick to maximum proportions in a few seconds. Darrel let it nudge at her thigh until she grew aware of it.

'Oh!' she gasped, peering down. 'What a lovely big one!'

'You'll soon know just how big it is!' he smiled. 'And just how satisfying.'

He saw the doubt flicker in her gaze, sensed her pain. 'I don't usually . . . I mean, you mustn't expect . . . you see, I can't actually . . .'

Darrel continued to look deep into her grey, flustered eyes. He saw the years of frustration, of despair. He pitied the lovers, made to feel ineffectual. He pitied her, made to feel inadequate. But now, all that was history.

'Oh yes, you can,' he assured her. 'And you will! Trust me. I know my job.'

He knew that would please her. Job satisfaction was something she could understand. But she needed something extra, something in the way of fantasy. It was obvious that the screens were doing nothing for her. She was hardly bothering to glance at them, keeping her eyes closed. It would all have to be done by hypnotic suggestion.

'What is your name?' he whispered.

'Shona.'

'A pretty name for a pretty woman.' He flicked across her nipple with his tongue and her clitoris with his fingertip. She writhed and moaned. 'Such a voluptuous creature! I would love to have you in my harem.'

At the magic word 'harem' her whole body twitched and he knew he had found the key to her secret fantasy. He moved between her thighs, let his glans nudge at her entrance while he continued to whisper to her, feeding her imagination.

'First I will have you dance for me, the exotic belly dance of the ancients. Like Salome you will perform the dance of the seven veils, revealing your beauty to me while I sit on silken cushions and drink potent wine.'

Darrel moved in, his shaft sliding between her oily love-lips. He stopped halfway, let her feel him filling her up, pinched her nipple till she moaned aloud, then continued. 'My lust will rise at the sight of your bounteous breasts with their rose-red buds. I shall long to feast upon them with more than my eyes, but I know I must wait until your exquisite undulating dance is over before I can touch you. How you torment me with your eyes, your thighs, your lips, your erotically swaying hips.'

He pressed further in, feeling her wet walls contract around his shaft, making him even more firm than he was before. Although he took no pleasure in the act it gave him satisfaction to feel her responding to his words as well as his movements. 'At last, my dear Shona, you allow me to approach your gorgeous, quivering, naked body. Your skin gleams with natural oils, your pores exude the scent of musk and subtly blended perfumes. I see your nipples stand erect and my member does likewise. I am unable to control my lust for you, the most alluring of all my women. You are my heart's desire, my chosen one!'

'O-o-oh!' Shona sighed, her hips thrusting impatiently now. Darrel thrust deeper, harder. His right forefinger found her love-trigger at the apex of her mons and pressed upon the slippery button of flesh until she moaned louder. 'Yes, there! Please don't stop!'

Then came the moment that Darrel lived for in his work, the moment when he knew beyond doubt that the unstoppable rise of his client towards an orgasm had commenced. It didn't matter how long he took over it, the result was inevitable. He had the woman perfectly under his control, like a well-tuned machine, and the path to success was assured.

But she needed the extra stimulation of his commentary to get her there. 'I tremble as I approach the beautiful temple of your body. I fall upon my knees and kiss your hand in supplication. Although I am the master, and have absolute power over you, nevertheless at this moment you hold me in thrall. Tenderly you press my face to your breast and I take your rosebud into my mouth, licking and sucking at it like a morsel of Turkish Delight. I enjoy both your jewels to the full, my dear heart, and feel I am entering Paradise.'

'More, more!' Shona moaned. Darrel applied more friction to her clitoris, thrust deeper into her quim, pinched her nipple harder, and continued his tale. It was a script he knew by heart.

'My burning spear thrusts against the pale drum of your belly, yearning to enter you. My fingers find you open and ready for me, your sweet channel filled with luscious juices. I bend my lips to the fountain and drink my fill, but my importunate tool will not wait. He must have his way. He must enter the dark cave and find the treasure he craves. Impatiently he rears against the entrance and at last you allow him in. He slides blissfully down the slippery slope and begins to move within your velvety walls, his head nudging against your secret chamber.'

'Ah, yes!' Shona moaned, near to the brink. Her heaving breasts were enormous now, taut, straining, while her face was flushed and her lips worked agitatedly. Darrel leaned forward and pressed his mouth to hers, knowing it was what she wanted. Their tongues met for the first time and the contact was electrifying in its effect. Like a rumbling volcano that shudders to the surface from the depths of the earth, the first spasms of her climax could be felt through her whole body.

Gathering force, the cataclysm rolled through her abundant flesh like a spring flood. She moaned and thrashed on the bed, which was vibrating wildly now to maximize the intensity of her orgasm. Darrel almost laughed at the grotesque enormity of her coming, the mounds of flesh like quivering jelly, the eyes rolling in ecstatic wonder, the mouth making inarticulate gurgling noises. If she had been in her death throes he would not have been surprised.

At last the earthquake subsided, the hills sank to a slow rhythmic heave, the valley lay still and the waters drained away. Darrel withdrew and wiped himself but Shona remained on the bed in a state of utter exhaustion, eyes closed.

When she finally opened them her expression was beatific, incredulous. 'I'd never have believed it! So . . . extraordinary!'

'That was your first time,' Darrel said. It was a statement, not a question.

Shona nodded. She looked excited, breathless and very girlish. 'When my friend suggested I should come here I laughed at her. I told her I'd had forty-three lovers and not one of them could get me off.'

'We aim to please. And we always succeed.'

'Evidently! I shall recommend you personally to all my friends.'

'How kind of you.'

But Darrel, envisaging more frustrated matrons like her, was not particularly enamoured of the prospect. Still, if it earned him more credits who was he to complain?

Some minutes after she'd gone the screen bleeped and his current credit status was displayed. He was doing well. Shona had given him a generous tip. Soon he'd be able to afford a holiday at the Plezure Beach complex. Darrel had visited the purpose-built leisure resort several times. It stood on reclaimed land off the Scillies and had everything you could possibly want in the way of entertainment, sporting and leisure facilities plus a guarantee of constant 'sunshine,' artificial rays that enabled you to acquire a healthy-looking tan without risking the dangers of real ultraviolet.

Yet there had always been something missing from his vacations. Sometimes he thought he was so used to giving pleasure that he'd forgotten how to receive it, and his few encounters with the female genies who were on vacation there had been less than satisfying. But though he often grumbled about the work to his colleagues, it wasn't a bad job: well-paid, undemanding, board and lodging provided. And at least he had the satisfaction of knowing that he was good at something.

In the highly competitive society he lived in, if you had no specific skill you had no hope of a decent life. The horror of life in the Alleys was always there, glimpsed when you travelled to your holiday destination, reported on at intervals in 'life-bytes' on the community screens. There human beings lived like animals, deprived of human dignity. Whenever Darrel felt stirrings of discontent he thought of the Alley-rats and immediately felt happier with his lot.

It was time for his half-hour recreation break. Darrel slipped back into his suit and went down the corridor to the communal restroom where he would be sure to find some of his mates. Three of them were sitting drinking in the far corner, near the screen. He grabbed a drink from the dispenser and joined them.

'Hi, Darrel!' Zal greeted him, his blue eyes vivid against his dark face. 'We're just in the middle of a discussion on how our genes could have made us more responsive. Any ideas?'

It wasn't the first time they'd speculated about their supposed 'sensual powers'. Darrel launched into a summary of his current thinking on the topic.

'Well, I downed a feature on perception the other day. Stereoscopic vision. Apparently each eye makes a rough approximation of an object from the data it receives, but it takes a conjunction of the images from the two eyes to get to a two-and-a-half dimensional model, giving an impression of the surfaces. Then the brain reconstructs the rest of the picture to get a three-dimensional view from all angles. So I drew an analogy from that. I reckon most men when they make love are kind of blinkered, 2.5D. Maybe some get to the 3D stage. But we genies, we must be in the fourth dimension. Some kind of super-sensory perception.'

'But to what extent are any of us aware of this?' Shin, the Eurasian, asked.

'We don't have to be, do we?' Zal said. 'Just as other people aren't aware of their perceptual processes when they use their eyes. They regard it as normal. If we do have these superpowers, then for us they're normal too. We don't have anything else to compare it to.'

'That's it!' Darrel grinned. 'All we get is feedback from our clients. I made a woman who'd never had an orgasm before come for the first time just now, but what did I have that the other guys didn't? Search me.'

'Maybe she just got off on the idea of having a genie do it to her.'

The others laughed. Zal said, 'I read that a "genie" in historic fable was a kind of spirit, often kept locked up in a container, like a bottle. If you freed him, you got three wishes.'

'That's how I feel, locked up in a bottle. The clients come in, they peer at you through the video-bubble. Sometimes I reckon if I ever got out of here whatever magic powers I'm supposed to have would just fade away and I'd get to be normal again.'

Shin said, 'Whatever normal is.'

Darrel finished his drink and pushed back his chair. 'They reckon everyone's bio-engineered these days, don't they? Except the Alley-rats, of course. That's what makes them so frightening. They're savages, out of control, outside the system.'

'I had a cousin who became one of them,' Jabez said. He had a quiet voice and never said much, but when he did the others bent forward to listen. 'He dealt in cocktails, illegal ones. Used to serve the genies here. But the Controllers found out he was using his own recipes. They turned him out and he ended up in the Alleys. I went to see him once, on vacation.'

'You *saw* him!' Darrel said, wide-eyed. 'You mean, you went into the Alleys yourself?'

'Not too far in. We met at a café on the outskirts. There were a couple of ex-Plezure girls there. They still had their skills, but they'd lost their looks. Gave me and my cousin a fantastic time. I wouldn't have believed it was possible to feel such things. I often think about it.'

He ended on a wistful note. The others stared at him. Then Zal said, 'What's their life really like? I mean, is it as bad as they make out?'

Jabez shrugged. 'They manage. There's a pecking order, according to how skilled you are – and how ruthless. They live by scavenging and bargaining. Biggest racket is illegal cocktails. There's a lot of fuzz heads out there.'

Before they could question him further, a sub-controller strolled up, fingering his iriscope. 'Which of you is Darrel, Room 301?' Darrel turned his head so the man could examine his eyes with his viewer. 'Okay, you got a special.'

A buzz of excitement went round the group. Although almost all of their work was conducted on the premises, occasionally a special job came up that required them to go elsewhere. They were always very well paid, to compensate for the slight element of risk in venturing outside the compound.

'Why me?' Darrel asked.

The man was reading from his visor-screen. 'Personal recommendation. Details on your screen. Don't worry, it's not urgent.'

He ambled off the way all the subs did, arrogant and cool, totally in control. They made Darrel's hackles rise, but he was always scrupulously polite to the bastards. It just wasn't worth getting up their nose.

As soon as the man was out of sight, however, he got to his feet. 'I think I'll go back to my room now,' he said, with a grin.

'Don't blame you,' Zal said. 'If I had a special I'd want to check it out *prontissimo*!'

'Good luck, Darrel!' the others said, enviously, as he left them.

The screen that had been displaying his credit status when he left was now giving him the details of his assignment. He was to accompany a female model called Franca to the 'Most Digitized Visage' contest at ten hundred hours, Standard Decimal Time. Darrel's curiosity grew. He touched the screen and more information was offered.

First he chose to find out more about Franca. A picture of the woman, devoid of make-up, showed her to be a real beauty with extraordinarily large blue eyes, sensual dark pink lips and a head of flowing auburn hair. It didn't look like the kind of face that needed much digital enhancement, but that was the way things were these days. A client could pick 'n' mix between girls, taking lips from here, eyes from there, tits from another model.

He flicked the zapper and her naked body appeared, giving him an instant hard-on. If that body was natural she was a real babe! Breasts like firm pink balloons and buttocks likewise. A waist you could get your hands around easily, slinky hips and long, lean thighs. She had only a small reddish mat of hair at her delta, trimmed to form a neat little triangle, and the pink folds of her vulva could be clearly seen beneath. He hadn't had contact with a babe like that for ages. They generally had no need to buy the services of a genie.

A bunch of statistics scrolled before his eyes, but he scarcely paid any heed. Instead he requested data on the event they were supposed to be attending together. The Awards Ceremony was to be held in the Dome of Honour and was being hosted by the Guild of Master Manipulators with Shed Lorrenge as compere. A big real-time event – he'd need to wear formal.

Darrel flipped back to the file on Franca. This time he activated her image, so that her low, sexy voice told him why she'd been nominated for the award. But as she proceeded to inform him how many times her various features had been digitally enhanced Darrel found himself gazing at her dewy open mouth, her darting tongue, her flirty eyes. His hand strayed idly to the thick rod between his thighs and his fingers fumbled with the strip-fastener. Soon he felt it proud and solid in his palm, the glans exposed and glistening.

He flipped back to the shot of Franca naked and pressed to see her move. She danced a little, slow and self-conscious, looking at the camera with shy, darting glances. Darrel fingered his shaft the way he liked it, just below the glans, and felt his desire accelerate. He moved the skin back and forth with rapid precision until, in a few seconds, his vision blanked and his lower body convulsed. Spurts of white gloop rained onto his thighs as he shuddered his way through the brief but intense orgasm.

Feeling relieved, he stepped into the shower cubicle and gave himself a good wash down, then put on his absorbent robe and lay on the bed. His satisfaction level was about the same as if he'd worked up a thirst and then had a long, cool drink.

It always amazed him what a fuss his female clients made when he serviced them, as if there was more to sex than having your system flushed through. Obviously things were different for women. He'd never experienced the kind of emotional rapture they seemed to enjoy. While he made love he was focused solely on his partner, on their reactions and responses, and although he was physically aroused he could be miles away mentally and his emotions just didn't enter into it. Perhaps that was what they'd meant when they said it was in his genes to be the perfect lover: while on the job he was never distracted by his own pleasure, as other men probably were.

Even so, the sight of Franca had got him going more

than usual. He glanced at the clock: eight hundred and twenty. Only one hour, fourty minutes to go, SDT. Darrel was looking forward to meeting her in the flesh. Maybe she would require more of him than merely escorting her to the ceremony. The prospect of making love to her intrigued him, since her body would be infinitely more attractive to play with than those of his recent clients. His pulse quickened at the thought, but he quietened down with a few deep breaths and decided to run his autogenic relaxation program for ten minutes.

'Don't get too excited,' he warned himself. 'She's just another job.'

Chapter Two

Franca met Darrel in the grand atrium of the Plezure Plaza, where fake palm trees and splashing fountains created an exotic ambience. He recognized her at once. She was sitting in an aluminium chair on a silk cushion, her elegant legs crossed slantwise at the ankle, her shimmering body-cape catching the light from all angles and turning her torso into a rainbow pyramid. Feeling self-conscious in his matt-black suit, Darrel crossed the marbled floor with a smile and she rose to greet him.

'You must be Darrel,' she said, her voice low and seductive, giving out a cloud of musk-laden *Jessamine* as their cheeks brushed in salutation. Her skin had the textured feel of high-grade bio-plastic but it might have been real. It was always hard to tell.

He stepped back from her and found himself subjected to a cool azure gaze that provoked a melting sensation in his bowels. The glossy lips were parted slightly, giving a glimpse of wet pink tongue. As he watched, her mouth curved into a smile. 'You'll do,' she said.

He acknowledged the compliment with an ironic bow, and offered her his arm. 'Is your car still waiting?'

'Of course.'

They moved out into the canopied courtyard where a sleek limo was standing, liveried chauffeur at the wheel.

At their approach the man leapt out, hastening to open the rear door.

'Nice,' Darrel commented. It was a long time since he'd ridden in any vehicle, let alone one as luxurious as this. The chauffeur was simply there for show, of course, but it was pleasant to have him usher you into the car.

He sank into the cushioning embrace of the upholstery, noting the discreet presence of the cocktail cabinet. Faint soothing music and a scent that complemented Franca's perfume filled the car as the computer kicked into action.

'Fancy a soother?' he asked his companion.

'I need something.'

Darrel grinned at her. 'You're not nervous, surely? You're going to win and you know it!'

Franca's eyes frosted a little. 'There will be some competition. I must be at my best. Please give me a slow unwinder.'

Darrel flicked open the drinks cabinet and surveyed the labels of the chilled containers. 'Will a Slack Sundae do?'

'Mm. That usually does the trick.' He handed her the small bottle with its integrated mouthpiece. She said, 'Now I'll choose one for you.'

She picked out a Pacific Pommagne and unscrewed the top half a turn to open the airlock, shaking it a little before she handed it to him. Darrel took a sip. The spritzy apple flavour lifted his spirits and relaxed him. He decided he was going to enjoy this particular job.

They cruised through the semi-deserted streets, catching glimpses from time to time of the chaotic underworld of the Alleys that cut swathes like ugly gashes through the serene beauty of the city's architecture. Rotting buildings, filthy streets, gutters crawling with unspeakable animal life appeared like flashbacks of a nightmare, then were gone in an instant. Darrel found the way that dark world was interwoven with the modern, prosperous one unnerving. It seemed primeval, a place of archaic horror, but since his conversation with Jabez he was aware of his dawning fascination with it. Were there really women out there who could give you more pleasure than you could ever experience in the sanitized environment of the Plezure Plaza?

Darrel glanced at Franca, whose flawless face remained expressionless as she sipped the soothing cocktail, her eyes on a skyline dominated by the vast luminescent mushroom that was the Dome of Honour. He felt his cock stirring at the sight of her, a frisky side effect of the Pommagne. Was her body as perfect as her face? he wondered. It might have been digitally enhanced for her screen presentation. More to the point, would he ever find out?

'Here we are, Sir, Madam,' the chauffeur said at last, turning towards them with an oily grin as the car slid into the vast forecourt. Darrel felt in his breast pocket for some creds. He was always embarrassed handling coins, but it was the only common currency among types like chauffeurs. The man opened the car door for them and tipped his hat with one hand as Darrel thrust the coins into the other.

'Thank you, Sir. Have a nice evening, Sir, Madam. When you need me again just tell the doorman lot seventeen.'

'Seventeen,' Darrel repeated.

'That's right, Sir. Remember it by the year the

Slammers won the Trophy Hat-Trick, Sir. If you're a Razorball man, that is.'

Darrel grimaced, then forced a smile. He was not a fan of that violent game. But Franca said, 'I'll remember. It's my mother's birthday.'

An old wound was suddenly reopened in him and he felt a burst of irrational envy at the thought that Franca knew her mother that well. But she was smiling at him so beautifully that he couldn't feel bad for long.

'Come on,' she urged him, threading her arm through his. 'Let's go into the Dome. I'm longing to see all the people.'

They were already moving in a steady stream through the entrance, men and women in their formal attire, rainbow-hued and glittering, like exotic insects amassing round a honey pot. The Dome was gorgeous in the setting sun, every facet of its surface reflecting the purple, orange and crimson glow of the sky. Darrel and Franca stepped onto the moving walkway and were carried through into the high, dazzling atrium where lackeys with iriscopes were checking everyone's identity against hand-held computers.

'Isn't it wonderfully exciting?' Franca smiled, pressing close to him.

Darrel was finding her increasingly attractive. She was coming out of her shell, drifting into little-girl mode as the sense of occasion filled her with exhilaration. Everyone seemed to be looking at her, some whispering to their companions behind fanned fingers, and it came home to Darrel that he was escorting a celebrity, a woman who was hotly tipped to win the 'Most Digitized Visage' award.

'Welcome, Franca dear!' an unctuous man said at the

inner door, taking her cloak. 'And may I tender, once again, my heartfelt congratulations on your nomination?'

'Thank you, Lars,' she replied, holding her hand out to be kissed. Darrel saw that, under the rainbow cape, she was wearing a figure-tight outfit with clear-vu domes around the high globes of her breasts. There was a band of gold around the base of each dome and an ornamental gold finial over the nipple. The rest of the garment flared from her hips into a brief frill of a skirt, exposing her thighs in their stretch-silk splendour.

As they made their way to their seats, Darrel murmured, 'Who was that?'

'My agent.'

She spoke dismissively, as if he was a necessary evil. Darrel grinned, helping her into her seat, then he sat down in his. The silver-grey cushions immediately moulded themselves to his body, making him feel as if he was sitting on air.

The great hall filled up swiftly, piling rank upon rank of jewelled creatures into the auditorium. At last the proceedings began, opened by the odious Web Pundit, Shed Lorrenge. The Guild of Master Manipulators was a technical association, and most of the ceremony was scattered with obscure references to the art of manipulating on-screen images. Awards were presented to editors, programmers, producers, cameramen. Conmen to a man, as far as Darrel was concerned. Nobody trusted any image any more. Even 'The News' was just another series of fake pictures in a virtual world, indistinguishable from the latest glamourized soap.

As the proceedings moved towards the Creative categories Darrel was aware that Franca was growing restless. A slight sweat had broken out over the pearlized pink of her upper lip and he found it extraordinarily attractive, perhaps because it was proof that she was made of flesh and blood after all. He took a risk when Lorrenge announced the Most Digitized Visage award and squeezed her hand. She flashed him a grateful smile, then her eyes swivelled back to the distant stage and the tiny podium atop the sweeping steps. Darrel gave a wry grin. Was she wondering whether she could negotiate her passage without tripping up?

'So here is the list of finalists, each one a perfect peach!' Lorrenge was saying in his oily voice. 'From the Zap agency, the lovely Lorian!' An image of exotic, brown-skinned Lorian Van der Veldt filled the screen behind the podium, to rapturous applause. 'And from Starshift Enterprises, the very feminine Franca!'

It seemed to Darrel that the applause for her was slightly louder. She appeared to be in a different world now, sitting upright on the edge of her seat with her eyes gleaming intently and her lips slightly parted, like a breathless child. He paid no attention to the remaining four names on the shortlist. Franca had to win. He could conceive of no other outcome.

And neither, it seemed, could the judges. After making some gratuitous remarks about high standards and the like, Lorrenge lifted up the silver microphone with a flourish and announced, 'The unanimous verdict of the judges is as follows: the winner of the Most Digitized Visage award for 2020 is ... Franca, of Starshift Enterprises!'

She moved in a dream, out of the cushioned security of her seat and into the wide aisle which she seemed to float down at high speed. The clapping and cheering reached its crescendo as she skipped effortlessly up the stairs and stood beside Lorrenge on the podium. He kissed both her cheeks and handed her the small gold trophy. She faced the crowd nervously, evidently wanting to make a speech. Darrel's heart was in his mouth. He was fielding the envious glances of men in the audience, men who evidently presumed that his relationship with Franca was an intimate one. Perhaps by the end of the evening, their jealousy would be justified. He did hope so.

'Ladies and gentlemen, I just want to say . . .' she faltered as the applause died away into silence. 'I just want to say . . . thank you.' For a moment her nerve seemed to fail her, and Darrel thought she was going to stop there. But she took a deep breath and continued, 'Thank you to everyone who has had a hand in my success. To my agent Lars and everyone at Starshift. To my late mother, for encouraging me at the start of my career. To the Guild of Master Manipulators, for arranging this wonderful evening and subsidizing the awards. And to . . . to Darrel, for helping me face this ordeal tonight! Thank you all, so much!'

Darrel felt his cheeks burn and his heart began thudding crazily. What the hell did she have to go and say that for? Now everyone would be wondering who this 'Darrel' was and he would be drawn into the publicity machine that surrounded these events. It was more than he'd bargained for and, as Franca made her way back up the wide aisle, acknowledging with nods and smiles the compliments thrown at her, he felt a surge of anger in his chest.

Worst of all, the minute she resumed her seat she leaned over and gave him a kiss on the cheek. 'That's for being so supportive to me,' she whispered.

'Are you crazy?' he snorted. 'I'm your paid escort, not your live-in lover!'

Flushed and excited, Franca looked like a woman in the throes of orgasm and his heart contracted at the sight of her. She gave him a cheeky smile which temporarily mollified him, but now he had the hots for her in earnest. If she didn't ask him to service her after this he would demand double his fee – or sue the bitch for breach of contract!

As the proceedings moved on towards a close, Franca showed him her trophy. It was a cleverly designed piece, consisting of a mask in which the various features – eyes, nose and mouth – were slowly rotated by a concealed motor. Others leant over the back of her seat asking to see it, and she showed it off proudly, like a kid with a birthday present.

Blaring music and loud applause signalled the end of the ceremony and people began to flock into the aisle. For a moment Darrel feared that his rôle as escort might be over. But then Franca rose, taking his hand. 'We have to go to the celebrity suite for the reception,' she said.

The crowd seemed to part before them as she led the way to the side of the hall and up some stairs to the mezzanine floor above. In a room whose walls were almost entirely glass people were already sipping luridly-coloured cocktails, their conversation bright and meaningless. Franca's entry was greeted by a brief round of applause. Then Lars appeared, his smile a tribute to orthodontics, and swept her into his embrace.

'Sweetheart! Felicitations! But the verdict was never in doubt, my dear.' He swung round to a passing waiter and took a tall glass containing a pink frothy concoction off the silver tray. 'Here, let me drink to your health and beauty!'

But she insisted on presenting Darrel to him first. Lars gave him the briefest of nods, his hostility barely disguised. Franca grabbed a blue drink in a frosted glass before the waiter moved on and handed it to Darrel with a smile.

Lars began to gush again. 'Franca, sweetheart, let me present you to the redoubtable Gregor, of NDS. I have it on good authority that he wants to use your face to launch a thousand shuttles.'

He led her by the elbow to the far corner of the room, where she was soon hobnobbing with a bald little man given to wild gesticulation, and Darrel was left to his own devices. He examined his drink briefly, not bothering to speculate about its name or psychogenic function, and downed it in one. A reckless mood had descended on him which he recognized as a combination of lust, anger and frustration. He wanted Franca and he wanted her now, but there was a whole queue of greaseballs and other obstacles between him and the attainment of his desire.

No one else in that crowded room interested him half as much as Franca, even though several attractive women smiled at him in open invitation. She drew his gaze constantly, the shimmering light on her semi-naked back turning her into an irresistible beacon. Slowly he made his way towards her corner, trying to appear casual as he took a morsel from the buffet and placed his empty glass on a trolley. He felt out of place in that crowd, an interloper, and was considering making a discreet exit when she suddenly turned and looked at him.

Her stare was compelling. Darrel moved towards her as if in a dream and was soon beside her. The bald fellow was describing his shuttle fleet with expansive movements of his chubby hands and Lars was ogling Franca with smug assurance. Darrel disliked them both. But then he heard her whisper out of the corner of her mouth, 'Rescue me!'

Before he had time to figure out what she meant, Franca sank to the floor with a low moan and lay spread-eagled, her eyes closed and her beautiful lips slackly open. The gold of her trophy flashed within the velskin bag around her wrist. Lars formed a barrier with his arms. 'Keep back! The poor darling has fainted! It must be all the excitement, the heat . . .'

Swiftly Darrel took control, knowing it was what she wanted. He scooped her up into his arms, finding her body surprisingly light, and began to stride towards the door before Lars or anyone else realized what was happening. As soon as they did, cameras began to roll. Darrel snarled at their intrusive lenses and continued on his exit route with stoical determination.

The curve of her bottom sat in the crook of his arm as if they'd been made to fit. He looked down at Franca's pale face, then at her taut breasts arrayed like delicacies beneath their plastic domes, and felt another spasm of lust. It was a long time since a woman had roused him like that. A very long time. And he meant to make the most of it. With an excited babble of voices following him down the corridor he strode forward, determined not to give up his quarry. On reaching the exit he told the doorman to page the chauffeur in lot seventeen. The man looked at him quizzically but when Darrel scowled at him he whispered into the button on his lapel.

For several anxious seconds Darrel stood at the entrance, fearing the rising tide of curiosity from those within. Just as the onlookers began descending towards him in a ragged mob he saw the hired car approach. 'Hurry, man!' he muttered, hastening down the last steps.

Despite the unconventional manner of their departure the chauffeur didn't bat an eyelid. 'Evenin', Sir, Madam,' he said as he opened the back door and helped Darrel slide Franca onto the back seat. She tucked up her legs to allow him access, dismissing any lingering suspicions of his that her fainting fit might have been genuine.

As they pulled swiftly away Darrel knew that a whole flotilla of lenses was capturing their flight. Enhanced images would flood the media next day, probably making him look as if he was embracing Franca sexually, and he would have his fifteen minutes of notoriety. But what would she gain from it? Maximum publicity for her award, of course. Cold anger seeped through him. 'It's all right, you can stop faking it,' he told her. 'They got plenty of shots of us. I hope you're satisfied.'

The sooty lashes fluttered open and she gazed up at him with limpid, azure innocence. 'It wasn't publicity-seeking, Darrel. I wanted to get away from those dreadful men, that's all.'

He wanted to believe her but she was caught up in the business of on-screen images and their interpretation, a business where 'exposure' was all and every shot or mention brought in more credits. 'Sure,' he said, cynically.

She cuddled up to him, the plastic around her breast crackling against his sleeve. 'I'll make it up to you, Darrel. In more ways than one.'

Franca was giving him that mischievous smile again and his heart vaulted dangerously. Was sex on the agenda after all? It was looking likely, especially when she told the chauffeur to program the computer-router for Parkside. 'That's where I live,' she told Darrel.

He was afraid she simply wanted to be dropped off there, but as the car turned into the tree-lined avenue and then cruised along the neo-Georgian block she whispered, 'You will come up for a drink, won't you?'

Try and stop me! he thought. But he just nodded.

It was Franca who tipped the chauffeur this time, clinking a couple of credits into his hand then leading the way up to the securidor. The iriscope scanned her eyes, then she punched in a code to admit Darrel and the simulated oak door slid silently open. Inside, an elevator whisked them to the third floor and the understated elegance of Franca's apartment. It was decorated in restful blues and greys, with a pervading scent of freesia from cloned blooms in an antique glass vase.

'God, I'm glad that's over!' she said, kicking off the gold bands from her feet and stretching out on the soft couch.

'Aren't you glad you won, though?'

Franca shrugged. 'It was more for Lars, really. I couldn't give a fart. As long as the work keeps coming in.' She looked up at him with huge, inviting eyes. 'Want to know why I asked for you to escort me?'

He sat on the fat arm of the couch, looking down at her. 'Yes. I'm curious.'

She laughed and rolled over onto her back, her hands on the plastic domes over her breasts. 'I'm curious, too, about you! I wanted to know what an ALM was like.'

Darrel felt his prick stir. So she knew he was an Alpha Lover, Male. But wasn't that classified information? 'You could have booked an appointment at the Plaza, like anyone else.'

'Did I say I wanted to know what you were like as a *lover*?' He shook his head, bewildered, disappointed, and she went on. 'No, I meant as a person, as a man. Granted I've not had a great deal of time to get to know you, but at least I've been able to observe you out of context.'

'You make this sound like some kind of experiment. Am I your guinea pig?'

She laughed. 'Nothing like that. Like I said, I was just curious. I know what it's like to be identified with your rôle and no more. I'm just a face and body, no one considers that I might have a mind. The people I work for see me as a collection of pixels.'

'Well, what's your conclusion regarding this ALM?' he asked, a note of bitterness creeping in, hiding his insecurity. He wasn't used to such complicated transactions and he felt out of his depth.

Franca reached up and cupped his chin with her palm. It felt oddly comforting. She smiled and said, 'The investigation isn't over yet. I think it's time to make some more intimate discoveries.' She slipped her cool fingers into the neck of his suit and stroked the hollow of his throat. Small flashes of fire sped down his oesophagus.

Darrel gulped. 'I thought you weren't interested in my . . . body.'

'Did I say that?' She gave him a wry grin and

33

unlatched some secret fastening in her bodice. The whole of the front came off, like a breastplate, exposing her exquisite bosom to his gaze. 'I just wanted it to be less . . . impersonal. I wanted to take you out of your familiar surroundings, loosen you up a little. I wanted to place you in unaccustomed situations to see how you would react. And I must say you stood up to the test very well. Very well indeed.'

There was a hot, heavy tingling in his balls and his chest felt strained so that the breath came in short bursts. Something very odd was happening to him. Usually when he was with a woman he felt totally in control, but now it was as if *he* was being controlled by *her*. It was uncomfortable, but also weirdly exciting. He couldn't take his eyes off the spherical perfection of her breasts. His fingers were itching to tease those pink, flaccid nipples into active life and feel the pale mounds on which they rested strain and swell under his caressing palms.

Franca was holding her arms up to him now, placing her hands around his neck in order to draw him down to her. Soon his lips were grazing on the smooth skin of her breasts, smelling the musky jasmine scent of her, feeling his endocrine system kick into action as the adrenalin coursed through his veins. The blood was pumping up his cock to a respectable erection but this time it felt less programmed, less automatic. Whatever stimuli he was responding to were subtly different from usual and he felt pleasantly disoriented, as if he'd mixed incompatible cocktails.

'Is this what you want?' he mumbled as she pressed his face into the sweet divide of her cleavage.

'It's what *you* want that matters,' he heard her say.

'You're not on duty now, Darrel. This is pure pleasure. Your pleasure.'

No one had ever spoken to him like that before. The effect was wildly heady, like a Triple Zinger. He opened his mouth and tasted the smooth cream of her flesh. At the same time he felt her nimble fingers stripping off his formal, peeling it off him like the skin from an orange until he felt the clingy material pooling around his ankles. His prick, finding itself suddenly freed from its confines, became jauntily erect and thrust itself against the silky mesh covering her thigh.

While Darrel found his way to her erect nipple and began to lick it, he felt her hands on his buttocks and moaned. It was distracting. So much so that he found he couldn't tune into her desires, as he usually did, but was obliged to focus solely on his own pleasure. She crossed her long legs and squeezed his waist with her thighs, making him shudder with sudden longing.

Then, before he realized what was happening, she had twisted round and bent her head to his cock, licking the glans with delicate precision. Darrel uttered a loud groan as sensations sweeter than he had ever known began to cascade up and down his spine, turning him into a quivering mass of hedonistic abandon. He sucked at her breast and licked at the nipple, feeling his shaft trying to inch its way between those warm, wet, cushioning lips.

No pussy could be more welcoming than her mouth, he decided, as she laved more and more of him with her agile tongue. Darrel could feel himself loosening up, coming apart at the seams, but it was no use fighting it. As the delicious arousal reached critical, crazy thoughts about Franca skimmed the surface of his mind: she was some kind of spy, sent to test him; she was a female genie getting in some extra-curricular activity; she was high on some aphrodisiac cocktail. One thing was certain, she was an expert cocksucker.

It wasn't the first time he'd had it done to him. Sometimes his women clients got off on it, as a prelude to their own satisfaction. But never before had he experienced such sheer sensual bliss. If this was what women got from him no wonder they were prepared to pay over the odds for it! Suddenly everything about sex seemed to make sense where before it had been an incomprehensible blur.

Darrel's restless mind drifted into vacancy as his libido took over, filling every corner of his consciousness. His prick was trying harder to thrust into her mouth now, needing more friction, but she artfully evaded him and kept him dancing on the edge, dreaming of full penetration. Her tongue was flicking his sensitive skin at amazing speed as her lips moved slowly up and down the glans area without descending to his shaft. His fingers strayed to his crotch but she caught them and wouldn't let him touch himself. He could feel the gathering momentum of his climax, like a great river contained by a huge dam.

Then he felt her fingers encircle the base of his shaft, no more. She squeezed him there lightly, her lips and tongue still working overtime on his glans. Darrel moaned as the inevitable moment of his release approached. He felt her move her fingers up his turgid shaft, just a centimetre or so, rubbing gently. Images of her pert breasts and hidden pussy teased him mercilessly, but he didn't have the will to do anything about it. All he could do was wallow in the hot tide of lust that was carrying him helplessly, like so much flotsam, towards his goal.

Then, just when he was wondering how much longer he could hold out, the open cave of her mouth enveloped him in moist velvet and he thrust deeply, joyously, into her throat. She was prepared for him and didn't gag. Her tongue, more restricted in its movements now, nevertheless managed to slide around his shaft to stimulating effect. Darrel's aching balls contracted, his whole body tense. The suspense was exquisite, tormenting. He reached for her breasts, like a drowning man seeking something to hold on to, and was reassured by the contact with warm, firm flesh.

Caught up in the unstoppable rise to orgasm, Darrel felt the hot sweetness pouring through his veins, filling his whole body with tumultuous energy. When the explosion came it felt as if his whole being was being ejected through the slitty eye of his glans. He roared aloud as the juice spurted from him in a triumphant arc, releasing all his tension in a long series of ecstatic bursts.

Afterwards he fell back, drained and limp, into Franca's waiting arms. For a while his head nestled between her naked breasts, feeling the steady heartbeat beneath his ear. The drowsy afterglow kept his thoughts at bay while his bio-systems returned to normal, but after a while his mind began to race again. He moved away from her, propping his head on his elbow, and she gave him a questioning look.

'I never knew . . .' he began awkwardly.

She knew exactly what he meant. 'You're not supposed to know. Your job is to give pleasure, not receive it.'

'But why? How? I don't understand.'

Franca smiled, getting up off the bed and pulling a silk top over her breasts. 'They told you it was all in your genes, right?' He nodded. 'Did you really believe there's a gene that makes you a perfect lover but inhibits your own responses?'

'I never questioned it. I was little more than a kid when they took me to the Plaza. It seemed like paradise at the time.'

'Sure. That's how they operate.'

'Who are "they"?'

'The Controllers. Once they set up the state brothel system they decided they couldn't have their monopoly challenged. So they had to offer "satisfaction guaranteed". And they needed sex workers like you to deliver that guaranteed service.'

'But if it's not in my genes, what's going on?'

Franca smiled, mysteriously. 'They've got you conditioned.'

'How?'

'Well, let's say that tonight, for a few hours, you were temporarily deconditioned. Those cocktails you drank . . .'

'You mean, there were special drugs in them?'

She nodded. 'I know a guy who deals in them.' She glided over to the wall and pressed a button. A screen slid back to reveal a shower unit. 'But that's enough talk. Time you showered and got on your way. They'll be suspicious if you stay away from the Plaza too long.'

Darrel knew she was right. His pass only entitled him to stay out until two SDT, and it was already gone one. While he douched himself, feeling the revitalizing energy flow back through his veins, Franca dialled for a cab. By the time he was dressed again the signal came that his transport was waiting at the door.

'Thank you for being my escort this evening,' Franca smiled, kissing his cheek in what seemed to Darrel an absurdly formal manner.

'I don't know how to begin to thank you . . .'

'Then don't. It was my pleasure, too. And I mean that. Goodbye, Darrel. I don't suppose we shall meet again.'

She spoke matter-of-factly, without a hint of regret, and he felt a sluggish disappointment seep through his heart. But he turned nevertheless and hurried back into the lift, down to where the sleek cab was waiting. There was no driver this time, the car was fully computerized, his route already mapped in its memory. As soon as he slid into the front seat the whine of the gears began and he was propelled smoothly out of the forecourt and onto the lonely highway.

Chapter Three

The experience with Franca had changed Darrel in some way. The effect was subtle, but nonetheless real. The minute he got back into his room he switched to the News channel and soon located a feature on the ceremony he had attended with Franca. He drank in the image of her as she stepped up to receive her golden trophy and saw himself sitting there, star-struck, when she returned to her seat. He replayed it over and over, fascinated by the woman. Was this what people had once labelled 'love,' he wondered, this exhilarating obsession?

Yet there was another side to it, a darker side, that he could not dismiss. His curiosity about her began to gnaw at him, and he wondered how many other men she had been with. You didn't perfect a technique like hers without a lot of practice. Was this corrosive emotion what they used to call 'jealousy'? He felt adrift, lacking a compass to direct his new emotional self. Life in the Plaza didn't include such feelings. Stepping outside the bland cocoon of its environment had proved to be a perilous experience, but not in the way he might have supposed.

And what of the things she had told him, about the system, about himself? Dark, unsatisfactory hints for the most part, enough to unsettle him without giving him many clues. Did she know what turmoil she had thrown him into, through a combination of her seductive sensuality and her teasing words? He wanted to go back and question her further, but there was no chance of that. After his regulation six hours' sleep he would be required to stay in his room, ready for any client who might fancy a 'servicing' before breakfast.

His first appointment was at ten, another vulgar old woman who made his heart sink as he saw her on screen, coming down the walkway towards him. She was plump and tarty, her sparsely frizzed hair dyed yellow, her chubby neck, wrists and fingers laden with cheap jewellery.

'It's just a job,' he told himself as the door slid open and she tiptoed coyly in.

'Welcome!' he smiled, through gritted teeth. 'How nice to see you. I'm Darrel.'

He held her sweaty palm for as long as he could bear. She simpered, 'And I'm Lianne. You were recommended to me by Shona.'

'Ah yes, Shona. Such a lovely lady. Well, Lianne, would you like a cocktail? I can recommend the Sweetly Passionate Subliminal.'

She giggled. 'What a fanciful name! Will it do exciting things to me?'

'No, Lianne,' he replied, solemnly. '*I* will do exciting things to you.'

He watched her blush and shiver a little with excitement, but it gave him no job satisfaction. All he could think of, as he fixed the drink, was how different this was going to be from his session with Franca. But this was work and that had been pleasure. Strange how the difference had never been so obvious to him before.

Lianne took the cocktail with trembling fingers and gazed at him with eyes of faded blue. She had once been pretty, but not even the anti-ageing serum that she'd obviously been injected with had been able to turn back the clock. She was probably around a hundred, but looked eighty. He knew the type. She would have gone through several husbands, wearing them out and amassing enough wealth along the way to have all the latest biotech treatments.

But Franca had been young and untouched by time or technology, her flesh wonderfully firm and natural. While Lianne sipped her drink, Darrel fell into reverie. 'Sweet lips,' he murmured, his mind on Franca's, remembering the way they had encircled his glans.

'What was that?'

He came to with a jolt. 'I was just referring to how your lips will taste when you're through with that drink. I shall sip the nectar from them, like a bee.'

'Oh!' She squirmed in her chair, recrossing her fat legs and showing a glimpse of a hairy vee. *Oh God*, Darrel thought, *the randy cow isn't even wearing underwear!*

The thought that he was under guarantee to satisfy this woman depressed him enormously. He'd never felt like this before, and attributed it directly to his experience with Franca. That woman had a lot to answer for. Whatever her intention had been she had succeeded in making it very difficult for him to perform professionally to his usual high standard.

'I can tell you are a delightfully sensual woman,' he went on, in quiet desperation. 'Would you like me to give you a massage with an oil of your choice?'

Lianne's pale eyes grew round with enthusiasm. 'Yes, please!'

Darrel went to the aromastat and selected three fragrances. She sniffed them ecstatically then made her choice: 'Erotic Caprice,' known in the trade as 'civetine' after its main ingredients, a synthesis of musk from a wildcat's arse and skunk oil. It was supposed to be irresistible to women who were turned on by a man's sweat.

Slowly he stripped off Lianne's gaudy clothes, exposing the fake-tanned flesh beneath. Her breasts stood out like mahogany razorballs, the skin taut and glossy in stark contrast to the rest of her. They must be recent implants. Age brought shrinkage problems and increased risk of infection. A woman her age probably had to have them renewed every five years or so. Remembering the pink perfection of Franca's breasts, Darrel surveyed them distastefully. Did he really have to handle those things?

'I suggest you lie on your front to begin with, Lianne,' he said.

She grunted as she stretched out on the four-poster, exposing her fat behind. As he poured the scented oil into his palm Darrel wondered what the fantasy key to her psyche would be. He needed all the short cuts he could find, but so far there had been no clues. Usually he could intuit them within a few minutes. His clients' eyes would flick across the screen images until they found the one that most pleased them, then their pupils would dilate. But Lianne had ignored them all. Was she like Shona, more easily aroused through the ear than the eye?

Darrel began to smooth his palms up her legs and she visibly relaxed, spreading herself out on the undulating bed with a long sigh. He found himself feeling sorry for her. Evidently she had no one in her life to do this for her, no husband or lover. Yet after his experience with Franca he found he could better understand the need that drove her to pay for his services. He started to knead the slack flesh over her buttocks, kneeling astride her, and she groaned loudly when his fingers slipped between her flabby thighs and teased her nether lips a little from behind. The scent of the musky amber was filling his nostrils, overpowering the background aroma that seeped through the ventilation system.

Slowly, Darrel made his way up her back with sweeping gestures until he was leaning over her shoulders. He decided to whisper in her ear. In a bid to evoke some secret fantasy of hers, he began by suggesting she should imagine herself lying on a tropical beach.

'Far from civilization, you feel all your inhibitions disappearing as you soak up the warm rays and smell the exotic scents wafting around you. The people here are friendly and sensual, the men especially. They love large, plump women. Their goddess is a brown-skinned beauty with enormous breasts and when a boy reaches puberty he has to make love to her image.'

Slowly the great bulk of the woman began to roll over, exposing her sagging belly and the enormous, surgically-enhanced breasts. Darrel felt half seduced by his own fantasy-weaving, seeing her as a kind of parody of that mythical goddess. Was he the 'boy' who had to make ritual love to her? The thought was chilling. He poured more oil into his palms and set to work on her arms.

As he continued with his tale his imagination began to flower. 'The boy is stripped naked. Then, blindfolded and bound by the wrists, he is led to the temple of the goddess where she awaits his initiation. Inside the giant statue hides a real flesh-and-blood woman, with whom he will mate for the first time.'

Lianne was growing excited. Her nipples were standing erect and her thighs had fallen apart in open invitation. What was turning her on? Normally Darrel would not hesitate to follow his instinct but now he felt unsure. Was she identifying with the goddess, or the boy? He moved across to her chest and began to anoint her breasts with drops of the warm oil. She shuddered as he rubbed it in gently with his fingertips, then rolled each nipple in turn between his finger and thumb, feeling the hard rubberiness grow even more rigid.

'Oh!' she moaned, making little thrusts with her pelvis and moving her thighs in restless longing. 'Oh, oh! This is blissful!'

But it was not yet enough to ensure that she would be satisfied. Darrel lifted one arm above her head and then the other, experimentally. The brown globes of her breasts were lifted too. He held her arms there by the wrists, watching her hips squirm voluptuously. Then, deciding to take a chance, he reached for the silken cord that was always hiding beneath the pillow and swiftly twisted it three times around her wrists before knotting it tightly.

Lianne's faded blue eyes flipped open and she stared at him with silent adoration. He began to caress her inner thighs with his oiled hand and her expression melted into bliss. His fingers moved up between the flaccid labia and found the narrow channel of her quim with its protruding nub above. She gasped as he found the trigger of her sex and began to press on it with his thumb, circling slowly, while his fingers dipped into the wet chasm below.

Soon she would expect him to drive hard into her, his virility a powerful aphrodisiac in itself as he lengthed her over and over with increasing vigour, taking her to seventh heaven.

And she had every right to expect that. After all, she was paying top credits for it. The only trouble was, Darrel was feeling anything but virile and his hitherto trusty tool was feeling anything but hard. Struggling to hide his dismay along with his flaccid penis, Darrel bent his lips to the woman's pussy and started to give her a good tonguing.

By now he should have had an erection like a crowbar, so what was wrong? He wrinkled his nose as the woman's knees gripped his head, forcing his face to remain at her crotch. Fortunately she wasn't aware of his predicament – yet. But then he had an idea. He wriggled out from under her legs and thrust one hand into her pussy to keep her happy while he reached up with the other one to the curtain-tie of the bed. Loosing one from its moorings he moved swiftly up and fastened it around her eyes before she knew what was happening.

'Oh!' Lianne squealed excitedly. 'What on earth are you doing, you naughty boy?'

'You'll just have to guess, won't you!'

Darrel's voice had come out as a snarl and she seemed to like it. 'Wicked man!' she chided him, happily. 'I hope you're not going to do anything *too* dreadful to me!'

'Well, now, that depends on how you behave yourself, young woman!'

On the way back down, he gave her breasts a brief

caress. They felt like burnished brass and looked like polished mahogany. It was hardly like flesh at all. Grimacing with distaste, Darrel resumed his manual stimulation of her cunny and she rocked around in the throes of ecstasy as she tried to buck and wriggle her way towards a climax.

'Give it me good and hard, big boy!' he heard her say.

His heart sank. This one wouldn't be satisfied if she didn't have at least eight inches of something thick and solid inside her. Darrel had heard of such things as dildoes but they were banned in the Plaza, since women expected the genies to satisfy them personally. He looked around the room in desperation, his finger waggling stiffly on her button. Then he caught sight of the hand pump he used to top up the air in the bed from time to time, and a slow smile spread over his face. If he unscrewed the valve he would be left with a thick plastic cylinder.

Reaching out he managed to grab the pump with one hand while maintaining his contact with Lianne's throbbing clitoris. His tongue took over as he used both his hands to prepare the pump to function as its designer had never intended.

Slowly he began to push the end of the cylinder into Lianne's wide-open quim. He was astride her, his limp cock dangling over her entrance, so it was quite possible for her to imagine that he was screwing her. She *Oo*-ed and *Ah*-ed a bit, then, when the thing was sliding all the way inside her, she exclaimed, 'Oh, what a big hard one you have! But why didn't you let me see it, you naughty man! The sight of it would have turned me on a treat.'

'I'd rather turn you on this way,' he murmured. 'Is it good?'

'Good? It's fantastic! I love being filled up completely!'

She began to move her hips, thrusting against his hand as he moved the pump in and out. Darrel kept his thumb firmly on her jutting clitoris and soon she was growing frantic in her desire for fulfilment. He brushed her solid tits with his left hand, tweaked the nipples and felt a shudder pass through her flesh. At the same time she began to moan, her voice rising to a crescendo as the climax broke.

Over and over again he saw her convulse with extreme ecstasy and knew that he'd succeeded. He withdrew the pump and threw it into the corner, then began stroking her belly as the rippling sensations subsided.

'Oh God!' she exclaimed, gutturally. 'That was the best ever! The best *ever*!'

Darrel should have felt his usual professional pride at a job well done. Instead he felt devastated. Not only had his tool failed to perform, but the fat cow hadn't been able to tell the difference! He felt useless, redundant. Although he put on a show of being pleased, helped the woman into the shower and acted grateful when she tipped him generously, he felt a complete charlatan.

After she'd gone Darrel felt he needed a different sort of company. He was due a break, so he went along to the restroom, where he found Shin and Jabez. They welcomed him warmly.

'How was your special?' Shin asked, his dark oriental gaze brightening.

'We saw the event on screen,' Jabez added. 'She looked a peach.'

'She was nice. Not at all vain.'

'And sexy?' Shin prompted. 'Did you get to find out?'

Darrel shrugged. 'There wasn't much time.'

He didn't know why he didn't want to talk about it. It seemed too intimate, too personal. But there was something more pressing that he needed to know. Something equally personal. He had to ask them, but how to broach the subject? They talked of other things for a while, then Shin gave him an opening.

'Women are easily pleased, aren't they? As long as you ring their bell . . .'

'Sometimes it's not that easy.'

Shin's dark eyes twinkled. 'We're genies, aren't we? Born and bred for the purpose, so they say.'

'But what if there's a glitch in the gene program? What if it starts to deteriorate after a time?'

'Are you saying you're having problems?' Jabez asked.

'No, no! Just theorizing.' He grinned, self-consciously. 'I was just wondering if we'd be thrown on the scrap heap when we couldn't get it up any more, or if they've ways of fixing it.'

The two men were staring at him with wary interest, their expressions incredulous. 'God, do you think that's possible?' Jabez asked.

Darrel shrugged. 'Who knows?'

'If that ever happened to me I don't know what I'd do,' Shin mumbled. 'Doesn't bear thinking about.'

'Don't think about it then, or you might lose confidence in yourself,' Jabez cautioned. 'I wish you'd never brought the subject up, Darrel. It doesn't do to speculate about such things.'

'Of course not. Sorry.'

Darrel knocked back his drink and was surprised to see a sub-controller coming his way again. The man came sauntering up with his iriscope and held it close to his left eye.

'Your break's over,' he said. 'Back to work.'

He knew better than to argue. On his way back to his room Darrel concluded that he must have another client due. Well, now he'd find out if his 'glitch' was temporary or not.

There were two girls already awaiting him in his room, which was presumably why the sub had singled him out. They were petite Polurasians, and looked like non-idents. When he entered they giggled and averted their eyes beneath their fan-like lashes. Darrel felt the sombre mood of the past few minutes start to lighten.

'Hullo, ladies. I'm Darrel, at your service. May I enquire your names?'

The one with the longer hair smiled shyly. 'I'm Mitsi and my sister is Teela.'

He put an arm around each slim waist and led them towards the bed. 'Tourists, are you?'

The Plaza got a lot of those. Women vacationing without their husbands, lovers. Unattached women looking for adventure. Women who couldn't bring themselves to tell their husbands that they were sexually unfulfilled. But they weren't usually this young, or this pretty. Darrel felt his libido rising along with his optimism.

'Well, my dears, what can I do for you?' he began, thinking he could trust them to tell him what they wanted.

Mitsi, who seemed the bolder of the two, gave him a slightly wicked smile. 'We're here for Teela, really. I just came along to keep her company.'

'I see.' Darrel gave her an amused smile, not believing a word of it.

'You see, altough neiter of us is a virgin our experience of sex has been rater ... different.'

'How's that?'

'Well ...' Mitsi overcame her nervousness and continued, 'Back home we bot got married togeter. We were sixteen, bot virgin. Dat is te way in our culture. But te man my parent chose for me was a good ... lover.' She giggled, shyly. 'I climaxed on my wedding night. But Teela was not so lucky.'

Darrel looked at the other girl. She was blushing, her pretty eyes sliding from his. He took her hand and kissed it, seeing her soften towards him. 'Maybe you could tell me about it, Teela,' he suggested softly. 'What happened on *your* wedding night?'

'My husban was ... rough wit me. He came straight into me, and it hurt. Since ten I ...'

'She cannot bear him to come near her,' Mitsi broke in. 'Dat is why I wanted her to come to a man who know how to make love to a woman. I want her to know what it can be like.'

'I see.' Darrel regarded Teela gravely. 'Do you trust me?'

She looked at him with frightened eyes. 'I don't know ...'

'It is hard for her to trust any man,' Mitsi explained.

'Then what she needs is to relax.' Darrel rose and fetched two cocktails, giving one to each girl. While they sipped them he was thinking about how best to approach the problem. His mind worked automatically, scanning through his options. At last he took Mitsi to one side and, speaking softly to her at the other side of the room, explained his plan. 'I should like your sister to see how a woman may be pleasured,' he began. 'Will you let me make love to you first, while she watches?'

Mitsi giggled. 'I don't know if my husband will like dat.'

'Does he have to know?' She shook her head. 'Then, if you care for your sister's happiness, you will do as I ask. You see, Mitsi, so far she associates sex only with pain, not with pleasure. She needs to know that you enjoy it, before she can relax enough to enjoy it herself. Not just to know it intellectually, but to see you enjoying it. Does that make sense to you?'

'Yes, I tink so.'

She went back and spoke to her sister in their own language. There was a brief exchange, with much frowning and questioning, but at last Mitsi said, 'She will agree. Already she is feeling better, I tink.'

'That's the effect of the cocktail,' Darrel smiled. He kissed her briefly, but then realized that he had been so absorbed in considering Teela's little problem that he had completely forgotten his own. His heart sank when he realized that he had just undertaken to service not just one woman but two, in succession. And so far his cock had shown no sign of life. What if it let him down again, even more spectacularly than last time? He began to panic.

'I think I shall have a drink too,' he announced, trying to sound casual. He found a can of Rubyfruit Reveille – the only one – and, praying that it would do the trick, glugged it down.

His panic subsided, but he had no way of knowing

whether it had worked or not. Only time would tell. He began to ease off Mitsi's loose top, laying bare her thin brown shoulders. She wore no bra and her delicate little breasts were attractively shaped with nipples like hazel-nuts. He brushed them with his fingertips and she gave another of her giggles, echoed by Teela. Darrel smiled at her over her sister's shoulder. 'Maybe you'd like to undress me.'

'I can?' The girl's eyes widened with a mixture of curiosity and fear that he found alluring.

'Of course. Anything goes in this room. No need to feel inhibited.'

So while he slowly undressed her sister, Teela tentatively peeled his suit off from top to bottom, exposing more and more of his hard flesh to her inquisitive gaze. He guessed she had never seen another man naked before, let alone a foreigner. Their culture was very prudish and strict with its women. It was surprising they were let out alone in a foreign country at all. Still, that was their business, not his.

Teela was stroking the taut globes of his behind as he finally removed the last of Mitsi's clothing. He kissed her breasts and felt her shiver slightly, his hands caressing her narrow hips. Although his erection had not yet grown Darrel was aware of an encouraging heat in his groin and a heaviness in his balls. The alien look and feel of the girl's body was a turn-on to him, too. She was so compact and small-boned compared to the women he normally serviced. What would she feel like inside?

At the thought of sliding into Mitsi Darrel felt an unmistakable stirring in his prick and his self-confidence grew. He parted her labia and pressed his lips to her little slit. She was moist already, and smelt pleasingly of musk. He tasted her juicy channel and the flavour seemed more shellfish-like than he was used to. Nice, though. As he began to lick and suck in earnest she started to make excited squeaking noises, like a mouse, and her sister began to stroke his buttocks more firmly. He could tell she was growing excited too.

The tiny clitoral button at the top of Mitsi's vulva was beginning to swell and he knew she was almost ready for him to penetrate her. He could feel Teela's fingers growing bolder, wanting to explore, and she started to stroke his naked thigh. Soon she would discover that his prick was still flaccid. A flash of anxiety returned, but then Darrel felt another stirring, this time more definite, and his erection grew to half-mast. By the time her questing fingers dared to touch his shaft it was fairly hard and, at the touch of her cool hands, suddenly increased its dimensions.

'Oh!' she squealed in delight. 'You have big one!'

Her praise was all that was needed to complete the process. Swelling with pride, his penis attained its full proportions in a matter of seconds and he knelt over Mitsi, straddling her thin thighs. She was now writhing and sighing loudly, her pelvis bucking and her breasts taut to bursting. Darrel reached up and squeezed them, then positioned his glans at the entrance to her cunny. Her pussy lips caressed him with evident delight.

'Oh, you are going into her,' Teela whispered in an almost reverent tone.

'Yes.' Darrel fixed his eyes on her and then brought her face close to his, to be kissed. His hands played briefly with her breasts. They were slightly larger, and a bit more pendulous, than her sister's. She closed her eyes and he knew she was trying to accustom herself to the strange sensations and emotions she was experiencing. This time, he knew how she felt. His own experience with Franca had opened his eyes to what it was like to feel real sexual pleasure.

Mitsi seemed to have no difficulty in responding to a man who was not her husband. Her naturally sensual nature seemed to be carrying her through. Darrel was so joyfully relieved at being able to perform that he thrust into her more vigorously than he'd intended and was afraid he had hurt her tight little vagina. He froze, trying to quash the urge to push in further.

But she seemed to love it. 'Mmm!' she murmured ecstatically, rotating her pelvis to maintain contact between the base of his shaft and her pulsating clitoris. He thrust again and again with increasing force and speed, each time eliciting a sigh or murmur of delight.

As he rammed his cock home, Darrel had to remind himself that his main task was to pleasure her sister. It would be all too easy to concentrate on Mitsi and make Teela feel left out. With an effort of will he drew the other girl into his arms and began to kiss her gently, fondling her ripe little breasts all the while. She was soon moaning too. It wasn't long before each sister was responding individually to him, each apparently oblivious of the other, each caught up in a voluptuous world of her own.

Soon he felt the tell-tale ripples caressing his cock in rhythmic clinches as Mitsi's pussy convulsed in orgasm. He saw her eyelids flutter and heard her moan with bliss as she gave herself up to the all-engrossing climax. At the same time he felt Teela kissing his neck with wild abandon and making little animal noises that sent tingles down his spine.

'Now me!' he heard her murmur, just behind his ear. 'My turn now!'

Darrel pulled out of her sister and found, to his relief, that his prick was still hard. Giggling, Teela came to sit on his lap, facing him, and he began kissing her deeply while his fingers toyed with her protruding nipples, pulling and pinching them until they felt like little rubber bullets. She squirmed on him like an impatient child and he could feel her open labia making wet marks on his thighs. While Mitsi withdrew into a dozy heap at the pillow end of the bed, Teela was evidently keen to take her place and as soon as possible.

After a minimum of foreplay Darrel lifted her under the arms – she was light enough to be easily manoeuvred – and carefully positioned her pussy over his genitals. Slowly he pulled her towards him until, like a docking spacecraft, his erect member made contact with the hollow of her sex. She gasped as his glans nudged her entrance, then, after one last adjustment, began to push up into the dark, dank cave of her cunt.

'There now, that wasn't so bad, was it?' he murmured, encouragingly. 'Are you sitting comfortably?' She nodded, a beatific smile on her face. 'Then we'll begin.'

But she was so hot that Darrel hardly needed to do a thing. He was amazed at the way shy, inhibited – and allegedly frigid – Teela suddenly took command and began to ride his cock horse like an equestrian champion. She wriggled her taut little bum and squeezed him with her tight little quim for all she was worth. Up and down she bounced, enjoying the long, hard length of him without the slightest qualm and as he caressed her smooth back and kissed her jutting breasts she moaned continually with an almost musical humming noise.

Darrel was dimly aware that Mitsi was now watching them with amused interest from her cross-legged perch on the pillow. But she didn't interfere. This was Teela's moment, and she must be allowed to savour it all by herself. Realizing that he was little more than her plaything, Darrel allowed her free rein to use him any way she wished in the wild quest for orgasm. She pushed his head towards her breast and he obediently sucked at her nipple. She pulled his hand round to her arse and he willingly invaded her cleft with his finger. She fondled his balls and rubbed his silky hair into her breasts. She made him rub her swollen clitoris until she almost shrieked with the intolerable arousal this produced. And then, with a shattering force that clenched his prick over and over in a series of vice-like spasms, she finally came.

Screams and loud moans rent the air as Teela experienced her first vaginal climax, thrashing and jerking so violently that Darrel was afraid she was having some kind of fit. But when all the shouting was over and she collapsed in his arms there was a blissful smile on her face and she murmured, 'Tank you, Oh tank you!'

'My pleasure!'

'You did it!' Mitsi grinned, moving up the bed to give her sister a hug. 'You really did it!'

But she was looking at Darrel, her eyes shining with a kind of admiration. To say that he felt great was an understatement. He felt terrific! Whatever demon had possessed him during his unfortunate session with Lianne had been well and truly exorcized, he was sure of that.

The two grateful girls hugged and kissed him, then went for a joint shower. When they came out of the cubicle and dressed in their exotic robes they were reduced to a pair of shy Polurasian maidens again. It was a remarkable transformation. They even bowed in native fashion, bending at the knee. Then they backed out of the room as if they were in the presence of royalty.

Darrel found it poignant rather than amusing. For an hour or so they had met at some primal male-female level but now their cultural differences had reasserted themselves and a gulf had widened between them. Perhaps it was just as well. Teela had come to him wanting something profound but impersonal. She had got what she wanted, and he would be paid handsomely for it. Best to leave it there and not dwell upon it.

Even so, when his credits came up on screen Darrel felt oddly degraded. He could remember feeling something like that when he first came to the Plaza, before he was used to the job. But it had soon faded when he started to realize what perks his credits could buy and how much better off he was there than in the hostel. Now that adolescent uncertainty had been briefly reawakened, perhaps because the girls had seemed so young and naive themselves.

'Stop this!' he told himself, as he grabbed a restorative cocktail. Introspection was not for genies. They were supposed to get on with the job no matter what, and thinking about it too deeply was bound to get in the way of their performance. Was that what had gone wrong when he was with Lianne?

The screen buzzed and Darrel glanced at it with apprehension. He didn't feel ready for another client just yet.

But he had no choice. There was his next challenge coming down the walkway towards his room. She was mincing along on impossibly tall and thin heels, twirling a long string of beads with girlish affectation, and his heart sank at the sight of her. It looked as if the redoubtable Shona had kept her promise to recommend him personally to all her friends.

Chapter Four

'Hullo, I'm Norella, and I just love to be spanked!'

Darrel smiled through clenched teeth and did his best to ignore the revulsion that her coquettish eyeing of his crotch induced. She was slavering over him like a wild beast at the kill. He went to fetch her a cocktail, choosing one that had a sedative effect.

'Norella, would you like to try a Luscious Laze?'

She gave him a vampish look. 'I'd rather have a Sweet Scorcher, if you don't mind.'

Sighing, he handed her the stimulating aphrodisiac and watched her knock it back. This one would be hard to handle at the best of times but with that stuff inside her she would be dynamite. Although she must be in her eighties at least she had all the vigour of an over-sexed adolescent. Fake, of course. She must have had hormone implants that were badly tuned, giving her way too much libido.

'You know, you're even more gorgeous than Shona described,' she said, licking her lips. 'I can't wait to see how gorgeous you are under your suit, too.'

She came at him like some rampant dinosaur. Darrel even put up his hands to defend himself, then turned it into an embrace. She felt hot and rubbery in his arms and smelt of scented lard. Her breasts poked into his chest like cone-beacons and she ground the hard shield of her pubic mound against his thigh. Darrel knew he would have to pull out all his professional stops with this one or sink under the sheer weight of her indefatigable lust.

'Shall we move to the bed?' he suggested.

'I thought you'd never ask.'

She guffawed in a raucous, masculine way that made his neck-hairs tingle. Nevertheless he sank onto the bed with her and the mattress began its gentle, programmed vibration. Norella squealed with delight. 'Oh, I've always wanted to try one of these. Help me off with my clothes so I can lie on it naked and feel it thrilling me!'

Darrel pulled off her vulgarly-bright garments and exposed acres of tightly-stretched flesh with the unmistakable sheen of a major bio-plasty job. It would be a miracle if she could feel anything beneath that hide. That early skin-tech had often seared the nerve-ends.

Soon Norella was lying face down on the bed, looking like a beached whale. Darrel wondered just what she expected him to do to her. She was bouncing around on the vibrating bed like a kid on a simulator ride. But then she grinned over her shoulder at him and said, 'Smack me, will you? On the botty. Hard as you like.'

Taking a deep breath, Darrel obliged. His palm struck the drumskin-taut flesh of her right buttock like the crack of a whip, making his hand sting. He repeated the action with his other palm on her left buttock and she gave a gratified moan. Then he slapped both together, and saw her bum clench. 'More!' she demanded, throatily.

It wasn't difficult to vent his frustrations on her in a frenzied series of whacks that had her rolling around on the bumpy sea of the bed in transports of delight.

Was she going to come? he wondered. So far his cock had shown no sign of life and his old-fear returned: what if he could only get it up for women he found attractive? Since such clients were few and far between, his future as a super-stud seemed doomed. His only hope with this one was that she had a perverse sexual nature and might not need penetration to reach her climax.

But his hopes were dashed as she heaved herself up onto her knees, her great moons lifted high into the air exposing the ragged wisps of her pubic hair beneath the drooping, wrinkled labia. 'Now poke me with your big cock!' she demanded.

Darrel moved close and began to stroke his way down her buttocks towards her cunt. With luck she would accept a finger instead of his prick. His other hand moved up to fondle the solid slope of her left breast and its turgid nipple. She gave a long, breathy sigh as his finger found her wet, open chasm and plunged in. Her quim was smooth and tight inside, probably toned by an electronic exerciser, and he was soon able to slip a couple more fingers in. She squirmed and clenched on him as his thumb found her outsize clitoris and began a slow massage. Had she been born with that monster pleasure-knob, or was it another artificial creation? If so, it was probably the result of hormonal rather than surgical intervention.

All that speculation was not helping his erection. He thought of Franca and the amazingly good head she'd given him, then of the sexy twins, but it only induced wistful regret, hardly conducive to the job in hand. He thrust harder, faster and deeper into the gurgling Norella with his bunched fingers hoping to make her forget it wasn't his prick in there.

There was a quivering, followed by a seismic shuddering, and the woman climaxed thoroughly, her juices streaming over his hand and down his wrist. Darrel pulled at her nipple to prolong the sensations and only slipped his fingers out when the last spasms had subsided. Norella sank down like a deflated balloon onto the gently undulating bed, her body covered in a light sweat.

He continued to massage her back and buttocks as she lay there semi-conscious, breathing in regular, rasping gasps like a steam vent. Silently he prayed that the manual orgasm would satisfy her, but it wasn't long before she was chirpily awake again and with her eye on his flaccid penis.

'That was wonderful for Lady Lovefuck,' she said, coyly. 'But what about Lord Pokewell? I can see he's looking a bit sorry for himself, a tot left out.'

'Oh, you don't have to worry about him,' Darrel answered, breezily. 'He can look after himself.'

But it was the wrong thing to say. 'Oh, he shouldn't have to do that! Let me look after him. Maybe he'd like a nice cuddle between my boobies.'

She heaved herself up and began to fondle his prick. Darrel did his best to hide his despair, but he knew that there was no hope of him responding with a lusty erection to this ghastly woman. He felt anxious and humiliated, his cock a shrivelled apology for a penis, his job on the line. Now she was moving her head down there, evidently thinking she was about to do him a favour, but after the memory of Franca her fellatio would seem like a cruel mockery.

Nevertheless he felt powerless to prevent her taking his tool into her rapacious mouth and giving it a good licking. Norella squeezed her bosom together with his prick in her cleavage, but it felt shrivelled and vulnerable between the grotesquely large and solid breasts. He guessed they had more silicon in them than the Plaza computer. She was squashing his delicate organ mercilessly, evidently under the impression that it was turning him on, and at last Darrel could bear it no longer.

'Norella, darling, I think I need a little pick-me-up,' he suggested. 'How about you?'

'You mean another cocktail?'

'Mm. Just to get the old juices flowing.'

'Mine are flowing perfectly well, thank you,' she said, reprovingly. Her brown eyes were surveying him with mild suspicion as she pawed at his obstinately deflated member. 'What's the matter, can't you get it up?'

Darrel stared at her in horror. Never before had those fatal words been uttered within the four walls of Room 301. It sounded like the knell of doom. He shook his head and improvised hastily, 'No, I just need to relieve myself. I'm a bit thirsty too. Please excuse me.'

Hurriedly Darrel leapt from the bed and into the safety of his shower cubicle. He took a leak then sat on the shower seat while the toilet flushed, wondering what the hell to do next. His worst fears were being realized: he had become impotent with clients he found repulsive. He knew very well what it meant. It was a condition of his work-contract that he took on all comers, irrespective of their personal appearance and habits. Before it had never bothered him. The job had been just that, a job, one he could do without thinking, but his encounter with Franca had somehow changed all that. Bitterly he decided it was all her fault.

There was only one excuse he could think of giving Norella for his disappointing performance. He made a great show of retching and spitting into the toilet, let it flush, ran taps, coughed and spat again. When he emerged he did his best to give the impression that he was suffering from an attack of nausea. He staggered to the bed and fell down onto it, gasping.

'What's the matter, are you sick?' Norella asked anxiously.

He nodded and rasped out, 'I . . . think so!'

She shrank away from him. 'Well, I hope it's nothing catching!' Norella got up and hastily began to dress herself. 'I think I'd better go now. Just in case, you understand. I can't afford to be ill. I'm only covered for the first hundred thousand credits.'

Darrel watched in distaste as she scrambled into her clothes, keeping as far away from him as possible. Her brown eyes were rolling and her breath came in ragged pants. There was sweat on her brow and the scent of fear exuded from her pores. 'I'll tell them at the desk that you're not feeling good,' she muttered as she made her exit.

Although Darrel was relieved that he had managed to ward off any real trouble he knew it was only a temporary reprieve. Sooner or later he would have to face the fact that his powers were waning, and then it was only a matter of time before he was thrown out of the Plezure Plaza onto the streets. He had no idea what happened to genies who didn't make the grade. Jabez had hinted that the Alleys were full of ex-genies, now hooked on various illegal cocktails, but that could just be idle gossip. He wouldn't put it past the controllers to spread such rumours deliberately, just to keep them on their toes. Still, he had no wish to find out for sure.

A medic appeared in a couple of minutes, armed with a neat case of drugs and implements. Darrel was scanned, his temperature, pulse and blood pressure taken, and pronounced fit.

'Probably a contaminated cocktail,' the medic pronounced, dismissively. 'If you threw up the emetic must have kicked in and you got it out of your system.'

'The emetic?'

'Yes. All cocktails contain one, didn't you know? It's only activated if certain toxic ingredients are present. If the stuff's pure it has no effect.'

'Really?' Darrel stared at him in amazement. 'They think of everything, don't they?'

'Yeah. It works if you try and OD on the stuff, too. Meant to stop kids experimenting.'

'I see. Well, I had a lucky escape then.'

'Looks like you did.'

When the medic had left Darrel looked at the screen and saw he had accrued the usual number of credits. At least Norella must have felt reasonably satisfied, despite the sudden ending to her session. She'd probably make a return visit, though. The prospect filled him with dread. He'd got away with it this time, but there was no way he could evade discovery for long.

The more Darrel thought about it, the more he wanted to see Franca again. Somehow she seemed to hold the key to his present predicament. She'd hinted that she knew more than he did about the set-up at the Plaza. He had to get a few more answers out of her, and soon. His shift ended in two hours, when he would call a cab and go to her flat.

The genies were not exactly forbidden to leave the Plaza, but it was not encouraged. In practice, few had the desire to roam. There were plenty of opportunities for making good use of their free time, with a vast leisure complex on site, and if they wanted a change of atmosphere there were many themed restaurants to choose from. Darrel tended to stick to those close at hand where he could be sure of meeting up with his mates.

Now, getting his pass from the front desk, he felt strangely nervous. When Jabez saw him there and asked him where he was going he floundered, not having thought of an alibi. In the end he said he was visiting a relative, then regretted it when he saw his friend frown with suspicion. 'But I thought you were brought up in a hostel.'

'I was.' Darrel added, desperately, 'But apparently I have a cousin. He ... er, contacted the controllers and they said I could meet him. Don't know how he found me, though.'

His lie seemed to convince Jabez. 'Hey, that's great! Maybe he can tell you something about your parents.'

'I doubt it. Still, might be interesting.'

He sauntered off towards the waiting cab but his heart was thudding wildly. Why couldn't he have said he was going to see Franca? Jabez would have understood. He'd seen her on screen, knew she was a stunner. Yet Darrel had wanted to keep his visit secret.

Not that he knew she'd even be at home when he called. Darrel had shrunk from using the vidphone because it was situated in the lobby where everyone could see. He punched his destination into the car's keyboard and the route showed up highlighted on the dashboard map. Sinking back into his seat, Darrel heard the familiar whine as the engine kicked in and soon he was speeding along the highway towards Parkside.

Once the now-familiar tree-lined avenue came into view Darrel felt his pulse racing. For some reason he believed a lot was riding on him meeting up with Franca again. The car cruised along the Neo-Georgian façades until it found the right number, then drew to a halt and the door clicked open letting Darrel out into the cool night. He coughed, unaccustomed to the thick, smelly air after the filtered atmosphere of the Plaza, then walked up to the entrance.

Frowning, he surveyed the securidor. He pressed the visitor button and an iriscope scanned his eyes. He punched in Franca's name and then waited while the computer signalled his presence. Impatiently he tapped his nails against the door, hoping and praying she would be in. Just when he was fearing that the long wait meant no response, a 'go' light flashed on the panel and a subtle click indicated that the securidor had been deactivated to allow him access.

Quickly Darrel slipped through into the dim hallway, breathing more deeply once his nostrils sensed the conditioned air. He remembered that Franca's apartment was on the third floor as he stepped into the lift. Soon his gaze was being subjected to another reading as he stood on the thickly carpeted landing, then her door slid open and he was inside.

Franca was waiting to welcome him. She looked

stunning in a very tight turquoise outfit with a metallic sheen to it, and a low V-neck that displayed her curves to devastating effect. However, it was her face that drew Darrel's gaze. After Norella's plasticized hide and coarse features it was so refreshing to see the delicate, satiny bloom of natural skin. Her full lips curved into a smile and he was reminded of how they had felt when they closed over his yearning cock. Within the confines of his suit he felt that same organ rouse and stir.

'Darrel, this is a nice surprise!' she greeted him, coming forward to kiss his cheek. He scented the lemony musk that was issuing from her cleavage and his erection solidified. A wave of relief passed through him. So he wasn't all washed up as a lover after all!

'I needed to talk to you, Franca. Things have been going a bit awry . . .'

'Really?' He was both surprised and gratified by her tone of concern. 'Nothing too serious, I hope. Come through and tell me about it.'

He followed her delightfully swaying butt through to the sitting room, whose cool blues and greys had an instant calming effect. Sinking into a lounger he shrugged off his footwear and put his feet up with a sigh. 'I've been worried, I don't mind telling you. Never had the slightest trouble before. But twice now I've had erection problems with a client, both of them unattractive to me. No trouble with the attractive ones,' he added, with a grin.

'Hm.' Franca's expression was grave. She was sitting at his feet, looking up at him. In other circumstances he would have found this appealing, but there was an undercurrent of anxiety in her that was fuelling his own.

'I didn't anticipate this. Must be a reaction to the drug I gave you. But there's no way of knowing how long it will take to wear off, and in that time you could lose your job.'

'Don't!' he groaned. 'I tried feigning sickness but you can't fool the medics.'

'Of course not. No, the only hope is another drug, an antidote. Or at least something that will mask the symptoms until your natural receptivity is restored.'

Darrel frowned. 'Receptivity? That's an odd way of putting it.'

'Well, it's accurate. You receive the signals and act on them.'

'Signals? Oh, you mean from my clients. Telling me if they're getting off on what I'm doing to them.'

'That's only part of the story.' Franca got up and, shifting his legs, perched on the footstool. She leaned forward, her eyes intensely blue. 'Darrel, can I trust you?'

He held her gaze, unwavering. 'Absolutely!'

'Well, you remember we talked a little about what made you tick, sexually. I told you that it wasn't in your genes, but that you'd been conditioned?' He nodded. 'That wasn't strictly true. "Controlled" would be a better word. Your superiors aren't called "controllers" for nothing, you know.'

Darrel felt realization strike him like some half-remembered dream. 'God, what are you saying – that I'm some kind of robot?'

'Some people might think so. But only one area of your brain is being controlled. The part that deals with sexual activity.'

A cold dread filled his veins. When they'd first taken

him out of the hostel to the Plaza they had run some 'medical tests', including a brain scan. He recalled being strapped down on a trolley near a giant machine, then there was a gap in his memory. All he could remember after that was waking up in the Plaza sick bay with a rather pretty nurse in attendance.

'What have they done to me?' he asked in horror.

'It's not just you, it's all the so-called genies. Look, I'm really running a big risk here. No one, except those on the other side, has any idea that I know this stuff. I've probably said far too much already.'

Her eyes were dark pools of uncertainty. Darrel wanted to reassure her. He was scared too. Suddenly the world he knew was toppling. He reached for the warm comfort of her hand. 'It's okay, Franca, I won't betray you. I always knew those controllers were bastards. So I'm hardly likely to say anything to them, am I?'

She gave a rueful smile. 'I suppose not.'

'Okay, tell me. Are we talking cochlea implants?'

She shook her head. 'No. They tried them but decided they needed something more subtle. Think in terms of a printed circuit embedded in a skull cap . . .'

'. . . a skull cap!'

'Mm. Inserted subcutaneously.'

Darrel's mouth dropped open. 'Are you saying they've implanted a whole capful of printed circuit in my *skull*?'

'Under the skin, yes. And remote-controllable. So when you're with a client you can be given feedback all the time.'

Darrel felt himself becoming more and more distanced from what he'd come to think of as reality. 'How?'

'The cap contains sensors linked to your central

nervous system. It can look through your eyes, feel through your fingers. That's how it monitors the tiniest reflexes in your clients – dilation of pupils, skin resistance, that sort of thing – and feeds it back into your system. All this is at the subconscious level, you understand. So you're responding all the time to her responses.'

Light dawned. 'And that's what makes me such a great lover, eh?'

She shrugged. 'Who knows? The controllers don't have all the answers. And they have to monitor the process, anyway.'

'What do you mean?'

'Every time you're with a client they're watching what goes on, making sure the system works. It's still in the experimental stage, you see. All genies are guinea pigs.'

'But . . . oh shit! That means they already know about my little performance glitch.'

To his surprise, Franca broke into peals of laughter. 'Of course! And you've given them a real headache trying to work out what went wrong with their program! It will never occur to them that you might have been subjected to a little outside interference.'

'Those cocktails you gave me, right?'

'Right. I have a contact who can produce drugs to temporarily disable the electrodes, put you genies back in touch with your natural instincts. He thinks that one day everyone will have one of these cranial caps fitted at birth, so they can control people not just sexually but in other ways as well. When that happens we'll need people like him, who know how to reverse the process.'

Despairingly, Darrel put his head in his hands and closed his eyes. His fingers were pressed against his skull but he could detect nothing abnormal. Of course, he didn't know what a 'normal' skull was supposed to feel like. But he could remember having odd twinges from time to time, and sometimes his head felt very hot. Was that to do with this business, or was he just imagining it?

For that matter was Franca telling the truth, or was this all an elaborate practical joke? He didn't want to believe it could be anything more sinister. The pieces of the puzzle seemed to fit. The way they always took kids from hostels and subjected them to medicals before putting them to work. He thought about the Controllers who were rarely seen, only referred to, and the confidence with which they guaranteed client satisfaction. The way he always seemed to know instinctively what his female clients wanted him to do to their bodies.

Cool fingers were stroking his brow. He smiled ruefully at Franca, who was regarding him with tender concern. 'Sorry, I'm just finding this difficult to come to terms with.'

'Of course you are. It must be a shock. But I felt compelled to tell you. I do hope I haven't put you in any danger.'

'Danger?'

'Well, the Controllers . . . you know. But as far as I know they have no idea that I'm privy to their little game. Or that I have access to the antidote.'

'Does it take a while to wear off? Is that why I had difficulties?'

'I don't know. I'm not a chemist, I leave all that side of it to . . . to my contact.'

'Do you have any of the antidote now?'

'Probably. But . . .'

'Then can I have some?'

Franca's eyes met his with a knowing smile. 'Are you sure? The effect is unpredictable.'

'That's what I love about it, the unpredictability. Can you understand that, Franca? For years my life has run like clockwork, and all because I was being programmed. I never realized. I thought it was in my genes . . .'

'Same difference, surely?'

She was grinning cheekily at him, enjoying her ability to disconcert him. Darrel gathered her into his arms and pressed his mouth to hers. The smooth, warm lips yielded at once and they touched tongues. A streak of fiery lust flashed down his spine and into his groin, making his cock jerk upright. *No problem there*, he thought proudly as his tongue slid into her mouth and tasted the sweet saliva.

They kissed thoroughly, savouring each other, while their hands explored the physical contours beneath their clothes. Darrel badly wanted to fuck her. The last time he'd felt like that was when he was a teenager, his rampant libido leading him towards the girls' hostel and all that sweet young pussy. Desire coursed joyously through him, a powerful force that blotted out all non-erotic thoughts, making it feel good to be alive. He fumbled at Franca's clothes, undoing the fastenings, and at last was able to put his hands on her smooth, pneumatic breasts where the nipples were already huge and stiff.

'Wait!' She put a temporary hold on his wandering hands while she went to her cocktail cabinet and brought out a silver bottle that she handed to him. 'Drink this. I want to be sure that you experience everything fully this time.'

Eagerly he glugged down the fruity-tasting liquid. There was an instant hit, the blues and greys of the room no longer quiet as his eyes registered vivid colours. All his sensations were heightened. As he moved towards Franca the subtle blend of her perfume took on the strength and complexity of an exotic garden where jasmine, honeysuckle, roses and lilies ran riot. He touched her, and it was like caressing the velvet skin of a baby. He kissed her, and tasted a very old, luscious dessert wine.

'God, Franca, this is amazing!' he groaned, as she slid out of her clothes and removed his. Soon their nude bodies were touching everywhere and Darrel felt his skin glow with the contact, activating every nerve beneath the surface. Delicious sensations sped through his veins, fuelling his desire, and he went slowly onto his knees before her. First his lips caught the jutting berry of her nipple, then they kissed the rounded swell of her belly before settling on the twin lips of her pussy.

Franca stood astride him and his palms caressed the silken planes of her thighs while his mouth kissed her labia, his tongue probing between them until it found her clitoris. He licked it, root to tip, and felt rather than heard her sudden intake of breath. His prick was surging uncontrollably now and he could hardly contain the urge that was building up in him, blotting out everything else from his mind.

'Let's lie down!' he growled, tugging at her hands.

She obliged at once, drawing him over to the minksim rug then pulling him down beside her. The contrast between the sleek, glossy fur and her velvety skin only increased his arousal. He squeezed her breast, eliciting little pleasure-gasps from her, and began to probe deeper into her vulva with his tongue. The love-juice was running hot and sticky in there, signalling her readiness for him, and Darrel knew that he couldn't hold out much longer.

When he moved to penetrate her she clutched at his hips in eager anticipation, spreading her thighs and thrusting with her pelvis to guide him in. Once his glans had nudged its way through her entrance he was unable to resist the urge to thrust all the way in. The long, smooth slide into bliss was incredible. Darrel felt her welcoming walls enclose and gently squeeze his shaft, drawing him down towards her cervix.

For a few seconds he just lay wallowing in the sensual heart of her, relishing the warm, wet, cushioning luxury of it. Then the craving for friction became too strong and he slid his cock back to the entrance in order to thrust back into her, hard and strong, his knees cushioned by the soft fur. He exulted in his power, shafting her over and over with increasing speed until he was ramming it home with exhilarating rhythm.

And she was loving every second of it, no doubt about that. Her breasts were huge and firm, the nipples remaining hard as he periodically pinched them, sending her into ecstasies.

Darrel didn't want it to end, yet he was driving towards a climax with inexorable force. His balls, taut and heavy, were slapping against her thighs, while his prick slid back and forth more or less on auto, and all the while she was opening up to him more and more, her cunt undulating up and down his shaft, producing the most exquisite feelings. The tension built up inside his stomach and his mind was in abeyance as he rode the cresting wave of his bliss like a surf-champ. His whole body was flooding with hot, sweet rapture and all he was aware of was the glorious thudding repetition of his journey up and down that honey-laden quim. His cock was in total control and he was happy to remain in joyful surrender to its command.

Then, just a few seconds after his sensory overload reached critical, Darrel's flesh began tingling all over with supercharged energy. Somewhere a valve opened, releasing the pressure, and the first ecstatic spasms of his orgasm propelled him into near-oblivion. A concentrated stream cascaded out of him, bringing a profound and sensual relief to his soul as well as his body. It felt as if he'd somehow been in exile from the human race and now had been brought back in touch with his own humanity again.

The mind-blowing climax lasted unbelievably long and, while it was in full spate, Darrel was oblivious of everything but his own phallocentric universe. As the paroxysms started to fade, however, he realised that Franca was quietly moaning and writhing on the furry mat, her face flushed with erotic arousal. He reached out and stroked her breasts. She shuddered, her moans intensifying, and he saw the flush spreading over her chest as her cunt clutched at him over and over, finally expelling his cock altogether.

'I'm glad you came too,' he grinned, taking her into his arms as he lay beside her.

'Where have you been, lover boy?' she grinned back. 'That was my third!'

He laughed and hugged her close. A deep and lasting

fulfilment had taken hold of him, satisfaction of a kind he'd never felt in the clinical world of the Plezure Plaza. He felt utterly relaxed and at ease with himself.

But after he'd been lying there for a few minutes on the minksim rug, feeling his breathing and heart-rate slowly return to normal, his thoughts turned to what Franca had revealed and a sudden realization of what had been done to him was followed by a sense of outrage. He sat up, troubled, and Franca's beautiful eyes flicked open, staring up at him.

'What's the matter?' she asked, sensing his distress.

It was going to be hard to put his feelings into words.

Chapter Five

Darrel tried to marshal his thoughts. After the carefree bliss of their love-making it was painful to have to face stark realities once more, but the implications of what had happened to him just had to be explored. He frowned, trying to make sense of it all, but it was like grappling with some weird change of identity.

'God, Franca, if that's how it feels to make love naturally . . .'

'We're lucky. Not everyone has the potential for that level of sexual experience.'

'But don't you see, what they did to me and the other genies is a wicked crime! They've deprived us of the ability to receive pleasure. We can only give it, and then only to order. We're like stud-puppets, for God's sake, dancing to their damn tune!'

'You could put it like that. Now you understand why some of us want to counteract it, in however small a way.'

'Who's behind it – do you know?'

'It started when Kleinstadt was head of Mirac, around ten years ago. As Minister for Information, Recreation and Culture he was given unprecedented powers. Nobody realized the full implications of linking IT with those other fields. They thought it was just an administrative convenience. But it was all part of a very ingenious plan to control people when they were at their most vulnerable, indulging in pleasurable activities.'

Darrel nodded, back in reflective mode now. His body still felt good, but his mind was striving to make sense of it all and his anxiety level was rising. 'What else are they up to?'

'We're not sure. My contacts have been concentrating on the sexual field because it's such a powerful instinct. But there's some evidence to suggest that competitive sportsmen are being wired up in this way too. Governments know how powerfully people identify with national teams. In effect they can act out World War Three within a stadium and make sure they control who wins.'

'Extraordinary! I still find it hard to believe. But without actually having my skull opened up, I don't see how I'm going to get any real proof.'

Franca's expression grew thoughtful, her mouth pursed into a pretty shape that Darrel longed to kiss, but his mind was too preoccupied. He was starting to wonder what her motive was in putting him through this. How many other genies had she drugged, seduced and then shocked with such revelations? But he wanted to trust her. He decided that, for the time being at least, he would give her the benefit of the doubt.

After some hesitation she said, 'There is a way you can find out more, but it's very dangerous.'

'Tell me.'

'Okay. I told you there's a monitoring process. The controllers sit at their screens all day observing the genies at work. If you could get into one of their control rooms you could see it all for yourself.'

'They're security-protected, surely?'

'Naturally, but that's not the main problem. We have ways round that.'

'I don't see how you could beat the iriscopes.'

Franca gave a knowing smile and got up off the rug. She walked into the next room and soon came back with a small wooden box. Kneeling beside him she pressed some hidden catches and the lid swung open to reveal a small metal cylinder, code-sealed. She clicked on the numbers, unscrewed the lid and, very gingerly, extracted something on the tip of her forefinger. It was a tiny convex disc of what looked like transparent plastic.

'What on earth's that?'

'A contact lens. People used to wear them to correct their sight.'

'What, like spectacles?'

'Yes, but the technology was soon superseded by ophthalmic laser treatment, just as that surgery is now being overtaken by gene therapy. Anyway, although they were an improvement on clumsy old specs, these things were still a bit of a nuisance. They had to be kept moist and scrupulously clean. They were inserted in the morning and taken out at night. And they didn't suit everybody.'

'So? How will this help me get into the control room?'

Franca smiled. 'Traced onto this lens is an exact replica of the iris of the man we call The Fat Controller. Put them over your own iris and you'll fool the scope into thinking you're him.'

'Brilliant!'

'But that's only half the story. Even if you were to trick your way into the room you'd still have to find a place to hide. We have a plan of the room, made with an infrared camera, but it's rather old. They may have rearranged the furniture and fittings since then.'

'I'll take that chance.'

'Will you?'

Franca's gaze was deep and clear, like some high-altitude mountain pool reflecting a summer sky. Darrel thought he could happily drown in those depths. He nodded, and her fingers strayed to his cheek, caressing him softly. His guts churned at the thought that he might be prepared to die for her. Just might.

'I have to find out as much as I can. If everything you've told me is true, my life won't ever be the same again.'

She looked sad. 'I know. I thought long and hard before telling you, but I knew you were the kind of man we need.'

'We? You keep saying "we" . . .'

'I can't tell you any more now. You're safer not knowing. All you have to decide is whether you want to take this next step. It will have to be done between shifts. The Fat Controller takes a ten-minute break at fifteen hours, SDT. That's the only one in every twenty hours that coincides with one of yours. Once you're inside you have to stay there until his next break, an hour later.'

'That could be tricky.'

'I know. I can only help up to a point.' She went over to her computer and soon a diagram was scrolling out of the printer. Smiling ruefully she came towards him holding out the paper and the wooden box. 'This is the room plan. Here are the contact lenses. The rest is up to you.'

He took them both, sunk in thought. What she was

asking him to do could have unknown consequences. If he was caught, it didn't bear thinking about. Yet Darrel was aware that he had started on some kind of quest. He could no more go back than he could forget about what she had told him, what he had experienced. Since knowing Franca his consciousness had changed so radically that there was no other way for him to go but forward, into the unknown.

She put her arms around him and rested her head against his shoulder with a sigh. Darrel felt gutted. His life had been thrown into turmoil and he felt ill-equipped to deal with the mixed feelings that his relationship with Franca produced in him. If only things could be as simple as they'd seemed just ten minutes ago, when he'd been lost in a sensual paradise.

He left the flat soon afterwards, with Franca's whispered 'Good luck!' echoing in his ears all the way down to the street, where his cab was still waiting. On the way back to the Plaza he was puzzling out how to achieve his goal of spying on the Fat Controller without being missed from his room. Was there any way he could avoid having to service clients for an hour? Normally he would have two or three at that time of day. That seemed the least of the obstacles, but it was the only one he could get a handle on. The idea of actually being inside a control room just seemed too far-fetched to contemplate.

For three days he puzzled and fretted over the problem while he practised inserting the fiddly contact lenses. It was hard at first. They made his eyes water terribly until he got used to them. When he was able to look at himself in the mirror the effect was strange. Nothing you could quite describe, just a slight difference about the eyes that made his expression seem a shade sterner. Yet he began to wonder if all his efforts had been in vain, since he couldn't figure out how on earth he was going to put his disguise into practice.

Then, on the following afternoon, he had an extraordinary stroke of luck. At two there was a buzz at his door and when he opened it a robomaid stood there with cleaning tools and a mechanical voice informed him that his room was due for its monthly servicing. Darrel had been given a schedule and should have remembered, but the events of the past week had erased it from his mind.

The opportunity could not be missed: he might not get such a chance again. The servicing normally took an hour or so and involved a more thorough cleaning and inspection than the daily ten minutes. Darrel would be assigned no clients during that time, so it was the perfect opportunity for his mission. Somehow he had to figure out a way to prolong the process for the robot, to make it last until four. That would give him time to get into the control room and remain there until the next break.

Darrel thought quickly then, while the robot was disgorging its array of tools and cleaning materials, he quickly pulled the knob off one of the screen terminals, twisted the switch within until it came off in his hand, then replaced the knob. It wasn't much but it might delay things a little. Then he went into the shower cubicle, as if he needed a leak.

In desperation Darrel scanned the fittings, looking for something he might vandalize. His gaze was drawn to the ceiling fitment that housed both the light and the shower. It would be fairly easy to disable. He waited until the toilet performed its automatic flush then prised off the cover. Underneath there was the lighting element, coiled around the rose. He pulled at the thin tube and it came away in his hand, then he unscrewed the shower disc and removed it.

'No light, no shower, that should freak the mother-fucker out!' he murmured with a grim smile. Under cover of the toilet flush, he proceeded to throw all the parts down the waste chute. There was a sickening crunching noise that continued for a few seconds after the flushing had stopped, and Darrel held his breath. There was no telling what the latest generation of robots might have programmed into them. They grew more sophisticated by the month. Was this one subject to a 'search and find' command that amounted to human curiosity?

When he emerged, however, Darrel saw that the robomaid was going about its business in the usual orderly fashion of such creatures, fishing down the drapes from around the bed and putting them into the sack it would drag behind it down the corridor to the soiled linen chute. A lot of its brief involved fetching and carrying. Once it noticed the missing parts in the shower it would simply requisition new parts and summon a mechanic to fit them. The fault in the screen control might take longer to detect and it was not just a question of replacing the part. Darrel had made sure of that. The mechanic would have to tune the screen in again.

'Okay, Roberta, I'm off to put my feet up,' he informed it with a grin as the door slid open. 'Have a nice day!'

Instead of heading for the restroom Darrel walked in the opposite direction until he reached the recreation area, where he was soon engaged in an exhilarating game of virtual tennis. He reckoned he needed to burn off some of his excess adrenalin. Just before three he hurried back to his room. There was a sign on the door asking him to call at the front desk. He grinned. It looked as if it was all going according to plan.

'I'm sorry, but Room 301 is not yet ready for occupancy,' the female clerk told him. 'There are some technical faults. We hope to have them repaired by four.'

To allay any suspicion, Darrel pretended to be annoyed. 'What about my clients?' he snapped. 'Do I have to lose a whole hour's credits?'

She stared at him blandly. 'You will be credited at the standard rate.'

'But I normally earn above standard. Really, this is too bad. An hour should be ample time to service my room.'

Unused to being challenged in any way, the clerk fiddled nervously with the frayed edge of the screen housing that was integrated with her desk. Her brown eyes flared at him. 'I agree, but certain abnormalities were found. It can't be helped. I am sure you understand that your room must be in perfect order before you can return to it. Now you are free to enjoy your extra leisure time in any way you wish.'

Still grumbling, Darrel wandered off in the direction of the recreation area. Once there, however, he continued on down the corridor that led to the Health Suite and, beyond that, the controllers' offices. Slipping into the men's toilet he took out the box containing the contact lenses and was soon putting them in his eyes. There were few people around but once he was in the lounge area he hesitated. To be caught in the next corridor would be to invite questioning. Then he started as one of the doors opened and a large, fat man with folds of skin around his neck and a greasy moustache appeared. The Fat Controller! Darrel recognized him from Franca's description. If he was only just going for his break Darrel had had a lucky escape. He'd expected him to have vacated his room by now.

Cheered by the fact that fate seemed to be on his side, Darrel watched the man trundle off towards the lift that gave access to the upper floors where no genies were allowed. That was where the controllers had their living quarters. Once the Controller was in the lift and the familiar mechanical whine had begun, Darrel hurried towards his door. The iriscope was to the right, a probing lens that would look deep into his eyes and try to match his iris pattern to that of the Controller. If it failed to do so an alarm would sound.

Warily, Darrel pressed the entry button and the iriscope whirred into action. It subjected him to a long, cool gaze and then a mechanized voice intoned, 'Access granted.' The doors slid open and he crossed the threshold into the Control Room.

A quick glance confirmed that Franca's map was more or less accurate. The furniture was arranged round a huge computer console in the middle of the room facing a bank of screens on one wall. There were a couple of easy chairs, as well as the swivel stool that the Controller used, and a large dispenser fixed to a side wall. Maps and diagrams were pinned to screens and there was a stand dripping exotically engineered foliage which failed miserably to achieve the desired effect of making the place appear user-friendly.

Most importantly, however, the hiding-place Darrel

had singled out for himself was still there: a large walk-in store recessed into the wall. And he noticed, to his great relief, that the door was slightly open. He hurried over and slipped inside. The light was on and he could see that there were shelves groaning with boxes of disks, memory chips, computer repair kits and other spares. There was also a large desk in the corner on which a spare computer screen stood. If anyone poked their nose into the place he could hide behind it.

Darrel looked around for the light-button. It would be best if he were in darkness. That would give him vital seconds of advantage if he needed to hide. He plunged the store into darkness and squatted down with the door open just enough to give him an unimpeded view of the bank of screens. Then he waited. It seemed a long time, and he got cramp in his legs so he sat right down on the ground. The screens were on hold, the numbers of the rooms they showed displayed against a darkly flickering background.

He was disconcerted to see his own room number among them. Of course he'd realized that he must have been spied upon as soon as Franca had told him what they were up to, but it still came as a shock to see concrete proof of it. What would they have made of his embarrassing failure with Norella? Then it occurred to him that no one could watch that many screens simultaneously. There was a chance that the FC, as he now thought of him, had been focusing on some other room at the time. Just a chance.

The door to the room slid open without warning and the man himself entered, chewing noisily, with the remains of a bun in his hand. The distaste that Darrel had already conceived for him deepened. What kind of a man would do such a job? How could he justify snooping on other people's sexual activity? Did he get off on it, or was it just the credit he was after?

The FC sat down on his swivel stool with practised ease and flicked a switch. At once every screen above him flickered into active life. Only a small proportion of them showed empty rooms. The rest were full of real-life pornographic images. Darrel's eyes flicked automatically to the screen he'd identified as his, and saw the robomaid shampooing the carpet while a mechanic tinkered with the screen control. Suddenly the image went blank. The techno must have disconnected in order to carry out repairs.

Darrel's gaze scanned the extraordinary images filling the wall. Most were of couples but there were a few threesomes. After the initial shock he got used to seeing his fellow genies on the job, thrusting into clients from all directions, licking breasts and clitorises, fondling buttocks. Some were administering 'special services', whipping, binding or blindfolding their willing victims. It all amounted to a bizarre exposition of human sexuality in action.

His eyes switched to the bulky figure of the Controller as he cleaned his sticky fingers on a fibro-wipe, threw it into the bin, then hit one of the buttons on the console in front of him. The bank of screens immediately vanished, to be replaced by one giant-size view of a particular couple. Darrel smothered a gasp. He'd had no idea that the controllers were able to focus in on the action to that extent. The FC hit another button and the screen split into a ratio of two to one, the larger picture being that of the couple while a third of the screen was taken up with a neural map of the genie's skull. Darrel was horrified. He squinted through the crack and almost jumped out of his skin as the FC shifted his huge buttocks on the stool and a loud fart echoed across the room. The whiff that followed had Darrel pinching his nose and holding his breath.

When he recovered he saw that the camera had zoomed in even closer, revealing the action in minute detail. The FC was actually humming now, enjoying his work as his piggy eyes surveyed the erect nipple of the woman, shown in all its tumescent glory, its pink hue almost exactly matched by the tongue of the genie as it licked around the pimply areola with its sprinkling of fair hairs. Darrel could hear the woman's soft, appreciative moaning as she grew more aroused.

The camera panned, showing the side of the genie's face as his mouth moved down the taut slope of a curvaceous breast. Darrel stared at the profile of the man in shocked recognition: it was Zal! Somehow it seemed worse to be watching someone he knew, but he had no option. Embarrassed, he saw his friend clutch at a pair of the nicest tits he'd seen in a long time and as the camera widened its view he saw that the woman had an attractive face, too. She was blonde and green-eyed, with full sensual lips. Darrel couldn't help wondering why she had to resort to the Plezure Plaza for her gratification. Maybe she got off on the idea of impersonal sex with a paid gigolo. He'd known women like that.

Suddenly his attention was drawn to the cranial map where a string of connections had lit up in red, just like the route-finder on the dashboard of an autocab. Darrel realized that the highlighted pathways were constantly changing as Zal responded to the woman's arousal. The neural network was incomprehensible to him but presumably the FC knew what he was seeing. Darrel felt some grudging respect for the man's expertise.

The camera moved on down, showing Zal's lips at the bud-like navel of his client, who was writhing and moaning with accelerating passion. Now her mound was visible, covered with a curly mesh of fine golden hair that proclaimed her a natural blonde. Why didn't he get stunners like that? Darrel wondered sulkily. Then he thought of Franca and felt better. He saw Zal's fingers tease their way through the tight pubic curls then probe the tumid lips below, and felt a pang of envy.

Soon he was licking her pussy, the camera moving in so close that Darrel could see the slick film of love-juice mingled with saliva glistening on the edges of her labia. Zal withdrew his face for a moment and kissed her smooth, lean thighs, allowing both Darrel and the Controller to get a complete view of the woman's wide-open crotch. Her clitoris was very obvious. Swollen and scarlet-tipped, it jutted proud from the swollen profiles of her labia.

Suddenly Zal murmured something indistinguishable in her ear and then she grinned lazily, turning over onto her stomach. He nibbled at her earlobe while his hands alternately clutched and caressed the perfect globes of her buttocks. Darrel could see his penis now, and noted with some satisfaction that it was an inch or so shorter than his own, although probably about as thick. When Zal got up onto his knees the organ reared aggressively, eager to be delving into that invitingly luscious flesh.

The cranial map showed increased activity now, with the pathways lighting up in quick succession. Zal hoisted the woman up by the waist and her shapely behind stuck into the air at a provocative angle. For a moment Darrel thought Zal was going to enter her anus, but his fingers groped beneath to find the opening to her cunt and soon he was thrusting in with his cock, teasing her arsehole with his finger as he did so.

The woman was groaning now, reckless in her abandon and gyrating her pelvis in an attempt to increase the friction on her clitoris. Sensing her frustration, Zal reached below and began to rub her with one hand while he tugged at her straining breasts with the other. Her groans grew deeper, more intense, as he began to thrust in and out, finding his rhythm. His expression was intense, concentrated. The activity on the surface of his skull was multiplied now, lightning flashes streaking over it in all directions. If that was a non-bio electrical circuit there'd be blown fuses by now, Darrel thought.

But the sight of so much lascivious activity was having an effect on him, too. He could feel his erection reaching its height, pushing against the constricting material of his suit, and he opened his fly to ease it. Soon the glans was poking out like an inquisitive animal, impossible to ignore. Darrel pulled the rest of his cock out and enclosed the shaft in his hand, relishing the warm, sensual reassurance that instantly flooded through him. He began to move the skin of his shaft up and down, working it very slowly and delicately between his finger and thumb.

On screen, the couple were approaching their climax and the woman in particular seemed very far gone. Her head was thrust right back, with her golden hair tumbling wildly over her creamy shoulders like the mane of a palomino. Darrel noticed the elegant curve of her neck and the sinuous way she was moving her hips below her arched back. She was lithe and lovely, uninhibited too. Although he still envied Zal, he could imagine giving the guy a congratulatory slap on the back. At least his friend was putting on a good show for him, albeit unwittingly, making his hour in the store cupboard pass very pleasantly indeed.

Darrel gave a soft, involuntary moan as the feelings inside him escalated. He stopped abruptly, afraid he'd been overheard, but the cries that were coming from the screen must have drowned out his feeble squeak because the FC remained staring ahead, his fat arse firmly squatting on the stool.

The illuminated map of Zal's skull seemed to have reached critical, with practically every connection flashing red. The FC seemed to be taking notes on a palmtop. He pressed a button and a printer spewed out a hard copy of the neural map on the screen. Seeing him distracted by his work, Darrel put more energy into his masturbation. It was becoming impossible not to. The woman was clearly on the verge of orgasm, screaming and thrashing as her body found the suspense unbearable. Then Zal pushed further into her arse with his finger, slammed right into her with his cock and bit into her left shoulder. The combination of stimuli was enough to trigger her into a climax and she threw her head back even further, rolling her eyes and half-screaming, half-sobbing as she repeated over and over, 'Oh my God! Oh my God!'

Darrel had no idea if Zal was similarly moved. His

eyes grew dim as his own efforts were about to bear fruit, his prick throbbing with intensely sweet sensations. Realizing that if he came through the slit in the door he might just attract attention, when the first rush of his orgasm began he turned around and soon he was in the throes of a real blinder, feeling the hot jets pulse out of him with satisfying force and incidentally spraying the contents of the store with a light film of spunk.

As his legs buckled under him Darrel chuckled, *sotto voce*, 'Swab that, Robomaid!'

He fell onto his knees, facing the door. Through the slit he could see the FC still intent on his work, and above him the giant image of Zal and his client in an exhausted embrace was still glowing. But the synapses in Zal's cranium had stopped firing and all over the map blue ripples licked gently, like small flames, a visual metaphor for the afterglow.

The Fat Controller switched to another camera, another room, and Darrel saw an Afrasian servicing a pudgy redhead. He was finger-fucking her and his map glowed a dull, sluggish red as if he was only marginally involved in his work. His mind was probably elsewhere, but his reflexes were functioning all the same, making his finger move faster or slower as his client's libido rose or fell. The FC made a few notes on his palmtop then flicked on through a series of other screens.

He came to rest on an image of a woman who was riding her genie with expert control, her graceful body rising and falling in a sensual rhythm. At first Darrel only had a view of her back from the waist down as the camera focused on the contorted face of the man. But then it panned, and the rest of her was visible. Darrel gave a loud gasp and was unable to stop himself from falling forward against the door. He froze immediately, scared to death that the FC had heard him, but the man continued his work, leaving Darrel struggling to contain his shock.

For the client who was taking her pleasure in Room 58 with such obvious relish was Franca.

Chapter Six

The shock of discovering that Franca had engaged the services of another genie almost caused Darrel's downfall. He pushed the door of the store-cupboard half open and stared in horror at her beautiful nude body as her anonymous lover thrust into her with lusty strokes, the look of ecstasy on her face compounding Darrel's jealousy. He only realized what danger he was in when the Controller slid off his stool and turned around. Then, with a sudden intake of breath, Darrel lunged back into the dark recess and made for the desk in the corner.

By the time the FC switched on the light Darrel was well concealed, but his heart was thudding like a dynamo and his mouth was arid. He peered between the legs of the desk and saw the man's big feet standing in front of one of the shelves. What if he saw the mess that Darrel had sprayed? But he didn't seem to notice anything untoward. He picked something up – Darrel couldn't see what – and after switching off the light he closed the door completely and returned to his desk.

Darrel waited in the darkness, his fear of the man not half so acute as the bitter jealousy in his heart. He felt betrayed by Franca, and now his suspicions returned in force. Just what was her game? She must have known he might spy her on the screen if she came to the Plaza.

Was that what she wanted, to humiliate him? Anger bubbled up along with the other emotions, and for a few seconds he fantasized about what he'd like to do to her. Yet it was difficult to believe that she could be that callous. Not after the intimate experiences they'd shared.

Hadn't she said that she was running a big risk, telling him about the way Mirac used the Plezure Plaza as a lab with human lab rats? Maybe she'd been lying, drawing him into this situation just to set him up. What if she was on the side of the Controllers, acting as some kind of decoy, or double agent? His blood chilled. Had he got himself into a trap?

Darrel pressed the button on his chronograph: almost time for the second break. But now the door was closed and he couldn't see what the FC was up to. He pressed his ear to the steel door hoping that, when the time came, he would be able to open it. Were these things designed to be opened from the inside? Almost certainly not, and if he was found he had no plausible excuse for his presence there.

There was a scrape of heels on the hard floor and then a few clicking sounds followed by the shuffling of papers. It sounded as if the Controller was preparing to leave. Darrel held his breath as footsteps approached. The door was opened a few inches and a hand came inside. For a few terrifying seconds Darrel was sure the Controller was going to switch on the light, but he merely tossed something onto the shelf and carelessly pulled the door to. Then his feet could be heard moving towards the exit.

Once he was sure the man had left, Darrel put the light on. He saw, to his relief, that the door had been left a centimetre ajar. Pulling it back he entered the control room where the screens were on idle, showing the room numbers. Resisting the temptation to access Room 58 again, he walked towards the main door and let himself out. Warily he emerged into the corridor, but there was no sign of the Fat Controller. Mindful that he was not supposed to be in that part of the Plaza at all, Darrel remained on his guard as he slipped along to the end and then headed for the recreation area, walking as slowly and calmly as he could.

When he was back in safe territory the tension in him lifted, but the memory of Franca's perfidy still rankled in him like a sour cocktail. He was tempted to go straight to Room 58 and see if she was still there. What would she say if he caught her *in flagrante delicto*? But it was strictly against the rules to visit another genie's room. They were supposed to meet only in the social areas. He would be severely punished and now he knew what sort of organization was behind the Plaza he was afraid of putting a foot wrong.

'Darrel?'

He swung round at the sound of the female voice. For one heart-stopping moment he thought it was Franca, but it was only the desk clerk. She'd seen him from reception and come to tell him that his room was now ready. 'You should find everything in perfect order,' she informed him, smugly. 'But if you have any cause for complaint just buzz and we'll send a mechanic immediately.'

'Thank you. You're so kind!'

His ironic bow was lost on her. She just nodded and went back to her desk while he fought the savage instincts raging in his breast and decided to return quietly to his room. But there was a reckoning to be made with Franca and, sooner or later, it would be done.

Room 301 was perfectly restored to its former state. Darrel sank into his relaxer and tried to get back to normal too, but he kept brooding on Franca and her revelations. Why did she have to reveal the truth to him about the Plezure Plaza and its controlled genies? Now things could never be as they were before. The focus of his anger see-sawed between her and the Fat Controller. The thought of him sitting there watching everything that went on, like an obscene spider in an electronic web, made Darrel want to puke.

The prospect of seeing another client was unnerving him too, since his little potency problem remained unresolved. The screen buzzed and, wearily, he turned his gaze towards the figure walking towards his room. She looked young, dark and slightly-built, evidently not another of Shona's disgusting cronies. When she entered he saw that she was quite a beauty, with glossy brown hair, lustrous dark eyes and a full-lipped mouth. Although her figure was slight she had large, well-shaped breasts and Darrel was relieved to find that he desired her. At least while he was with this girl he could forget Franca for an hour or so. His smile was genuine as he went into his greeting routine. 'Good afternoon, Madam. Would you care for a cocktail?'

'No!' she snapped, adding more softly, 'Thank you.'

She sank into the relaxer that Darrel had just vacated. Her manner was nervous and he wondered why she'd refused a mood-bender so emphatically, since she didn't seem to be in a particularly good mood right now. She gazed aimlessly at the surrounding screens that were displaying scenes of varied debauchery in exotic locations. His eye was caught by an image of two dusky, full-breasted maidens paying lip-service to their handsome captive, and Darrel found his libido increasing. But even more he craved the attention of this gorgeous but distant client, wanting her sultry brown eyes to focus on his face.

He decided on a direct approach. 'I'm Darrel, by the way. What's your name?'

Disappointingly, she replied without looking at him. 'Annis.'

'Well, Annis, I think we might make ourselves a bit more comfortable, don't you?'

A look of urgency seized her and she grew agitated, fingers working restlessly in her lap. When she glanced at him her mind was obviously elsewhere. Darrel found himself wanting to claim all of her, mind and body. He wanted to make love to her badly, longed to see her look of unease melt into one of joyful abandon. But just what was bugging the girl?

Suddenly she rose from the chair and threw herself onto the bed, her arms flung above her head. 'Make love to me, quickly!' she demanded. 'Strip me and take me, just as if we were both dying for it. Make it look real.'

Darrel frowned, aware of some subtext that he couldn't interpret. But he chose to assume that she was living out some fantasy and began to strip off his suit. Her facial expression showed that Annis was still in her enclosed, agitated world, but her body was limp and complaint. She took no notice of his burgeoning erection but continued to lie looking at the drapes while the bed rocked and hummed. Convinced that she must be lost in some erotic world of her own making, Darrel began to take off her clothes.

Her feet were tiny, but he noticed that the soles were callused. When he exposed her legs he saw that there was a huge scar down her inner right thigh as if she had been slashed with a knife. He glanced at her face but she remained staring upward, indifferent. Her pubic hair made a thick, black mat at the base of her concave stomach while above her jutting ribs the voluptuous breasts reared in stark contrast to the rest of her, heavily rounded with huge flat brown nipples. Following a powerful urge, Darrel lifted them both with his cupped hands, his tongue moving irresistibly towards the already cresting peaks. He took her right nipple between his lips and sucked until it puckered, firming up into a hard knob of flesh.

She moaned as if in pain, but would not look at him. His hands moved down her sides, felt the bony hips and the hollow bowl of her pelvis. Suddenly she glanced at him, her eyes still anxious. 'Now!' she murmured, urgently. 'Do it now!'

He knelt between her contrasting thighs, the one so smooth, the other hideously disfigured. His prong was pointing at her pink slit but he decided it was best to check the condition of her pussy before entering. His fingers probed between the tight labia and she felt dry, unprepared. His mouth bent down, ready to perform cunnilingus, but again he heard her voice exhorting him, 'No, just come straight in!'

It must be hurting her, he thought, as he thrust in with his hardened prick and found resistance all the way.

His professional pride was affronted at having to enter her so roughly, but since it was the way she wanted it he must oblige. Although she winced a couple of times Annis made no attempt to slow or stop him and, once inside, he felt her start to moisten. But she showed no sign of enjoying the experience and he wondered just what her game was.

'Is this all right?' he whispered.

'Yes!' she gasped, drawing him close so that her mouth could reach his ear. 'Just go on fucking me,' she murmured. 'This display is for the camera. It was the only way we could get a message to you.'

'A message?'

'Ssh! Don't talk, just listen. And, whatever you do, don't show any surprise. Smile, if you like.' She added, ironically, 'As if I was whispering sweet nothings.'

Darrel faltered in his rhythm only for a moment. Annis groaned, but when he resumed his deep thrusting she seemed more responsive, moving her hips in time with his. 'The message is from Franca,' she went on. He was not surprised to hear that. 'She needs to debrief you at her place, tonight. Did you get into the control room?'

'Yes.'

'Good. We need people like you.'

'Who's "we"?'

But she was no more forthcoming than Franca had been. 'Just a group of us who are trying to resist the conditioning.'

Suddenly Annis seemed to catch fire. Her eyes darkened and she began to thrust urgently, clasping his erection with her pussy. She threw back her head and gasped, her breasts huge and ripe beneath his hands. He caressed them and pinched the nipples softly until she came, arching into the undulating bed, her face and chest glistening with perspiration. He could feel her still throbbing inside as she subsided limply and he withdrew at once, taking her in his arms. While he lay beside her damp, pulsating body his mind was in a whirl. Somehow he seemed to have been drawn into this 'group' that included Franca and Annis – seduced into it, to be more accurate. But what, exactly, was he letting himself in for? Doubt and suspicion assailed him, but it seemed unfair to question Annis in her present state.

'What time does Franca want to see me?' he whispered. The memory of her fickleness still rankled with him, but now he was inclined to believe that she'd had some ulterior motive in coming to the Plaza, like Annis.

'Whenever you can get away.'

'I'm on for another four hours. I'll try to come after that. I just hope they won't be too suspicious.'

Her eyes flickered and he recognized the naked fear in them. 'We all take risks. You don't know how dangerous it is just for me to be here.'

Darrel had already sensed that she had put herself in jeopardy by coming to see him, but he wasn't going to pry. If she wanted to tell him she would do so in her own time. Yet the girl fascinated him. She had been through something horrific, he was sure of that. Not just because of the scar on her thigh but the way she had steeled herself to let him make love to her. He wanted to do it again, right now, to awaken her with slow tenderness instead of taking her with brutal haste the way she had insisted on before. Something told him that her orgasm had been as much of a surprise to her as it had been to him, and he was thoroughly intrigued. She was obviously one hell of a complicated woman.

Annis sat up, rubbing her eyes, and reached for her clothes. 'I have to go now,' she murmured, pulling on her top.

'Won't you take a shower?'

She shook her head vehemently, continuing in a whisper, 'No, I've been here too long already. But look as if you're still acting professional. Do whatever you normally do at the end of a session.'

He helped her off the bed and retrieved the rest of her clothes. When she was dressed he gave her one of the complimentary combs and she pulled it through her tangled hair, restoring its glossy smoothness. She gave him a smile and, this time, it didn't seem forced. 'Thank you, Darrel,' she said aloud. 'That was very nice.'

'See you again, perhaps?'

'Perhaps.'

Annis grinned coquettishly at him, then turned to the door. He stared regretfully at her retreating rump, realizing he hadn't had a chance to examine it closely. Their encounter seemed unfinished, and Darrel was filled with a deep yearning to see her again, under different circumstances and in another context. She intrigued him, no doubt about that.

The rest of the afternoon was quiet, with only two more clients. They were both Shona types, although neither admitted to knowing her. Darrel managed to get away with giving one of them a hand job and the other a tonguing, but it was hard to disguise his cock's lack of enthusiasm. One of the women commented, 'Are we having an off day, dear? Or should that be a day off?'

She cackled hilariously at her own wit while Darrel hoped she'd forget that what she was laughing about was no laughing matter.

He clocked off at six and sauntered along to the front desk where the same girl was on duty. She regarded him suspiciously but he gave her a broad grin, saying casually, 'I'd like a pass, please.'

'Visiting your cousin *again*?' she said, eyebrows raised. 'Not female by any chance, is she?'

'Not by any chance! He's six-foot-four and works in Maintenance.'

'Can't think what people do when they visit each other,' the girl said, reaching for a pass card. 'I mean, you can chat on the vidphone if you want to see someone.'

'We play chess,' Darrel said, off the top of his head again.

'You can do that over the vidphone too.'

'Ah, but it's not the same. The clink of the ancient wooden pieces, the smell of the board, the minutes just ticking by. You have no idea, my dear!'

She regarded him with renewed suspicion but handed him his pass anyway. He exited with a cheery wave. Bravado was best in such situations, he concluded. He dialled a cab and one arrived within seconds. After punching in his destination he was whisked smoothly away towards Parkside.

Apprehension seized Darrel as he waited to be admitted to Franca's apartment. His involvement with her was beginning to take on a nightmarish repetitive quality, weird as *déjà vu*. He was also aware that each new meeting increased the danger of discovery, since he was now sure he must be under suspicion at the Plaza.

What if the FC had known he was spying on him in the control room? What if they had sensors so sensitive that they knew his every movement, his whereabouts at any given moment?

'Stop, this is sheer paranoia!' he muttered as Franca's door slid open, giving him access.

She seemed to be expecting him. Dressed in a stunning black velvet robe that made her skin look pure and creamy, she kissed his cheek as he entered and drew him with gentle fingers towards her sitting-room sofa. Darrel surveyed her grave, lovely face, aware that now he was comparing her with Annis. Franca was the more classically beautiful, her features in perfect symmetry, but there was something more appealing about the other woman's sultry charm. Or was it just that she seemed more elusive, less accessible to him?

'So you made it into the control room,' Franca smiled. 'Well done! What did you see in there?'

The memory of how shocked he had been to see her on the screen for Room 58 returned in full force, filling him with sudden jealousy. 'I saw you,' he said, his voice icy.

Her face fell. 'I see.'

'What were you doing there?' he growled, his heartbeat quickening. 'No, don't answer that. I *saw* what you were doing.'

She turned her big, beautiful eyes on him. 'I was rather hoping that wouldn't happen. I didn't know exactly when you would be in the control room, or what you would see. But if you saw me, then I can understand why you're upset.'

'Can you?'

Franca nodded. 'I can explain why I was there. The question is, would you believe me?'

'Try me!'

She sat down at his feet, like a supplicant. Her auburn hair, with its golden glints, fell luxuriantly to her shoulders and a part of Darrel longed to reach out and stroke it. But his cold anger prevented him.

Franca clutched her knees to her chest and spoke quietly, staring at the carpet. 'I know it must have looked as if I was there to enjoy myself sexually, but I can assure you I wasn't. My session was all in the name of duty. Just as Annis was doing her duty to the group when she visited you.'

Darrel's anger was compounded. How dare she say that about Annis! Yet something about her tone rang true. She went on, 'It's the only way we can glean vital information. For me it was easy. No one at the Plaza knows me as anything but a client. The genie I was with is someone I've been working with for some time, because he's friendly with someone important to us. Don't ask me to say any more right now.'

'I don't know what to say. Or what to think.'

She knelt up and placed his arms around her neck, looking at him with imploring eyes. 'You said you trusted me, Darrel, as I trust you. Now will you tell me everything you saw when you were in the control room?'

There seemed no reason not to tell her. Although Darrel didn't quite believe her story he realised that she was entitled to some secrets. The thought that one of his fellow genies might be involved with the group was intriguing, but he accepted that she couldn't say any more. Besides, now that his earlier distrust had gone his old desire for her was starting to return. She looked so gorgeous in black velvet. He hoped that if he told her as much as he could she might show her gratitude in time-honoured fashion.

As he related everything he could remember Darrel saw her warming to him. She seemed particularly pleased by the news that the FC recorded everything on a palm-top. 'Computers are not inviolate to our agents,' she smiled. 'We have some of the finest digital engineers in the business working for us. They have ways of hacking that are completely undetectable providing they know where the machines are situated and what models they are dealing with. Can you remember anything about the one he used?'

Darrel screwed up his face as he struggled to recall what he'd seen on the grey box. A lion logo sprang to mind. 'I think it was a Leo – yes, I'm pretty sure of that.'

'Good. That's incredibly useful to us, you've done well. Annis will be pleased . . .'

'Tell me more about her,' Darrel pleaded. 'She seemed so scared when she came to me.'

'That's not surprising when you know her history. Annis was once a genie, an ALF. She lived at the Plaza like you, but when she started to question the system they tried to alter her circuitry so they could control her better. She escaped, and one of the guards slashed at her leg, but we rescued her. She was crippled for months, and we nursed her in a safe place.'

'*Guards?*'

'Yes, didn't you know? All the staff at the Plaza are trained in martial arts. If any genie tries to leave without a pass they're forcibly prevented. So don't try anything foolish, will you?'

'But what happened to Annis? Why didn't they recognize her when she went back?'

'She was scared they would, but she's had extensive bioplasty by our own surgeon.'

Darrel gasped. It was hard to believe such a lovely face could be a complete fake.

Franca continued, 'She visited you not just to deliver my message but to test whether they would recognize her. That's why she was so scared. But none of the staff knew who she was. Now she can go back from time to time, doing the work that I do.'

'Which is?'

Franca sighed, resting her head on his knees. Her hair flowed down like liquid copper and Darrel couldn't resist fingering a lock of it. It caressed his hand coolly while she spoke. 'It's my job to gain the confidence of key genies. Some of them are unwitting helpers. Others, like yourself, are treated openly as allies, given explicit information.'

'And used as spies?' Darrel uttered the word with distaste. He felt abused. He'd thought he was doing Franca a personal favour, but now he realized he was just a tool of her organization and the way she had seduced him began to seem like a calculated ploy.

'We prefer the word "agents" but I can understand your suspicion. You don't have to do anything you don't want to, you know. If you wish you can go back to the Plaza and never see or hear from me, or Annis, ever again.'

To his surprise, the prospect dismayed him. Now that

he was being given the chance to go back to square one, to forget about this mysterious group of rebels, he found he didn't want to. Somehow he had been drawn by these two fascinating women into a world that was as compelling as it was dangerous and he didn't see how he could back out now.

'I should hate that,' he murmured.

'Good.'

She nestled against him, with feline sensuality, and Darrel felt his libido jolt into action. So what if she and Annis were using him, pleasuring him to gain his co-operation? Anything was better than living as some kind of controlled robot, acting as a paid gigolo for ugly rich bitches who couldn't get their jollies any other way.

Darrel lifted a great, heavy swathe of her hair and covered his face with it, revelling in the cool silkiness. Franca leaned forward and put her arms around him, her breasts heavy against his chest, then lifted her face. His mouth bore down ruthlessly on hers, his tongue forcing her lips apart, and he savoured her sweet helplessness as he filled her mouth, his hands groping within the neckline of her robe to find the deep fleshiness of her cleavage.

His cock wanted to be in there, to be cradled in that safe haven. He fumbled with his own clothes for a few seconds but Franca soon realized what he was trying to do and, to his relief, gave him a helping hand. Soon his erect organ was thrusting into the open, wild and free, searching for some contact, some friction. To his amazement, she seemed to know exactly what he wanted. As she guided his prick into the open vee of her dress Darrel wondered if she was somehow in touch with his wired skull, if she was privy to all his secret desires.

All his speculation ceased abruptly, however, as his cock slid its way down the ravine between her breasts. Lodged between those satisfyingly plump mounds, his erection grew to mammoth proportions and Franca began to squeeze and manipulate her bosom in such a way that Darrel was sure he would soon come. He gasped as the exciting massage stimulated him towards a climax, and his fingers crept down to pinch at the nipples that were now protruding stiffly through the velvet. Franca moaned too, evidently finding the experience as gratifying as he did. Through half-closed lids he could see that her eyes were closed and her face wore an ecstatic expression as she kneaded his prick with undisguised enthusiasm.

Darrel would gladly have exploded into that warm, fleshy divide if Franca hadn't suddenly whipped off her clothes and straddled him. Startled out of his climb towards orgasm, Darrel was at first disconcerted. But when she lowered her delightfully wet quim onto his glans and proceeded to descend, very slowly, onto his shaft until she had him completely enclosed in her inner sanctuary, he knew that there were even greater pleasures in store for him.

Franca began a long, slow pumping of his organ that soon had him moaning in grateful surprise as his former arousal level was restored, and then surpassed. He seized hold of the tits that, seconds before, had been nurturing his cock and grabbed handfuls of the firm, warm flesh, his thumbs flicking back and forth over the hard knobs of her nipples.

She began moaning softly, squeezing him with her cunt and rocking gently. Darrel thrust upwards, into the secret, wet recesses of her, and felt his orgasm gather and build, filling the whole of his groin with tingling fire. He bent his mouth to hers, raiding her store of sweet saliva with his tongue, and the pressure rose in his balls as she caressed his rigid prick with her softly molten pussy.

When the valve that was holding back his love-juice burst open, letting forth a stream of hot liquid, Darrel let out a loud cry of release. He felt the juddering spasms rack through him as the spunk pulsed out. Over and over he suffered the exquisite pangs of his climax, spurting forth until his bursting balls were reduced to dry sacs again. Then he collapsed onto Franca's heaving body, dimly aware that their flesh was slippery with sweat and cooling rapidly. He moaned into her ear, 'That was amazing!'

'Mm,' she murmured contentedly. He surmised that she must have come too, although he'd been so taken up with his own bliss that he hadn't noticed. Next time it would be different, he vowed. He would take pleasure in her satisfaction before he sought his own. He wanted to see her light up like a Christmas tree.

Suddenly Franca rose and walked abruptly into her shower. He heard the water gushing as she sluiced off every trace of him from her body, and a deep sadness overtook him. Were these snatched moments all they could share? He found himself longing to spend a whole weekend with her, exploring every subtle facet of their mutual desire.

It was a very strange feeling. Up to now, Darrel had seldom wondered what it might be like for people who had steady partners. Granted, there were few of them left in the hectic, amoral world he inhabited. But some still clung to the old values, went through a formal marriage ceremony and endeavoured to stay true to their vows. Never before had such a prospect seemed attractive to him, but after the bombshell that Franca had dropped into his consciousness he knew that nothing could ever be the same again, and the idea of restoring some stability into his shattered life was an attractive one.

Franca emerged from the shower with her hair tied back severely and wearing an industrial-looking suit with lots of pockets and zippers. It was the kind of outfit maintenance workers wore and it made her look some-how anonymous, but strangely sexy too.

Seeing his puzzled expression, she explained, 'I have to go and meet my co-liberationists now. You could come too, if you like. But we'll have to make you look less conspicuous.'

She sounded matter-of-fact, but her words struck terror into Darrel. If he went with her now he would be in deep, deeper than he'd ever intended to go. Yet his curiosity was overwhelming. 'Where do we have to go?'

'Into the Alleys.'

'The Alleys!'

His dread increased, but she said at once, 'Don't worry, it's not half as bad as the controllers would have you believe. The people are quite friendly. They have to be. It's the only way they can survive.'

'But if I'm late back to the Plaza . . .'

His words hung between them, sounding mean and cheap. What would happen to him, after all: the with-drawal of privileges, curtailment of his leisure time, a small fine? He looked into Franca's cool blue eyes and knew that she was in far deeper than he could ever be. If she was prepared to risk all for the sake of freedom, surely he could take a tiny risk himself. He would just have to think up some excuse for being late back, that was all.

'Okay,' he said, gruffly.

She darted back into her sleeping quarters and came out with another industrial-type overall. Darrel put it on over his clothes – it was several sizes too large – and immediately felt alien and weird. Franca giggled, drawing him over to her mirror. Darrel grinned back at his reflection, the image of a Grade Four Maintenance Clone.

'A wolf in sheep's clothing if ever I saw one!' Franca said. Then she seized his arm. 'Come on, we have to go. The shuttle leaves in five minutes.'

'Shuttle?'

'Yes, we'll be joining the late shift and getting off at Mobility Junction. Don't worry, we'll blend in perfectly. No one will notice us.'

Darrel's heart began to race again as they left the flat and went out into the quiet street. Franca led the way at a fast pace, striding down the road to where the shuttle track snaked between the elegant boulevards of Parkside. Soon after they arrived at the small boarding station the blind face of the shuttle appeared on the horizon, swaying on its chassis. As it drew near and slowed, Darrel saw that it was crammed with service workers in overalls of various types and hues, garnered from their work in the plazas, malls, parks and apartment blocks of the well-to-do.

Franca swung into the slowing vehicle and several men moved aside for her, their expressions brightening as they saw her blue eyes and lustrous lips. Darrel followed, almost losing his step but just making it in time. The shuttle never stopped, only decelerated.

'Oh, by the way,' Franca murmured, as they clung to the overhead bar with the carriage jerkily accelerating again, 'To preserve anonymity you'll be known as Brother Dee.'

Before he could reply the shuttle plunged into a black hole and all the internal lighting failed. Darrel hoped it was not a bad omen.

Chapter Seven

The shuttle led them through a long tunnel and when they emerged it was obvious that they were on the other side of town, the side where the Alleys were more numerous than the respectable neighbourhoods. Darrel stared down through the vehicle's plexidome into the dark gashes between the blocks, where shadowy buildings in various stages of decay lined streets littered with plastic cartons, cardboard boxes and paper wrappers. You hardly ever saw such packaging in the better areas and there was a certain gruesome satisfaction to be had in trying to guess what they had contained.

Another archaic feature of the Alley lifestyle was the bicycle. Darrel was amazed to see how many there were, wobbling unsteadily through the garbage with their crouched riders perched precariously on battered saddles. It was like something out of a historical fantasy. Was he really going to enter that bizarre world? The prospect made him feel queasy.

'Come on, this is us!'

Franca grabbed his arm and pushed him towards the exit as the shuttle began to slow. When the doors slid apart she jumped onto the platform and urged him to do the same. He held her hand tight, feeling like a child again as he landed unsteadily and then followed her and two workers down the moving walkway to street level.

Soon they were making their way through a compacted sludge that stank horribly. 'You get used to it,' Franca grinned, seeing his nose wrinkle in disgust. 'Not far now.'

A teenage boy on a bike wobbled past. 'Hail, friends!' he called.

'Hail, friend!' Franca replied. She explained that was the form of greeting used in the Alleys. It only increased Darrel's sense of stepping back in time to some bygone, more primitive, age. If there was danger lurking in these alleyways, however, he didn't smell it. Despite the disorder and decay that was evident all around he felt completely safe. Perhaps because his guide seemed so confident.

Franca led the way through a maze of narrow streets where the shuttered buildings gave no hint of life within. Yet Darrel had the impression that all kinds of activity was taking place behind those barred doors. They came to a large intersection, where traffic sped on from one salubrious area to another without a thought for the teeming half-life of the Alleys. Darrel paused, dazed by the sight of so many cabs and limos, with the shuttle track running at a higher level alongside.

'This is Mobility Junction,' Franca said. 'Parkside is in that direction. Tabor Sound is that way. The house we want is down there, to the right and through the underpass.'

The track under the highway was even worse, since it was evidently used as a public lavatory. Franca strode on unconcerned, her neat rump filling out the seat of her overalls most fetchingly. Despite the squalid surroundings,

Darrel had the hots for her. The memory of their last encounter was making his cock harden, making him wonder when they would next get a chance to screw. Thanks to her, his libido had been liberated and now sex was no longer merely work but a source of great personal pleasure. He felt like a kid once again, discovering some new and thrilling pastime.

They finally reached their destination: a large, decayed house standing in isolation on some scrubby wasteland, the shuttered windows and door covered in peeling green paint. From the outside it seemed deserted, but when Franca tapped out a rhythm on the door panel there was a shout and footsteps approached. After much unlocking of chains and sliding of bolts the door creaked open and the face of a man appeared. There were heavy lines between his brows and around his mouth, but although he was completely bald he couldn't have been more than thirty-five. A small gold flame in a circle hung from his left ear.

'Sister!' He gave a gap-toothed grin and his grey eyes lit up. 'We're expecting you. Everyone's here except the Maybury team.'

'Is there trouble in Maybury?' Franca asked, anxiously.

He shrugged. 'No word yet.'

Darrel followed into the dark hallway, stepping gingerly over the unsteady floorboards, and then they descended into a cellar. When his eyes grew accustomed to the dim light Darrel was surprised to find the place had been made quite habitable, with the stone walls covered in bright drapery and a few striking paintings. There were benches and assorted chairs set round a large pine table on which a lamp was burning, and every seat was occupied. Blinking with surprise, he calculated that there must be about fifteen people down there.

'Friends, I bring you Brother Dee,' Franca announced, much to his embarrassment. He glanced up and at once met the gaze of Annis, who was sitting at one corner of the table with a glass in her hand. She raised it with an ironic smile and his guts lurched with sudden longing. God, she was beautiful! The shadows cast by the lamp were painting her features in *chiaroscuro*, giving her the air of a Leonardo Madonna.

Darrel smiled, but the desire he felt for her was more complicated than plain lust and made him uneasy. He recalled the strange sounds she'd made as she came, more like cries of protest than pleasure, and he felt a deep hunger for her, one that he was unsure she could ever satisfy. It was quite different from what he felt for Franca, whose own desire fuelled his in a continuous loop of feedback.

A man stood up. He was over six feet tall, with an impressive mane of black hair and piercing blue eyes. His body was hard, lean and muscled, his expression alert. A warrior type, Darrel decided. The thought filled him with sudden dread.

'Welcome, Brother!' His voice was deep and sonorous, echoing round the cellar. The fierce blue eyes fixed Darrel with an intent look as he continued, 'Every one of us is glad to see you here. We believe you have already done us great service.'

'Yes, he penetrated the control room at the Plaza,' Franca confirmed. 'Tell Brother Jay what you saw, Dee.'

Darrel gave his account to a silent, rapt audience. At first, seeing everyone's eyes upon him, he felt nervous.

But Franca prompted him until he had remembered all the details and at the end admiring murmurs broke out, making him feel good. His eyes swivelled towards Annis, still wearing that dark, ironic smile, and pain momentarily gripped his heart.

Jay shook him by the hand with a broad smile. 'You have helped us more than you know, Brother. Please, be seated and join in our fellowship.'

A chair was found for him and liquid refreshment offered. Darrel sniffed at the glass of dark red liquid, his suspicions growing into astonished recognition when he finally took a sip. 'This is wine!'

The company round the table broke into a roar of laughter. Jay explained. 'This was once a wine cellar and there are still stocks of the stuff, dating back to the end of the last millennium. It's good stuff, too. Whoever lived here knew what he was doing. But go easy. If you're not accustomed to alcohol it can be quite a shock to the system.'

Darrel could only remember sampling the stuff once before. Jabez had smuggled a bottle of beer into the Plaza after one of his visits to the Alleys, and they had all taken a swig. Gassy and sour it had tasted, enough to put him off for life. But this was different. Very different.

One more cautious sip unleashed a feast of delicious flavours: soft fruits, vanilla, hints of mint and lime. Darrel took a large mouthful and swilled it round to let the tastes develop. The others watched him, awaiting his reaction. He swallowed, savouring its warm progress down his gullet, then said, 'Unbelievable!' They all laughed.

'Take it slowly,' Franca advised. 'But we must press on. This is a business meeting, Dee. First our various teams report on their activities, then we plan for the next week or so. I'm sure I needn't stress that all this is highly confidential.'

'I'm flattered that you trust me.'

Suddenly Jay was looming over him. His face grew dark. 'It's *you* who must trust us, Brother. One word of betrayal and your days are numbered. Don't be foolish enough to doubt that.'

Darrel's blood chilled. He didn't doubt it, for one minute. Everything about this organization suggested they worked with speed and efficiency, using a tight network of communication. He had a feeling they couldn't afford to behave otherwise.

He listened in fascination as they ran through tales of espionage and sabotage. Each group had a particular target area to work in. Franca and Annis worked together in the Plaza; a couple of men reported on their success amongst the maintenance bosses; a man and a woman told of an important new recruit in the ranks of those who served the controllers. It seemed the group had managed to penetrate all areas of government to some degree.

As they went on to discuss plans for the coming week, however, Darrel began to feel uneasy. What if they had some special assignment for him? It seemed he had become a member of this movement by default, and a part of him was annoyed that he'd been seduced into it. Then he thought of the crime that the controllers had perpetrated, not just against him but against all the genies, and his anger was redirected. What else could he do but join these people in the fight against such evil?

Darrel looked at Annis, her face now solemn, a study

in light and shade. She'd suffered far more at the hands of the controllers than he had and for her, too, there was now no other option. He admired her bravery

'More wine, Darrel?'

There was Franca with the jug of seductive dark red liquid. Darrel was developing a taste for it. He quaffed his glass immediately it was filled, then she gave him some more. Before long his head began to feel as if it was stuffed full of raw wool, clinging to the barbed wire of his nerve-endings. The buzz of conversation all around was like the insistent rattle of beads in a box and began to irritate him intensely. He felt his head loll to one side and was powerless to stop himself from slumping forward onto the table.

'Too much alcohol . . . not used to it . . .' were the last words he heard before total blackout occurred.

Darrel came out of oblivion into hazy awareness that he had been moved to a different place. The room was still dimly lit but he was lying on a bed with his hands unaccountably bound behind his back. He was also aware that he had a raging erection. When his eyes could focus properly he saw Annis sitting beside him on the bed with a faint smile. She was naked, her full breasts only slightly sagging and her nipples taut and red as cherries.

'Feeling better?' she enquired, her fingers sweeping delicately over his chest and stomach, making his muscles contract with longing.

'My head hurts. Why are my hands tied?'

Her smile widened. 'So you can't touch me, but I can touch you. Without fear . . .'

She reached for his prick and held it within her cool

palm. It leapt eagerly, wanting more contact. He guessed she had been handling it already while he was unconscious, making it big.

'You're a strange girl, Annis.'

'Life has made me that way. I was quite an ordinary girl once, just as you were an ordinary boy. Until *they* got their hands on us. Now I can't really let myself go unless I feel safe.'

The thought of lovely, wounded Annis letting herself go made Darrel melt all over – except for his cock. She was stroking it gently now, too gently really, making him squirm on the edge of arousal. The idea that he was completely at her mercy was both stimulating and scary. She moved down the bed and bent to kiss his naked toes. Exquisitely ticklish feelings sped up his legs to his groin as her wet, capacious mouth enclosed his big toe completely.

'Ouch! That tickles!'

She ignored him, her eyes half-closed, her expression rapt. He looked at the swinging globes of her breasts and groaned, longing to take them in his grasp. The wet mouth moved, snail-like over first one foot and then the other, leaving a trail of moisture that tingled as it cooled. Her long hair swept against his shins and then her mouth was there too, kissing him with the same intense attention.

'You're so lovely, Annis,' he murmured, cajolingly. 'If only you'd let me give you some pleasure too.'

She lifted her face for a second, her eyes liquid chocolate. 'This is pleasure.'

From the hard appearance of her nipples he was inclined to believe her. Then, to his amazement, she raised up her slender hips and slipped his erect big

126

toe right inside her slippery wet vulva.

Darrel gasped as she squeezed his toe with her inner muscles, wresting sensation from him with evident satisfaction. She continued to kiss his thighs with tantalizingly soft, wet lips, making his penis rear impatiently. With one hand she took his toe and rubbed it against her clitoris with abandon, making little throaty gurgles as the friction took effect.

'That's it, make yourself come!' he urged her, but she stared up at him coolly.

'Not yet!'

'Well, make me come then!'

Her face grew sly. 'Not yet!'

'Teaser!'

She ignored him, but her frantic rubbing of herself with his toe ceased and she began to slide up his leg, her open vulva leaving an even wetter trail than her lips had done. Her breasts were expanded to bursting now, great ripe fruits each topped with a tawny calyx. Darrel wanted to kiss that creamy skin and take those brown nipples deep into his mouth to suckle.

Annis was bent almost double now, her tongue lapping at his belly button while she worked her open pussy round and round against his thigh, making a sticky patch. Darrel strained at his bonds, wondering if she had been careless and tied them too loosely. He began to fantasize about breaking free and taking control, pinning her down and spearing into her with all the force of his pent-up frustration, but it was soon obvious that she had made no such mistake. His wrists were securely tied and he had to submit to her ministrations, remaining in her sweet power.

His dick was red and angry now, straining at the leash while Annis planted her moist, titillating kisses all around his stomach. Her trailing tresses brushed lightly over his glans from time to time, increasing his maddening desire to fever pitch. His pelvis shivered as her mouth sucked gently at the black hairs on his stomach, moving upward in slow, siphoning movements of her lips until she was flicking over his nipples with the tip of her tongue, sending spirals of hot flame throughout his nervous system, filling his balls with tingling fire.

Now Darrel's mouth was watering as the dark nipples dangled almost within his reach at the tip of those pale, enormous globes. Annis seemed to sense his desire, for when she'd had her fill of his chest she wriggled around and presented her right breast to his eager mouth while she continued to rub her vulva on his stomach. The long nipple bobbed in between his lips and out again, teasing him. Next time he caught it more firmly and sucked on it hard, making her gasp. *Good*, he thought wickedly. His teeth grazed against the smooth surrounding skin and then he nipped the dark areola softly while his tongue moved rapidly back and forth over the rubbery tip.

She was breathing fast now, in a series of accelerating pants that had him hot for her. His prick was like a firebrand, pulsating with desire, and it was with a profound sense of relief that he felt her thighs inching down, down until she could straddle him at the hips. She pulled his shaft towards her open labia, still breathing heavily, and at last his glans made contact with the hard bud of her clitoris. For a few seconds she rubbed him against herself then, able to stand it no more than he could, she raised herself up on her knees so that she could slide the stiff cock right into her cunt.

Darrel moaned aloud as his shaft moved into her lubricated interior, gliding easily into the warm, wet heart of her. Annis began to ride him with rapid strokes, her small bottom moving with practised ease over his thighs, her tits jolting heavily against her chest. He closed his eyes, unable to bear the sight of all that untouchable flesh, and at once the sensations grew more intense, more concentrated.

In the dark world of his own imagination, Darrel could see the pair of them locked in endless copulation, making love in as many ways as their fertile minds could devise. But most of all he saw himself on top, plunging recklessly into the steamy tropical paradise of her quim while his fingers pressed her love-button and his lips teased her nipples, triggering climax after climax. He saw himself taking her from behind, caressing her small, shapely buttocks with one hand while he stroked her swaying breasts with the other. He wanted to give her the ultimate orgasm, to make her come again and again in one long frenzy of mutual gratification.

But he was not in control, she was. And now Annis was teasing him mercilessly, moving to the sensitive tip of his shaft where she squeezed him gently with her labia, but not enough to bring him off. Tingling arousal filled his whole body, making his breath come in tortured spasms, and his balls felt ready to burst. She was grinning down at him, exulting in her power, feeling her own huge breasts expand still more beneath her supporting hands.

Then her fingers moved to tweak at her erect nipples

and Darrel thought she was taunting him, reminding him that his hands were tied. His hips thrust upward in a vain attempt to get her pelvis moving again, to bring the fuck to a swift conclusion. His buttocks were clenched tight with the strain. Now when he looked at Annis her eyes were closed in bliss as the gentle friction against her clitoris sent her into ecstasy. He was pleased for her, yet he would rather have played a more active rôle in her arousal. She was using his cock like a dildo, that was all.

Then, with a sudden groan that sounded more like agony than pleasure, she rammed her cunt down hard on his rigid organ, sending his libido into overdrive. After a series of rapid journeys up and down his shaft which brought him to the brink of coming, Annis slowed again and began to squeeze him with her inner walls, undulating up and down his erection, making him gasp and moan with lust. His eyes flickered open and he glimpsed an erotic vision of her, head thrown back, breasts covered in a fine film of sweat with her brown nipples shining like chestnuts. Unable to satisfy her with any other part of his body, Darrel willed all his strength into his penis, thrusting up into the hot wet cave of her cunt until she began to flush rose-red and the wild undulations of her pussy changed to a slow, rhythmic throbbing that had her half screaming aloud.

Darrel felt his own orgasm arrive in slow motion too, starting way down at the root of his balls and travelling up his cock until the explosion happened, sending hot waves of bliss throughout his entire body. He bucked and strained at his bonds, feeling the liquid fire accelerating through his system until he lost consciousness for a few seconds. An overwhelming floatiness took possession of his mind, taking him way beyond any sense of where, or who, he was.

Coming down, he felt a new looseness in his hands and realized that his bonds had been untied and his arms were lying limply at his sides. Annis was by his side too, stretched out in exhaustion, her breasts falling slightly to each side and a small rivulet of perspiration running between them. Darrel tried to take her in his arms but she resisted him, rolling over to the edge of what he now realized was a rather large bed.

'Please' she murmured. 'I can't bear to be touched . . . afterwards.'

Disappointed, Darrel kept his distance. His body felt good – warm and relaxed, still buzzing slightly from his climax – but his mind was disturbed. He wanted to prove to Annis that she could trust him, but sensed that it would take a long time. She had obviously been badly hurt, and not just physically. The external scar on her thigh was there for all to see, but he could only imagine the scars on her soul.

After a while she got up and dressed in a loose blue robe. 'I'll get Franca,' she said, as if it was the obvious next step. Before Darrel could question her she left.

Glancing around the room Darrel caught sight of a large poster on the peeling wall opposite. It showed a naked man and a woman entwined and rising out of flames, phoenix-like. The caption read: 'Humanity will always rise again.' He linked the image with the earring of the man who had opened the door, but did this group have a name? Possibly they mistrusted titles, labels, but their symbolism was certainly impressive.

Franca appeared, still clad in the overall. Her face was

flushed and her eyes bright, but Darrel sensed the stimulus was not sexual but emotional. She was high on brotherly love, not the other kind. Seeing him in his nude, sated state she gave a wry grin. 'I see you've recovered from your hangover, then.'

'Hangover?'

'Too much wine.' She sank down onto the bed beside him, her hand absently caressing his arm. 'You're doing Annis a lot of good, you know. When she was given that assignment to pose as your client at the Plaza she went white, but she knew she had to do it. We'd just lost the girl who was scheduled for that job.'

Her tone was casual, but it sent a chill down Darrel's spine. Just what did that little word 'lost' mean? He didn't want to enquire too closely.

About Annis, though, he was less restrained. 'What happened, to make her this way? It wasn't just being wounded by the guards, was it? She has some deep sexual hang-up too.'

Franca's blue eyes clouded. 'Yes. It was while she was working as a genie. She used to have a regular client, someone high up in the system, who used her horribly. He devised all sorts of ways to satisfy his evil lust on her poor body. It was that experience that made her start to question the system, try to find out more. Eventually she made her bungled escape bid and was in great danger, but we managed to rescue her. After she'd been de-conditioned and remodelled we hoped she'd start to recover emotionally, psychologically, but it was hopeless.'

Darrel looked at her disgustedly. 'Is that why you sent her to me? To force her to have sex again?'

'Not entirely. We had little choice at the time. We

needed to find out urgently if you'd succeeded in your mission. The fact that she had sex with you was incidental.'

'It may have been – to you!' Darrel snapped, still angry on Annis' behalf.

Franca squeezed his hand. Her eyes met his, at once sympathetic and distant. 'Don't get involved, Darrel. It's the first rule in this work. We lose people all the time, so we can't afford to get too attached.'

He didn't want to let Franca know how far the other woman had got under his skin. They were both special to him, but Annis had the greater hold over his heart. He wanted to heal her, to help her back to normality, and such an urge was far more powerful than the straight-forward lust he felt for Franca.

She gave him a bright smile. 'Ready to go back and meet the others? I thought you might like to have an informal chat with Brother Jay.'

It was not quite what Darrel wanted right then. His blood was still hot for Annis, and he was left with a sense of unfinished business. But he rose from the bed and, after hosing himself down in the antiquated shower cubicle, put on the uniform again.

The crowd had dispersed and there was no sign of either Franca or Annis when Darrel made his way down-stairs to the room he supposed had once been a kitchen. Seated at the table was Jay, sipping from a thick-lipped brown goblet. An old-fashioned notebook and pencil in front of him, the pad a mass of indecipherable symbols.

'Brother Dee, won't you join me in a pot of tea?' he smiled.

'Tea?'

His blue eyes positively twinkled. 'An old herbal drink that we've rediscovered, like wine. This is made with elder flowers, garnered by some of our women. It's very pleasant, taken with honey.'

Darrel stared, barely comprehending. It was as if he'd suddenly been whisked back into the middle of the twentieth century. But he tried the fragrant, steaming brew all the same and, after wrinkling his nose at the smell, pronounced it drinkable.

He pointed to the squiggles on paper. 'What's that – hieroglyphics?'

Jay laughed. 'You could say that! It's another long-lost skill. They used to call it shorthand, back in the days before computers. Women learnt it, to take down the sacred words of their master as fast as he spoke them. Then they would be typed up into letters or reports later on.'

'And you've learnt it too?'

'Yes. It's perfect for security, don't you see? I can record all my plans this way and no one will ever know.'

'I see! But you must be afraid your plans will be found. Has this place ever been raided?'

Jay's smile vanished as quickly as it had arrived. 'Not yet, but it will be one day. You can be sure of that. We're only ever one step ahead of them.'

Darrel asked, quietly, 'Aren't you afraid?'

'Constantly. But fear only matters if it makes you careless. We have faith in our early warning system. By the time the enemy gets this far the place will be deserted.'

'I wish I had your confidence.'

'You will. When you see what we can accomplish, working towards our common goal. You will join us, won't you, Dee?'

It was scarcely a question. Again Darrel felt he was the victim of a *fait accompli* but this time he scarcely minded. To be on the same side as the likes of Franca, Annis and Jay he deemed an honour. 'I don't see how I can back out now, do you?'

Jay grinned. 'I knew you'd see it our way! Which is just as well because we have plans for you. Just one more small job, then you can hide out on Malaku for a while. You'll like it there.'

'Malaku?'

'It's a very special place. In the old days they used to build penal colonies on remote islands like that, but this is a self-styled Republic of Freedom. Probably the only place on the planet where people of all races can overcome their conditioning and live together in harmony.'

'And no one's tried to stop it?'

'The authorities know about it, of course, and they don't like it. But to take the island and crush the people they'd have to use an enormous task force and, even then, it could be a prolonged siege. Hardly cost-effective and it would mean bad publicity too. After that Eurasian debacle they want to clean up their image.'

'Sounds like heaven on earth.'

'There's many would agree with you – some of them have even been there! It's certainly a vast improvement on what we have here, anyway.'

'Have you been there?'

He shook his head. 'Too much to do here.'

'What about Franca, Annis?'

'They'll probably go with you, when this next phase is over.'

Darrel gave a lazy grin. The thought of a holiday on

that island paradise with those two beauties was already giving him a hard-on. But he knew he'd have to earn it first.

'What do I have to do to get to heaven, then?'

Jay grinned. 'Become impotent.'

'What?'

'Temporarily, of course. Just to get the FC even more interested in you than he is already. Don't worry, it can all be done chemically. And you'll be in good company. Annis and a friend of hers will visit you in the Plaza as if they were clients. But, incredible as it might seem, you won't be able to get an erection.'

'I don't understand ... I'm already having some trouble in that department. At work, I mean. Here, and in Franca's apartment, things are different of course.'

Jay's black brows lifted sardonically. 'Of course! That's because you've been de-conditioned. But now we're going to put you back even further than you were before. I know you've been having trouble getting it up for your usual clients ...'

'Those ugly old bitches, you mean! Hardly surprising, is it? I just couldn't stomach them, after Franca.'

'Precisely. But from now on you will have trouble with attractive, nubile young women too. That should shake them up in the control room. They'll want to give you a thorough examination, try some new wiring. You'll be a kind of human lab rat.'

The phrase angered Darrel. 'What the hell is the point of that?'

'The point is we'll be able to take you apart again, so we can see exactly what modifications they've made. After that we'll put you to rights so you can really begin to enjoy life. We need to know about their technology, Dee, and about the way their minds work. Remember what I said about being one step ahead?'

Darrel considered the prospect glumly. There were risks involved, obviously. What if the controllers grew suspicious and discovered his involvement with the group? What if he became irreversibly impotent? What risks were there for Annis, too, making a second sortie into the lion's den? He was even more concerned about her.

'Of course it's risky,' Jay went on, reading his mind. 'We all face danger, all the time. If you want to back out, say now. You can return to the Plaza and never hear from any of us again.'

Darrel didn't hesitate. 'No, I'll do it! I want to help, any way I can. If women like Franca and Annis are prepared to put their lives on the line . . .'

He fell into brooding silence, thinking of the ordeal that Annis had already been through. What had she looked like before the expert reconstruction of her features? It was a question that had begun to torment him. Had her personality been changed forever, too? Did that explain the dark mystery that seemed to be at her heart?

'Thank you, Dee,' Jay said, rising from his seat with his long fingers pressed onto the table. 'Now if you'll come with me into the lab we can get you fixed in no time. Then you can return with Franca on the next shuttle.'

Chapter Eight

Darrel thought he would have trouble thinking up an excuse for his lateness, but in the end it turned out better than he'd expected. There was a new girl on the desk, one susceptible to his line of banter, and she accepted without question his story about his cousin falling sick while he was visiting and needing help from a medic. *So much for their security*, he thought wryly.

But Darrel knew that he mustn't let this give him a sense of false security. Lax they might be as far as exit-pass procedures were concerned, but since so few genies ever left the Plaza they could afford to be. In his case he had the uneasy feeling that they might be keeping tabs on him in other ways. If they could wire his brain for sex, why couldn't they implant a tracer too, letting them know exactly where he went on his little extra-curricular jaunts? The idea was chilling, but it wouldn't go away. He would raise it with Jay, next time he saw him.

Back in his room, Darrel felt depression fall on him like a snowy blanket, fogging his mind. It seemed as if he had been away weeks, not merely hours. As he logged on, his current credit rating showed on screen. His balance was very healthy but, for the first time ever, he found he really didn't care. Unless there was a favourable exchange rate with whatever currency they used on

Malaku, he just didn't give a damn. There were more important things in life than credit.

A woman came for his services just ten minutes after he arrived in his room. Darrel saw her coming down the corridor with a swinging stride, carrying her cocktail purse, and his curiosity was roused when he saw that she was neither old nor ugly. There was something oddly familiar about her. He wondered if he had seen her somewhere in the Alleys but was pretty sure he hadn't.

Then, when she entered, he was convinced that he'd met her before somewhere. Furthermore, she seemed to know him. Confidently smiling she held out her hand.

'Darrel! Good to see you again after all this time!'

He felt wary, unwilling to say anything that might hint at his secret life outside the Plaza. The woman dropped her beaded bag onto the bed and sank into the chair, slipping out of her heels. Then, with her arms stretched along the arms of the relaxer, she gave him a cheeky smile that lit up her heart-shaped face and jogged his memory even more. 'Remember me?'

He looked into her greenish eyes with the spiky black lashes, scanned her small red mouth and said, hesitantly, 'Yes . . . somewhere . . . long ago and far away.'

Her grin widened. 'Fernlea, to be exact.'

'Oh God!' He clapped his hand to his temple, his mind suddenly slipping back ten years or more and letting her face slot into context. She'd been one of those randy adolescent girls in the female hostel, the ones he had pleasured on his illicit nocturnal visits. He even remembered her name now: Cleofa.

He threw back his head and laughed, loudly. 'Well, I'll be damned!'

140

'On the contrary, you look as if you've done rather well for yourself. I might have known you'd end up as a genie, you Romeo, you! Well, you had plenty of practice – on us poor unsuspecting maidens.'

'Half the time you lot were seducing me, and you know it!'

She leaned forward, the neck of her red suit gaping to show a generous amount of cleavage. 'We couldn't get enough of you, Darrel. Me and the rest of the dorm. You were all we thought about, night and day. Remember when you had six of us at once?'

Darrel laughed. 'Could I ever forget? My big toes were in two of you, my fingers in two more. Someone else was sitting on my chest so I could lick her pussy and, as I recall, you had the pleasure of actually being fucked by me.'

'And what a pleasure it was! I had my first multiple orgasm that night. I don't mind telling you, nothing's been quite as good since.'

'And you expect a repeat performance?'

Her smile grew wistful. 'Nothing can ever be the same as the first time, can it? Not when you're so young and randy. But I've often dreamed of seeing you again, Darrel, I can't deny it. When I heard you were working here as a genie I couldn't resist the urge to seek you out.'

'I hope you won't be disappointed.'

'Isn't satisfaction guaranteed in the Plaza?'

'That's what they say . . .'

'I don't expect miracles. Just a good fuck. Do you have some decent cocktails, or should I mix my own?'

'I think we probably have something to suit you. Something hot and subtle, like a Sweet Seducer, perhaps?'

'That sounds promising.'

Darrel turned to make her drink, but his heart was starting to beat quite erratically. He was nervous, afraid that he wouldn't make the grade and Cleofa would report him to the authorities. Someone had done as much all those years ago, and although he hadn't wanted to harbour any suspicions she was certainly someone who might have betrayed him.

Then he remembered that being reported to the authorities was exactly what Jay wanted to happen to him. They'd rewired his brain, and now he was part of their experiment. Was Cleofa part of the same experiment too? It was impossible to find out without giving the game away, and that was far too dangerous.

When he turned back to her, Cleofa had removed the top half of her suit and was sitting there bare-breasted. Darrel stared at the budding pink nipples, which were still those of a young girl, perched on small high tits. 'Do you like them?' she asked, sipping the drink he'd given her. 'I had their development arrested when I was sixteen, I liked them so much then. It was very expensive. I had to sell all my inherited credit, but I've never regretted it.'

'I don't blame you. They're very lovely.'

Her bosom was unreal, like a porcelain replica. She saw his incredulous gaze and said, 'You can touch them if you like. Pretend I'm sixteen again!'

Darrel reached out and felt the soft, smooth skin of her breasts, the taut, delicate nipples. 'Did you have any other part of your anatomy arrested?'

She shook her head, grinning wryly. 'Couldn't afford to. My cunt is that of a twenty-four-year old, but I do daily exercises to keep it in trim so I don't think you'll have any complaints. Oh, you're turning me on a treat with your fondling! I can't wait to see how your body has developed after all this time. Have you had bio-plasty?'

He shook his head. 'I've always kept myself in trim. But I'm not the sex-starved boy you used to know.'

'I should hope not – you only ever lasted ten minutes at a time!' Cleofa stood up, slipping out of her lower garment in an easy movement to reveal that she was wearing nothing underneath but a dainty brown muff of carefully-trimmed pubic hair. 'Shall we move to the bed? I think my cocktail's beginning to take effect.'

Aware that, at some level, this woman terrified him, Darrel nonetheless let her lead him over to the bed. It began to undulate as soon as they lay down, triggered by their combined body-weight. Cleofa sprawled unself-consciously, revealing her plump labia with the dark slit between, and reached out to open Darrel's fly. He knew that he was far from an erection, that he would not be able to have one due to the anaphrodisiac effect of Jay's drug, and his nervousness reached crisis point.

He cleared his throat. 'I love to suck pussy,' he de-clared, boldly, in a desperate attempt to divert her attention from his cock. 'Will you let me lick yours?'

With a silent smile she opened her thighs. The glistening folds of her vulva parted to reveal her erect clitoris, red and proud as a miniature cockscomb, and the dark hole of her vagina just below. Darrel felt a thrill of unaccustomed terror strike him. Nevertheless, he bent his mouth to the fleshy petals and began to probe be-tween them with his tongue, eliciting a sharply indrawn breath of pleasure from Cleofa.

'Mm, so good!' she murmured, sighing and stretching voluptuously. Emboldened, Darrel began to explore her more thoroughly and was soon tasting the exotic sweetness of her love-juice as it poured from her.

In the old days, he reflected, he would have had a stonker of an erection by now. Yet he could feel his cock lying like a soft rag between his thighs, his balls loose in their sac. Was it Jay's drug working, or was it a recurrence of his recent problem?

Resentment stung him and he was perversely angry with himself for letting himself be experimented on in this way. He'd let the glamour of the group seduce him; their dedication and the undercurrent of danger had been exciting to him, and his experiences with Franca and Annis had helped draw him deeper into their web of intrigue. But only now did he realize just what had been done to him. His sexual responses had been so disturbed that he wondered if he would ever be able to return to normal again. His career as a genie seemed over for good.

Could this all be an elaborate plot to tie him to one or other of those women, to make him behave even more recklessly in his infatuation? As he licked with feigned enthusiasm at Cleofa's sturdy love-nub he wondered just how far they would go to ensnare and use him for their cause. *Mustn't get paranoid*, he reminded himself. His hands moved down Cleofa's smooth thighs and she moaned, shifting restlessly. He reached up to feel her taut, virginal breasts and her moaning intensified. Catching the bead-like nipples between his fingers and thumbs he attempted to stimulate her there while he performed cunnilingus.

'Oh, you've lost none of your old skills!' she

exclaimed, delightedly. 'Fancy you remembering how I like it! You're incredible!'

Darrel was surprised, since he had only been using his routine approach to clients. Her praise made him feel good, even so. Not that it had any effect on his cock; his erection was still non-existent. He would have to make Cleofa come with his mouth or she would report him to the authorities and put him in danger once again. Jay had explained that to be called to the FC's office too soon would be disastrous for their experiment, so the visit of Annis and her friend would be timed exactly. Or had Jay been lying to him?

Darrel forced his mind back on the task in hand and redoubled his efforts. Soon Cleofa was straining and groaning with the rise of her impending orgasm. When she began to gasp loudly and grew red in the face he knew that her climax was upon her. The juices gushed out of her, and she grabbed his head and squeezed it so tightly between her thighs that his ears felt as if they would drop off. When she eventually released him he had a weird buzzing in his ears for several seconds.

'Ooh, that was so-o-o good!' she exclaimed, sinking back in exhaustion. 'Come and lie beside me, Darrel. Let's reminisce about old times. You never know, it might get you in the mood again!'

Gently he stroked her breasts as her breathing returned to normal and they talked of the other girls in her dorm, girls that she had mostly lost touch with. But she said there was one, who worked in her office.

'I'm going to tell her all about you!' she grinned. 'And you can bet your life she'll want to take advantage of your services too.'

Darrel tried to seem enthusiastic, but he was full of trepidation inside. He hadn't bargained for this sudden resurrection of old ghosts. Did Cleofa hold some hidden threat to his security? It seemed too much of a co-incidence that one of the girls who had been indirectly responsible for getting him sent to the Plaza should have come back into his professional life right now, just when he was getting involved with a group that was dedicated to overthrowing the Controllers.

'Ooh, I'm going to want you inside me soon!' Cleofa breathed into his ear, putting him on full alert. Her long fingertips caressed his balls to ticklish effect, making him squirm with a discomfort that hovered on the edge of eroticism.

'I'm not sure there's time for that . . .' he improvised.

'There is if I pay more. I could book you for a second hour. How does that sound?'

'I . . . er . . . have a client with a regular booking next.'

'Lucky her! How about if I take out a regular booking too?' She snuggled up to him, her fingers reaching play-fully towards his limp cock. 'Mind you, I'd have to have proof that this little gent is going to take some interest in me first. He doesn't seem too keen right now.'

'I came while I was licking you,' Darrel lied. 'It takes a while to recover, you know that.'

'Mm. We'll have to see what we can do, then.'

She slid down his body and put her warm, wet mouth around his flaccid glans. The feeling was mildly pleasant, but Darrel wasn't in the least aroused. *How am I going to get out of this?* he wondered. There were another twenty minutes left in the session. He gritted his teeth and stared at the images on the wall-screens for inspiration. The girl masturbating in the shower didn't do anything for him. Neither did the couple who were enjoying a slow screw in various contorted positions in a woodland setting. The three lesbians rubbing cream into each others' breasts gave him a bit of a twitch, but that was all. And unfortunately Cleofa's determined efforts to resurrect his penis reminded him of nothing more erotic than slurping down seafood from the shell.

'You never used to be so slow,' she chided him, looking up with a wry grin.

'You know how it is, when you get older.'

Her brightness dimmed a little. 'I suppose I'm just another job to you. The fact that we used to know each other in the old days means nothing to you now, does it, Darrel? I should have realized.'

She looked so crestfallen that he took her in his arms. 'It's not that. Of course I have fond memories of you, and the other girls. But things are different now. Being a genie isn't all it's cracked up to be, you know. People think it must be wonderful making love all day, but they don't see the types we have to work with . . .'

He stopped, afraid he might have said too much already. What if she was some kind of *agent provocateuse*, sent not by Jay's lot but by the controllers, to test his loyalty? If so, he'd probably blown it good and proper by now.

But she cuddled up to him, kissing his nipple. 'Maybe we should meet somewhere else. Outside the Plaza, I mean.'

This time he was more careful. 'I'm afraid that's not permitted.'

She giggled. 'You didn't let rules and regulations bother you once upon a time!'

'I was young and foolish then.'

She touched the wrinkled shaft of his organ with a frown. 'And now you're old and past it, is that what you're saying?'

'I wouldn't say past it, exactly.'

'So prove it!'

'I can't function to order.'

Her face darkened. 'I thought that was exactly what you genies were supposed to do. What's wrong, Darrel – is it because you know me, is that it?'

He shrugged. 'Possibly.'

'I've a good mind to ask for my money back, you know.'

'Oh no, don't do that – please! It could cost me my job.'

'Would that really be the end of the world?' Cleofa sidled up to him again. 'I'm in good credit, Darrel, and I live in a nice big flat over on Parkside. You could come and live with me, be my lover. I'd soon get you up and running again in the sex department. I'd regard it as a challenge.'

He listened to her in silent horror. Then, doing his best to disguise his feelings, he said, 'It's a very flattering offer, Cleofa, but I don't think it would work out. I'm used to the life here. I went straight from one kind of institution to another and I've never lived independently. I don't think I could cope.'

Cleofa rose from the bed, her expression petulant, and began to dress. 'Well, you won't have a life here if you go on like this, will you? There's no future for a genie who can't get it up! I won't say anything this time, Darrel. Maybe you're a bit off-colour or something. But next time I shall show up with my friend and if you can't satisfy both of us I really will have to make a complaint. Better get your act together soonest, lover boy!'

She swept from the room before he could respond, leaving him feeling really low. Everything seemed to be running out of control, and he didn't know how much of it was coincidental and how much was planned. Paranoia set in as he wondered again if Cleofa had been sent deliberately, a ghost from the past to torment him. Her offer to keep him had not appealed at all, yet he knew if Annis or Franca had made a similar offer he might have been tempted. Was he becoming emotionally involved with those two women? Darrel was so confused. He'd never had to deal with such complicated feelings before.

He showered briskly, feeling as if he was washing away remnants of his dark past that had surfaced like unwanted flotsam. Within a few minutes of him spraying on some cologne his screen buzzed again, and this time he regarded the approaching figures with a mixture of excitement and relief. Annis had arrived with another woman, and they were heading his way. He peered at her companion, who was small and boyish with a cap of wavy blonde hair. His fleeting impression of the extraordinary chiselled beauty of her face was confirmed when his door stood open and the pair entered. But the androgynous looks and figure gave her a special attraction that both intrigued him and left him cold.

Annis was looking pale and rather strained, yet her heart-stopping looks still had the power to move him even when placed against the cool beauty of the other girl. She saw him staring at her friend and gave a wry smile.

'This is Zee,' she announced, softly.

His paranoia increased as he looked into Zee's pale blue eyes and she gave him a knowing wink. Here was just one more person who could betray him. He was beginning to have the uneasy feeling that this conspiracy was directed not towards the controllers, but at him.

'I've heard a lot about you, Dee,' Zee smiled, but her eyes were still distant. 'I think we're going to have fun together, the three of us.'

'Would you like a cocktail?' he asked them. They both shook their heads.

'No drugs, no bugs!' Annis said softly. It sounded like one of the group's mottoes, something they repeated to strengthen their resolve.

Darrel turned his back to drink some spring water and when he looked again the two women had begun to undress each other, totally absorbed. He sat on the bed watching them as first Annis's large breasts were revealed, their nipples darkly pointed, then Zee's small, pear-shaped ones, their delicate pink tips just budding into firmness. Her eyes smouldered as she lifted one of her friend's full globes to her lips, holding it reverently between her palms, and took the tumid nipple into her mouth.

Annis moaned, arching back until she fell almost on top of Darrel. He moved over to make room for the pair as they collapsed in erotic abandon on the bed. With Zee, Annis was showing none of the inhibition, none of the pain that she'd displayed when making love with Darrel. She was behaving like a sensual animal, her eyes and mouth large and open and moist, her body lithe and relaxed. Watching her revel in Zee's kisses, he felt a stab of jealousy.

As the girls grew more absorbed in their lovemaking Darrel was determined not to be left out. Despite the total lack of interest showed by his cock he nevertheless began to strip Zee of her loose-fitting trousers, revealing a small and peachy backside. His palms felt the velvety smoothness of her buttocks as he rolled the material down and soon he was caressing them boldly, running his fingers down her crack and soon finding the wet declivity between her slim thighs. She moaned aloud as his finger slipped right into her quim from behind, finding it both tight and moist. He thrust deep into her and reached the cervix with his fingertip, making her gasp.

Zee moved to kiss Annis on her rounded belly, leaving her friend's breasts free for Darrel to play with. He shifted so that he could continue to stimulate Zee's avid pussy while his lips roamed around the generous slopes of Annis's breasts, moving in a spiral towards her protuberant nipple. In passing he stroked Zee's smaller tit, pinching the hard nub as he went and making her wriggle in delight at the sudden surfeit of sensation. The feeling that they were like young animals, cavorting together in imitation of adult activity, was strong in him now.

The two women seemed oblivious to him and perfectly at ease with each other. It was obvious that they'd made love together before and, from the amount of enthusiasm they were putting into it, from choice rather than duty. It seemed to fit with the strange world they inhabited, a world where love had to be snatched on the wing, a few moments of pleasure to lighten the terrible tension they must be living under.

After Darrel had been trying, rather ineffectually, to join in, they suddenly turned their attention to him. Giggling and winking at each other they untied the belt at his waist and stripped him quickly and efficiently. Then they began to give him an all-over massage, Annis working down from his head and Zee working up from his feet, in gentle rhythm. He lay back and relaxed into it, relishing the sight of Annis's huge, bell-shaped breasts swaying above him and Zee's elegant little posterior raised into the air as she worked away at his thighs.

Once he would have been turned on a treat by such a sight, he reflected. And a part of him wanted to be, wanted to see his erection kick into action with the promise of a long, wet dive into one or other of their hot, welcoming pussies. Yet everything had become so confused for him since he discovered that his sex drive was being artificially stimulated and directed. He had no idea what was natural for him any more. To be in a state of impotence was almost preferable to the kind of fake experiences he used to have.

'Just relax!' Annis cooed, seeing his fists clench at the thought of the controllers and what they had done to him. She leant forward, her breasts pressed meatily against his chest, and whispered in her conspiratorial tone, 'They'll see you're not getting hard and wonder why. It's all part of the plan, Dee. Don't worry!'

He knew they couldn't talk properly, so he just smiled and stroked her cheeks. She placed her breast in his palm with a grin and he squeezed it gently, then pulled at the long nipple until she uttered a contented sigh. Moving his mouth close to her ear he murmured a single word: 'Malaku!'

She laughed knowingly and slid down his body, her lips finding the moist tip of his glans. Although they all knew it was futile, Annis proceeded to lick him there while Zee stroked his balls. Only a faint, sensual tingle wound its way through his nervous system but it was better than nothing. Darrel lay back again, a smile on his lips, and watched Zee take hold of her friend's breasts from behind and squeeze them into pneumatic splendour once again.

When his obstinate penis refused to come out and play, the girls made a show of pouting disappointment for the camera and eventually turned to each other again for relief. Darrel sat back and watched as Annis wriggled down towards Zee's open crotch and applied her generous mouth to the wet opening. Since she was lying half on top of him Darrel was able to stimulate her small breasts with his fingers, and soon the girl was thrashing and moaning with extreme arousal. Yet her moans seemed more frustrated than anything, and it was soon obvious that she needed something more than Annis's lips and tongue to bring her off.

'Fuck me!' she yelled, in torment. 'Find something to fuck me with, for fuck's sake!'

Annis giggled and picked up her bag which was slung on the floor. She opened it and brought out a large pink dildo fashioned in neoplasty. A flick of a switch started it humming and jerking and spewing out gobs of white lubricant. She thrust it in between Zee's trembling thighs and was rewarded with a long sigh of relief, 'Aaah! Oh that's so much better! I'm full right up now!'

Despite himself, Darrel felt a deep shame that he was unable to satisfy her himself. He knew that, in other circumstances, it would have been no problem but that didn't make it any easier to sit by and watch her come through artificial stimulation. Gently he rolled her hard little nipples until at last she gave some loud, choking gasps and her face grew cherry red. She thrust her chest against his hands and he stroked her tits and pulled at her nipples with increasing speed as the intensity of her climax increased. Then she sank, panting, into a sweaty heap on his belly.

'That was good, wasn't it?' he heard Annis say as she withdrew the slimy pink dildo. He saw Zee nod, then whisper something in her friend's ear. Both girls giggled, then they suddenly seized his arms and legs, taking him completely by surprise.

'Over he goes!' Zee said as his body was twisted and turned, making him lie face down. Then she announced, loudly, 'We'll teach you to let us down! We've paid for this session and we expected satisfaction from you, not from each other. We can do all that at home!'

'W–what are you going to do to me?' Darrel asked, genuinely frightened by the sudden turn of events.

Two pairs of hands landed on his bum and he felt his cheeks being parted. His arse opened up with a soft fart and he heard Annis whisper, 'Don't worry – it's well lubricated!'

'No!' he moaned, trying to clench his sphincter but to no avail. The slippery nose of the dildo was placed at his anus and he knew that his body's last remaining virgin territory was about to be violated. 'No, no!' he protested softly. But then, feeling his puckered hole stretch to accommodate the glans-like tip, he gave a low groan and settled for, 'Please be gentle with me!'

'Easy, easy does it!' Zee cooed as the dildo was turned gently round and round, slowly boring further into him. It was certainly well greased, both with whatever lubricant was inside and with the juices that Zee's cunt had added to it. It slid into him with insidious ease and he felt himself expanding around it, opening up to it. He was praying he wouldn't give another fart.

Then, when it was about halfway in, the girls let it slip out again. Darrel felt a rush of dark sensuality as the thing slipped through his sensitive inner walls and then slipped back up into him, more smoothly this time. He arched his back, hoisting his bum high in the air, and began to relish the unaccustomed stimulation of his back passage and the sensual massage of his prostrate that this produced. Although his prick remained limp he could feel some hot tingling in his balls and guessed that some kind of reflex was being triggered.

'Good, isn't it?' he heard Annis say, close to his ear. He could feel her heavy breasts dangling on his back, the nipples brushing against his skin, and then she began to kiss his neck with tiny, nipping kisses that aroused him mercilessly even though they had no effect on his cock. Zee was fondling his balls, moving them around in their sac and squeezing gently in a way that he found very exciting. The dildo moved faster, gliding in and out with ease now, and Darrel felt the pressure build inside him. Yet it felt very odd, without an erection, and when he finally experienced a brief squirt of semen it was a peculiar kind of relief, sensual without being sexual.

He collapsed face down on the bed while the girls

wrung out a towel in hot water and cologne and proceeded to give him a delicious rub-down. His arsehole ached horribly, but they sprayed some antiseptic into it and soon he felt only a pleasant numbness. Satiated both physically and emotionally, Darrel sank into a warm fog of contentment for a while and when he came to his senses again he realized, to his amazement, that he was alone. Dimly he heard the insistent buzz that indicated a message had been screened and he rose, bleary-eyed, from the bed to view it.

He'd half expected the summons but even so it was a shock to see it there in writing. He was ordered to present himself at the Chief Controller's office, Block Three, immediately. A chill snaked down his spine as he recognized the success of Jay's plan. It had all gone like clockwork, even allowing for the appearance of Cleofa – which might have been scheduled in any case. Feeling uncomfortably like a pawn in a chess game of global significance, Darrel got into the shower and attempted to stimulate his brain cells with a douche of tepid water. He would need to be on full alert for whatever lay ahead of him now.

Chapter Nine

'Ah, Darrel – good to see you. Please take a seat.'

The dulcet tones of the Fat Controller didn't fool Darrel in the slightest. He knew that no one was called into this office unless something was wrong, badly wrong. The man's polite veneer was a ploy, designed to put him at ease, that was all.

'I expect you're wondering why I want to see you,' the FC went on, his eyes gleaming in his pudgy face. 'We thought it was time you had a bit of a check-up, that's all. Nothing to be alarmed about. Think of it as your thousand-mile service. I suppose your cock must have travelled around that number of pussy-miles by now.'

Darrel was alarmed by the salacious language, delivered in that same unctuous tone. He decided to challenge him. 'Is anything wrong?'

'Nothing wrong, no. But we like to make sure that any minor hitches are corrected before they have a chance to grow into major ones. It's good medical practice, as I'm sure you appreciate.'

'Medical?' That word always alarmed him. Never more so than now,

'I'm sure there will be no need for elaborate treatment, but a physical examination will be necessary. Of course, it will take place under anaesthetic.'

Darrel knew he was meant to feel reassured by that last remark: no pain, no blood, nothing for the squeamish to worry about. But, knowing what he knew, the thought of how they might tamper with his brain once he was unconscious was terrifying. What if they turned him into some kind of gibbering idiot, by accident or design?

'W–when?' he stammered.

'Immediately. We've made sure you have no more clients for the rest of the day. So if you'll just follow me, Darrel, the sooner we get started the sooner you can get back to work again, earning all that lovely credit.' The FC put his greasy hand on Darrel's shoulder, and he fought the urge to shrug it off. 'We've been very pleased with you, you know. Your record is exemplary and we want you to go on giving satisfaction for a very long time to come. After this little examination I'm sure you'll feel on top form again.'

Like a lamb to the slaughter, Darrel allowed the FC to lead him through an inner door to a gleaming white room with an adjustable stainless steel couch and a huge bank of computer-controlled instruments. Two figures dressed completely in white, their faces half masked, waited by the couch. It was impossible to say whether they were male or female. Terror gripped Darrel, making him want to piss.

'Can I . . . relieve myself?' he asked, his voice coming out disconcertingly squeaky.

The FC gave his avuncular smile. 'Don't worry about a thing. All bodily fluids will be evacuated when you are under anaesthetic. The only thing we want you to do is to take your clothes off and put them in this container. I shall take my leave of you now.' He turned to one of the attendants, saying in a low voice that Darrel was not intended to hear but which he managed to catch, 'I'll be monitoring. This one interests me greatly.'

For a few seconds Darrel considered making a sudden dash for it through the still-open door to the Controller's office, but he knew it was useless. He was a long way from any exit and there would be plenty of time to sound the alarm. Besides, he knew if he made an escape bid before anything was done to him he would be letting the others down. Jay had explained that they needed to see how his electrodes had been modified, so they could decondition people more effectively in future.

Even so it was hard to submit to the unknown at the hands of these frighteningly anonymous individuals. When he had undressed, one of them took the container away and the other helped him onto the couch where he lay on the absorbent pad, feeling utterly alone and helpless. He scarcely had time to register his feelings before a mask on the end of a long tube was placed over his nose and mouth, bringing almost instant oblivion.

Darrel came to in his own room at the Plaza. He felt extremely groggy, as if he'd mixed a slow unwinder with a super-stimulator, and his head ached horribly. When he opened his eyes the room looked alarmingly fuzzy, but as his vision cleared he glanced from screen to screen and found they were all blank: that disturbed him even more.

Looking down he found he was still wearing a white, high-necked surgical robe that reached to his elbows and knees. Impatiently he tore it off, searching his body for signs of invasion, particularly around the genital area, but there were none. Whatever operations they'd performed on him must have been confined to brain surgery. There was still a close-fitting plastic cap around his skull, which was now throbbing with nervous activity.

After a while Darrel managed to get his stiff limbs into motion and he took a shower. The warm water revived him, but several times he felt giddy and had to sit down. His stomach was empty, but he felt too sick to contemplate eating anything. All he wanted was to be left alone, but he was afraid they wouldn't let him. They would want to know that their surgery had worked, and that would mean making him take on another client. Right now he felt he couldn't fuck another woman to save his life.

What he really wanted was to be with the others again. At the thought of Franca nursing him back to health, cradling his head against her ample bosom, his cock gave a definite twitch. Darrel grinned, despite his pain. And what of Annis? His last, strange encounter with her had only deepened his curiosity about that woman.

Was he fit enough to leave the Plaza and travel to where they were? His longing was acute, yearning for the comfort and companionship that only Franca and her kind could give him. It was no use looking to Zal, Shin or Jabez for support: they could only betray him now. He began to dress in the maintenance overalls that Franca had obtained for him and that he'd hidden behind his wardrobe. He pulled the cloth gingerly over his body, put the floppy hat on over his plastic skull cap and then walked up and down the confined space of his room to test his legs. Only when he was satisfied that his muscles could support him adequately, and his head was clear enough to make the attempt, did he leave his room.

The foyer was quiet, the girl on the desk absorbed in some game show on the screen in front of her and hardly aware of him. He mumbled something about 'maintenance crew' and she waved him on. It seemed ridiculous that security could be so lax, but when he tried to get through the exit an alarm sounded, freezing him to the spot. The girl pressed a button to switch off the annoying buzz, then came hurrying up from the desk.

'Can I see your pass?' she asked, in a peremptory tone.

'Mm.' He showed her his genie ID. She frowned at it. 'This won't let you out. You need an exit pass.'

'Oh, sorry!'

He pretended to search his clothing, unsure what to do next. A male guard came shuffling up and Darrel knew he had to think of something fast. 'Must have left it in my room,' he mumbled.

'Is he giving you any trouble?' the guard asked the girl.

Someone was coming in through the door, a client. She was moving hesitantly – perhaps it was her first visit – and stood still for a few seconds, framed in the open doorway. Darrel decided to risk it. He rushed up to the door, muttered 'Excuse me!' and pushed the surprised woman to one side. Behind him he heard the guard shout, 'Hey! Stop!' and the desk girl gave an excited squeal, but he was free!

Despite his enfeebled state Darrel managed to put on quite a sprint and was soon running alongside a shuttle car. It was due to slow down in a hundred metres or so. Panting, he struggled to keep up with the vehicle and was relieved when it began to brake. As soon as the car slowed to walking pace the door slid open and Darrel swung on board.

He didn't look too out of place among the other maintenance men. A guard glancing in at the window would not pick him out, he was confident of that. Only if they boarded the shuttle and searched it thoroughly would his identity card give him away. A slow exhilaration filled his veins as he realized that he stood a good chance of completing his getaway. Although he was puffed and exhausted from his brief flight he knew that he would soon recover once he was in a safe place.

Darrel recognized the stop where he and Franca had left the shuttle before and hopped off. The path to the safe house was easy to remember but he went warily, trying to ensure he was not being followed. It would be an appalling tragedy if he unwittingly led the enemy to his new friends' door. At Mobility Junction he crossed beneath the highway, wrinkling his nose at the smell, and soon saw the derelict house standing on its scrubby patch of land. He deliberately veered to the left then dodged behind an abandoned cabin and waited. After several minutes, convinced that no one was tailing him, he cautiously approached the house.

Darrel tapped on the door but no one answered and there was no sound at all from within. Suppose the place was empty? He knocked again, louder this time, but after a while crept round to the back where a flight of mouldering steps led down to the cellar. Peering in, he found the window obscured by a dark cloth. He hammered on the door, calling out Jay's name, and Franca's, but there was something absolute about the silence inside and he had the distinct impression that no one was there.

Darrel cursed softly. He was feeling utterly exhausted now, unable to go a step further. The hope of succour had driven him on, but now despair was weakening him, sapping his energy and replacing it with throbbing pain. He crumpled into a heap on the filthy ground, rested his head against the rotten door and closed his eyes with a groan, knowing that if he stayed there for any length of time he would make himself really ill. Yet he had no idea where to go – and no strength to get there even if he had.

His sleep was fitful and every time he drifted awake his body was racked with torment. Then, several hours later, when he opened his eyes to find the sky dark above him, he was aware of a figure bending over him and a solicitous hand on his shoulder.

'Dee – is it really you?'

He blinked up through his pain and recognized the pale oval of Zee's face. He tried to speak, but his voice came croaking from his desiccated throat.

'Don't try to talk,' she said, hastily unlocking the door. 'I'll get someone to help.'

She returned in a few seconds with a beaker of liquid and a man who Darrel vaguely recognized as one of the group. After he'd taken a few sips of the warming drink the man lifted him under the armpits and, with Zee holding his feet, they took him into the refuge. He felt soft cushions beneath him, a blanket being pulled up, then drifted back into darkness.

Darrel must have slept well into the next day. When he awoke Franca was beside him, a bowl of something savoury steaming in her lap. She smiled fondly at him.

'Thank God – I thought you'd never come round! Try some of this. It's nothing special, but it's hot and nourishing and should help build your strength up.'

He did his best but could only manage a few spoonfuls

of the soup. Franca wiped his brow with a deliciously cool cloth that was scented with herbs and had a revivifying effect on him. When he was sitting up, Jay appeared.

'Our hero!' he declared, wryly. 'But did you have to do a bunk like that? You've got half the Plaza out looking for you.'

'I couldn't help it. I was so sick of that place!'

Jay nodded. 'No matter. We'll ship you out as soon as you're fit, in any case.'

'Out where?'

'Malaku, where else? It's where all conquering heroes go to their rest, didn't you know?'

Despite his pain, Darrel felt his heart lighten. 'Really?'

'Annis is going, too,' Franca smiled. 'Just for a while. She's been quite the heroine and she deserves a rest.'

'I know. It must have been terrible for her, going back into the Plaza.'

'Not just that.' Franca's face bore a strange expression, half frowning, half amused. 'You haven't guessed, have you? Not even after she came to you with Zee.'

'Guessed what?'

'That she and Zee are lovers.'

'She's lesbian?'

'Bisexual.'

'I did wonder!'

'But she's very wary of men after what they've done to her. So now you see how particularly difficult her assignment was. Fortunately she found you relatively easy to cope with.' Franca gave a wicked grin. 'Probably because you'd been chemically castrated!'

'But why her? Surely you could have found someone else, someone who liked men more?'

'There are few women in our movement, as you must have noticed. The rest of us were needed elsewhere. If Annis had made a serious objection she would have been excused, but she regarded it as all in the line of duty. I'm sorry if that makes you feel bad.'

'No, it doesn't.'

And that was the truth. Hard as it must have been for her to contemplate sex with him, Darrel felt sure she'd responded to his basic sympathy. And the way she and Zee had performed in his room had been more than just professional. They had no doubt been lovers a long time. Wistfully, he realized that he could never win that woman's complex heart. But he still cared for her. 'How is she? Where is she now?'

'With Zee, in a safe place. You won't see her again until you're in Malaku. But first, our chaps have some unfinished business with you.'

'What are they going to do to me?'

'Basically, take your brain apart.' She laughed at his horror. 'Don't worry, it's not as bad as it sounds! I mean the parts they've wired up. They're setting up their equipment now, upstairs.'

'Will I be conscious?'

'No. I have to give you this. You might as well take it now.'

She handed him a small bottle with a spout from which the cover had been removed. He drank the bitter-tasting liquid down obediently and was soon feeling drowsy again, but the pain had gone and the floaty feeling was very pleasant. He drifted with it for a while then sank into darkness.

* * *

Coming round for the second time, Darrel felt perfectly normal. He blinked open his eyes and found himself in the familiar surroundings of Franca's apartment. 'What the . . . !'

At the sound of his exclamation the door opened and Franca appeared, carrying a tray. She set it down beside the bed with a smile. 'Ah, good. How does it feel to be back in the land of the living?'

'Surprisingly good, actually. But how did you get me here?'

'Special delivery.'

Darrel grinned, stretching his limbs beneath the soft, warm covering. It occurred to him that not only was he feeling normal again, but he was ravenously hungry – and not just for food! He reached up and touched Franca's hair as she poured him a drink.

'Feeling randy?' she smiled. 'That's not surprising, considering what Jay and Em have done to you. We'll have a chance to test out their handiwork later on.'

'What do you mean?'

'Never mind, just drink this. It's complete nourishment. Then have a bit more rest. I'll be back in an hour or so.'

He dozed his way through another hour and was relieved when she returned, this time with Jay and another man he vaguely recognised.

'You're looking fine, Dee,' Jay smiled. 'This is Em, our biodigital engineer. He did a bit of reverse engineering, found out what they'd done to you and reconstructed your circuitry to bring you back as close to normal as we can manage. Not that you can recall how "normal" used to feel, I suppose.'

'I was pretty randy as a teenager,' Darrel said, thinking

166

of Cleofa. What had happened between them seemed light years ago now.

Jay grinned. 'Weren't we all? I'll just take your pulse and temperature. Then we can leave you and Franca alone.' He winked. 'Got to test that your system's working properly again. She'll be wired up too, for experimental purposes, but don't let that worry you. I'm sure it won't get in the way.'

The very thought of it made Darrel's pulses race, but Jay didn't seem bothered as he checked the rate. After the physical checks he and Em left the room and Franca came to sit beside him on the bed. She was wearing a semi-transparent turquoise robe with a deep V-neck and Darrel was relieved to find that he had a pretty sturdy erection. She eased back the covers.

Her face lit up when she saw his rearing prick. 'I thought so! Looks like they've got it just about right.'

She touched his shaft with her cool, smooth hand and it twitched eagerly. Within seconds they were kissing, deep, luscious kisses that sent his libido soaring upwards along with his temperature. Franca seemed happy to do most of the work and straddled him comfortably, her thighs alongside his. He felt for her nipples and stroked them softly, aware of the full weight of her breasts against his chest.

Her lips moved down to enclose his glans and he sighed with a mixture of relief and pride as his erection reached maximum proportions, thrusting into the wet opening between her lips. His glans pushed hard against the roof of her mouth and he felt her tongue flick around the sides, then up and down the shaft. With his sexual potency came a resurgence of his male pride, a wonderful feeling of well-being. Those uncomfortable episodes back at the Plaza had disturbed his self-esteem more than he'd realized. Now that he had it back again he felt great.

And now, more than ever, he wanted to prove himself in a woman's cunt, to push his way into the soft, sensual heart of her and make her come.

Franca was fondling his balls now, her fingernails scratching at the sensitive spot beneath them and rousing him to frenzied desire. His palms caressed the generous curves of her behind as she squatted over him, then his fingers found their way between her buttocks and down, past her tight little anus, to her wide-open vulva. Darrel stroked the wet labia, making her gasp, and then proceeded to tease her bulging clitoris until he could feel it throbbing beneath his fingertips.

'Oh, you . . . !' she gasped, at a loss for words.

Unable to hold out any longer, Franca hoisted herself up and engaged his straining cock in the mouth of her pussy. She remained still for a few moments, letting both of them enjoy the contact, before starting to caress him with her inner muscles. His journey into her was slow and delicious, letting him savour all the delights along the way until at last they were fully locked together, his glans hard up against her cervix. She continued to squeeze him in lazy rhythm, her vaginal walls undulating up and down his sturdy erection, reminding him of his regained potency.

'You're so big!' she murmured, leaning over so that her gorgeous tits swung heavily against his chest again. He caught them full in his hands, and tweaked their long, stiff nipples. 'I don't remember you being this huge before. You're filling me up completely!'

'Good!'

Darrel's voice was a guttural bark. He could feel himself on the brink and he didn't want to spoil things by letting go too soon. Yet it was very difficult. After his recent problems the temptation to thrust home as hard as he could was strong. He sensed that Franca wanted more stimulation and pinched her nipple hard, making her moan and move her pelvis.

Slowly she rose to the tip of his cock, poised there like a bird on a wire, then she slid down suddenly and their pubic bones collided. She began to wriggle around, pressing her mound, with its distended clitoris, hard against the root of his erection so that he made closer contact inside, too. They moved in graceful harmony for a while, enjoying the grinding of hip against hip, the slide of thigh against thigh.

Then Darrel looked up to see her face contorted with intense concentration and knew that she was nearing her climax. She was lost in an erotic world of her own and he wondered what fantasies might be going through her head, turning her on. Had she enjoyed making love with Annis too? Was she also bisexual? The thought of those two beauties enjoying each other's horniness increased his own and, after a few jerking thrusts, he was in the throes of a gutwrenching orgasm that allowed him to spill out all his frustration in one tremendous burst of hot energy.

There was a lot of fluid, too. Darrel heard the squelching as they uncoupled and sank down beside each other on the bed.

'Wow! I hope you're satisfied!' Franca giggled. 'Because I am!'

'It was good, better than I had any reason to hope. I

thought I'd still be groggy after they'd been messing around with me.'

'You needn't worry – Em's the best! I've seen him patch up the most unbelievable cases.' She kissed him, then gave him a long, earnest look. 'Everything's going to be all right, you know. I can feel it in my nipples.' He laughed. 'No, really! They're very sensitive and they've never let me down. You and I will be having a ball on Malaku before you can say "Fat Controller"!'

But at the thought of what he had left behind, Darrel was filled with sudden fear.

'They'll be wondering where I am,' he said, sombrely. 'I tried to make sure no one was following me, but what if they've put a tracer bug inside my skull?'

'Don't worry, Em would have found it. I think you took the controllers completely by surprise. They weren't expecting you to make a dash for it so soon.'

'What had they done to me – do you know?'

'Roughly. They put in some new circuitry. Em said it was very interesting, a kind of three-way switch that enabled you to be linked up not only with your client but with a third party too. The details are bit too technical for me, though, you'll have to ask Em. I'm sure he'll be pleased to explain.'

'What happened to this . . . circuitry.'

'Em thought it might come in useful so he didn't remove it altogether, just disabled it. He can activate it any time, but he would never do so without your permission. That's one of our cardinal rules: group members must know exactly what they are letting themselves in for when on a mission.'

Darrel grinned ruefully. 'I'm not sure I knew exactly

what would happen to me when I last went back to the Plaza.'

'Well, you weren't *exactly* a group member then. More an honorary associate.'

'So am I now?'

She nodded. 'Oh yes. You've proved yourself, absolutely. And only bona fide members are allowed to make it to Malaku.'

'I can't wait!'

She sighed. 'You'll have to, I'm afraid. There's a kind of halfway house you must visit first, so the final experiments and adjustments can be made. Em doesn't have enough of the right equipment here.'

Darrel sat up with a frown. 'This is the first I've heard about it!'

'I only found out myself this afternoon. And I've another mission to perform, so next time we meet it will be on Malaku. But I've no idea when.'

The news had taken the wind out of Darrel's sails. He felt cheated, as if he'd been led to believe that the end was nearer than he supposed. Now he had some other ordeal to go through before he could claim his reward. It wasn't fair!

He realized there was nothing he could do about it, though. His life at the Plaza was over, and he'd thrown in his lot with this bunch, for better or worse. By the time Franca left him and Jay returned with Em, he was in a more resigned mood.

'You've made excellent progress,' Jay said at once. 'A little fine tuning should get you into fit a state to be operated on, sometime in the future. But first we shall send you to Geosan.'

'Geosan?'

'Didn't Franca tell you?' Jay's blue eyes were sparkling with amusement. 'You'll go on the shuttle to meet our contact there. You'll spend a few nights being tried out in a place like the Plaza, women only. They do things more . . . crudely over there. But the conditions will be right for us to test our circuitry.'

'I'm just a human lab rat to you, aren't I?' Darrel blazed.

Jay's eyes darkened to a serious ultramarine. 'No, Dee. You are one of our most successful agents, and for that we honour and respect you. Make no mistake about that. But we need as much information about the controllers' technology as we can get, and you just happen to have rather a lot of it wrapped around your skull. Sorry, but that's how it is.'

Ashamed of his sudden outburst Darrel said, 'Of course, you're right. I'm sorry.'

Jay smiled. 'That's okay. Now I think you've had about enough excitement for one day. We want to measure your blood-sugar levels, pulse, metabolic rate and so forth but it will be easier for us to do that while you're asleep. Drink this. It will give you some well-earned rest.'

He did as he was told, wondering how many more artificially-induced sleeps he would have to endure. It sounded as if he wouldn't have to do anything he didn't want to when he reached Malaku. He had an image of a place that was some kind of paradise, such as he'd only seen on screen. He hoped he wouldn't be disappointed.

When he awoke he found Franca and Jay at his bedside. A small case had been packed for him and he was told that, after his shower, he must be on his way.

'We have your new contact lenses and false papers,' Jay said, briskly. 'The details have been entered into the computer at frontier control by one of our master hackers. You will be identified as a Caucasian named Star. We anticipate no problems. All your needs will be taken care of while on the shuttle and you should arrive at Geosan feeling quite refreshed. Our man will meet you at the spaceport. His name is Choi. That's really all you have to remember; he will see to the rest.'

There was a sense of urgency, and of impersonality, in Jay's tone that made Darrel feel he really was on a mission this time, truly was one of them. It was daunting, but exciting too. Franca led him into the shower and helped him off with his robe, then disrobed herself. 'I thought you might need a little help in here,' she smiled.

Darrel let himself wallow in sensuality as she soaped his body all over, paying special attention to the crevices of his penis and arse. He gasped when her fingers slipped into his crack and began a gentle massage of his anus while her other hand played with his erect prick, raising it to substantial proportions.

Darrel took the soap tube from her and sprayed her breasts with it, then rubbed in the slick liquid, feeling her nipples harden into long, rubberized points beneath his fingers. One hand slipped down and found her crack open and dripping, the thick walls giving his fingertip an encouraging squeeze when he ventured in.

'Take me standing up!' she breathed in his ear.

He needed no further encouragement. Pressing her against the smooth shower surround, Darrel pushed his cock straight in between her labia, which she was holding apart. He found her entrance and slid in with ease, groaning with the sudden pleasure of being enveloped by warm, velvety flesh. They kissed, their mouths filled with watery saliva, and their tongues danced together while he stabbed into her with rapid, slight movements of his penis.

Franca clutched fiercely at his buttocks to keep herself from slipping down, digging in her nails, and Darrel was surprised to find he relished the slight pain. The water continued to shower over them in a long, warm stream, washing away any sweat they exuded the minute it appeared so that he felt clean and fresh. It was very exhilarating, making him feel healthy and athletic, the way he used to feel when he played Razorball for his hostel.

Suddenly Darrel felt himself coming and fell against the wall as a tidal wave of exquisite bliss washed over him, weakening his body from the waist down. Franca's cunt was rippling in response, her climax inspired by his, and they slowly sank down the wall together as their knees gave out. She giggled, starting him off, and they ended up in helpless laughter on the slippery floor until the last spasms of their mutual pleasure were spent. Then they clung to each other, aware that this would be the last time, for a while at least, that they would be able to make love. Darrel felt the urge to say something momentous, but all that came out was, 'Thank you, Franca.'

'That's all right.' She smiled weakly at him. 'We'll do even better on Malaku. More time, more space. No worries. It'll blow your mind, and that's a promise!'

But first, as Darrel was only too well aware, there was Geosan.

Chapter Ten

The transit car accepted Darrel with a sigh from its open-ing doors, then closed them with a grunt. This little train was whisking him towards no terrestrial vehicle, but a space-bound one that would zoom up through the at-mosphere, turn in space and catapult down again any-where on Earth – in this case Geosan, the quake-proof marvel of modern engineering that had sprung up from the ruins of Tokyo.

On board the shuttle the flight attendants were all Eurasian, small and slant-eyed with gentle voices and superbly jutting breasts. They must have been chosen for their figures, Darrel decided. He wondered how many of their bounteous bosoms were natural. His personal slave was a bob-haired beauty called Soo who smiled at him through peach-coloured lips and touched his hand or shoulder at every opportunity. He accepted a cocktail from her and she bowed prettily. He was going to enjoy this flight.

When he was asked to put on his helmet, however, Darrel grew nervous. What if the antigrav stabilizers interfered with his own circuitry in some way? But he was sure Jay and Em would have thought of that. The idea that this flight might itself be part of the experiment, however, was less than reassuring.

The sedative effect of the cocktail was beginning to kick in when the countdown began and Darrel's body lost some of its tense rigidity. He sank into the form-fitting cushion of his seat and closed his eyes. Visions of Malaku immediately surfaced – his vision, at any rate, which included nubile natives of the dancing-girl variety. Somehow they all seemed to resemble the delectable Soo.

Seeing the Earth rush away from him at a rate of knots was both terrifying and liberating. Darrel had only travelled this way once before, on a 'plezure flight' as a reward for servicing his thousandth Plaza client, so he was not as blasé about it as most of the other passengers, who looked like businessmen. Soon the Japanese coastal outline came into view and the pilot announced that they were going into 'spiral orbit'. A few minutes later the dizzying descent began. This was where people usually needed their vomit-bags but although Darrel felt very queasy he managed to avoid throwing up.

After a few minutes the landing dock was clearly visible and the craft drifted towards it, appearing to accelerate alarmingly during the last few seconds. Darrel only realized he'd been holding his breath when the ship finally clunked into place on the landing cradle. There was a long wait while various safety checks were made, and then they were given permission to disembark, row by row. Soo smiled winsomely at Darrel when she reached him and he wondered, idly, what the chances were of meeting any of these tempting women off-duty.

He was reminded, however, that he had a date at the Geosan equivalent of the Plezure Plaza. All he could hope was that the women there were as attractive as the flight attendants. He shuffled along at the back of a snaking

queue and began to go through the control points with
scarcely a qualm. His faith in his forged documents and
lenses had been strengthened after he'd passed so
smoothly through the outward system. But just as he'd
passed through the iriscope (here called 'Iridiscan') an
official called out: 'Mr Star! One moment, please!'

It took Darrel a few seconds to realize they meant
him. His heart was thudding when he turned back, afraid
that those seconds of hesitation might have given him
away. But the Asian was regarding him with a pleasant
expression.

'Would you step this way please, sir?' he said, bowing
slightly. 'There is a Mr Choi waiting for you in the reception lounge.'

Relieved, Darrel followed the official through the
bustling hall and into the luxurious suite reserved for
travelling VIPs. Jay and his friends were certainly well-
connected, he thought wryly. The thick carpet seemed to
caress his travel-weary feet as he walked over to the
panoramic window where a short man was rising from
his recliner.

'Mr Star?' the man beamed. He had an interesting face.
The almond-shaped eyes were hazel and his short, dark
hair had a distinctly red tinge, although both that and
his eye-colour could have been faked. Nowadays people's
appearance told you more about how they wanted to see
themselves than about their genetic inheritance.

His handshake was firm, lingering just a few seconds
longer than normal as if he wished to convey some
hidden message. Darrel smiled and nodded, acknowledging the secret agenda they shared. Choi went on, 'I
trust you enjoyed your voyage to the stars and back?'

Darrel concentrated carefully on his response. 'It was brief, but exhilarating. Almost as good as you-know-what.'

Once the coded phrases had been exchanged both men visibly relaxed. Choi even put a friendly arm around Darrel's shoulder as they moved towards the door. 'My limo is waiting in the carport, and we shall go straight to the Orchid Palace,' he said.

Darrel grinned. 'Sounds like a restaurant.'

'We do provide food, but our tariff of "refreshment" is a lot more interesting than any restaurant menu.'

Darrel was beginning to warm to the man's urbane manner and dry wit. He spoke little when they were in the limo, however, confining his remarks to a few comments on passing landmarks. The Geosan environment was dazzling, like a great bauble hung in the sky. Everything was on different levels, the road they were driving along at about level three with a further couple above. Down below the lights were starting to come on, turning the grids and blocks of the computer-designed city into something resembling a huge motherboard aglow with electrodes. Up above the sky was putting on a show too, sunset hues of pink and purple and gold. Despite the fact that there wasn't a sign of plant or animal life anywhere Darrel found it incredibly beautiful.

The remote-controlled car slid off onto a slip-road that wound down through the levels below and finally came to earth. Here the human element suddenly surfaced, like an anthill with the top removed. Darrel was surprised to find the streets teeming with life, people ambling in all directions, few of them rushing.

'It is the pleasure hour,' Choi explained. 'The time

between work and home. Male workers require a buffer zone between the two, and that is where our establishment comes into its own. We're always busiest between six and eight.'

It was Darrel's first inkling of the so-called 'Eastern Attitude'. Here wives expected their husbands to use prostitutes. It was regarded as normal. They also liked their lives to be as orderly as possible so the whole business was institutionalized, with independent soliciting incurring heavy penalties. Jay had explained that the Orchid Palace was a private enterprise run under licence, and so had a bit more leeway than the state brothels. It catered for a better class of client and was correspondingly more expensive.

The architecture of the Orchid Palace was very impressive. An effective mix of oriental and Neo-Art Deco, the phallic columns and breast-like pink domes with gold finials were suggestive of the sexual characteristics of both male and female. Darrel followed Choi through the heavy brass doors and found himself in an atmosphere of calm and luxury. A pretty girl in a tight skirt and transparent blouse that gave a glimpse of small, pale breasts glided daintily towards them. She bowed, offering hot towels from a tray.

'Welcome to the Orchid Palace,' she smiled at Darrel, then bowed again to his host. 'At your service, Mr Choi. What may I do for you?'

'Thank you, Mai. Please have Mr Star's luggage taken to his room, then escort him through to the preview lounge and provide him with any refreshment he requires. I shall join him there in a few minutes.'

The dainty creature took Darrel's hand and led him

along the hall. 'Is this your first visit to the Orchid Palace, Mr Star?'

'Yes. And to Geosan.'

Her face brightened with genuine enthusiasm. 'Oh, you will love our beautiful city! Please take a tour of the sights while you are here. You will not be disappointed.'

'I'm sure. I've been most impressed already.'

The large room she took him into was warmly lit, with little tables all around the walls flanked by thickly-upholstered recliners. A small stage stood against one of the walls, visible from all parts of the room, and beside it a smartly-dressed older woman sat with a permanent smile on her surgically-smooth face. The place was three-quarters full, men in business suits being attended to by a bevy of pretty girls in topless costumes who glided back and forth with trays of food and drink.

'Would you like anything special, Mr Star? A cocktail, perhaps?'

'Do you have an Oriental Sunset?'

'Of course,' she smiled. 'Perfectly appropriate.'

While he was sipping the sugary mixture of mango, ginger and saké flavours, Choi appeared. 'I had some business to see to,' he explained, sinking heavily onto the couch. 'But now I can relax with you, and enjoy the show. I want you to see what we have on offer here before you make your choice. Don't worry about hygiene – a stimulating shower is always included. Or a massage bath, if you prefer.'

'Sounds delightful. But could you please fill me in on my agenda? I know very little about why I'm here.'

'We must be discreet.' Choi moved closer to him, lowering his voice. 'I will talk in terms that we both understand. Your time here will be brief, which is why we must get down to things straight away. I understand that this is merely a stopover on your journey to somewhere even more congenial. But you know why this visit was necessary, do you not?'

'Yes, that much I do know.'

'Everything will be taken care of behind the scenes. All you have to do is behave as nature intended, if you take my meaning.'

Darrel grinned. 'Absolutely!'

'Your presence here is a wonderful opportunity for our people. So choose the girl you most desire. That will make sure you maximize your performance and give the greatest degree of feedback, if you understand me.'

'There's only one thing I can say to that – bring on the dancing girls!'

As if on cue, the background music increased in volume and everyone's eyes turned expectantly towards the stage, Darrel's included. The voice of the middle-aged woman began the proceedings.

'Welcome once again to the Orchard Palace, gentlemen. Whether this is your first visit, or your hundred-and-first, may I wish you a delightful and satisfying encounter with one or more of our beautiful girls. Before we begin our little show, a few essential details. Every one of our ladies is given a daily health-check to ensure your complete safety. However, if any of you are still wary of physical contact may I remind you that we have a complete range of virtual-reality experiences available at modest prices. If you prefer this style of encounter, please indicate to one of our hostesses who will take you to the Palace of Virtual Delights.'

She paused while two men sheepishly gestured and were led out by two of the girls. Then the woman went on, 'Please press the Start button of the screens that are now being lowered.'

Darrel looked up to see a stylish black box descending from its hidey-hole in the ceiling. It hovered before him, and he pressed the button. At once an image of the Orchid Palace filled the screen.

The madame continued, 'This computer contains full details of all the ladies you are about to see in the flesh. If you are interested in any of the girls please press the red button and your selection will be recorded. You may choose as many as you like. After the viewing session you may review your choices in order to make your final selection. Once you have decided which girls and which services you require please tell one of our hostesses, and she will debit your account. Thank you for being patient, gentlemen. I know you are eager to see the wonderfully talented young ladies we have assembled for you here tonight. If you have any questions, or are in any difficulty, please call over one of our hostesses who will be pleased to be of service.'

The lights dimmed, the music changed to a sultry beat and the scent of jasmine filled the air. Darrel sat back in his seat and prepared to enjoy himself. A curtain to one side of the stage was drawn back and the first courtesan appeared.

To his surprise, the girl was black. Her lower body was draped in a kind of sarong, with two straps of the same gaudy material criss-crossing between her ample breasts, each crested with a dusky nipple. Her eyes were black and sultry, her hair oiled and braided, and her full lips were painted a burnt-orange colour that Darrel found very alluring. She stood rather self-consciously on the stage, swaying her full hips, while the madame sang her praises.

'If you like your women hot and passionate, Kuru is the girl for you,' she began, in a sing-song tone that suggested she had learnt her spiel by heart. 'She is particularly proud of her fine breasts and protuberant buttocks, which are typically high and round.'

To prove the point, Kuru turned her back to the audience and lifted her sarong, displaying a behind with the characteristic *steatopygia* of her race. You could almost rest a glass on her shelf-like buttocks. Darrel felt his cock harden. This was most promising! The madame went on to detail the services this gorgeous babe had to offer.

'Kuru will give you a special mud bath, if that is your desire. Her expert fingers will massage the volcanic mud into all parts of your body, giving you a uniquely sensual experience, and if you wish you may return the compliment. Another of Kuru's specialities is a secret tribal ritual guaranteed to restore a man's potency. Of course she is open to all the more conventional pleasures too, including anal, and her uniquely voluptuous body, plus her extraordinary technique – part learned, part instinctual – will make your encounter with Kuru the sexual experience of a lifetime!'

Darrel was so absorbed in observing the girl's erotic movements that he forgot to press the button on his screen. He cursed, but as he was about to signal to one of the hostesses the next woman appeared on stage. This time she was a dazzling Amazonian blonde, whose tanned breasts jutted like firm, ripe pumpkins over her slim waist. While Darrel gawped she brushed her fingers casually over them, making the nipples stand out like giant berries. She wore a minuscule black leather skirt, with a waistband bristling with hardware and a short whip. Her long legs were encased in black latex to mid-thigh, high heels adding several inches to her already impressive stature.

'Gentlemen, may I present to you the lovely Ysa,' the madam said. 'Her obvious assets are complemented by some very special talents. She is an expert dominatrix, skilled in the art of bending men to her will and also in the subtle art of corporal punishment. If this is your preference, your experience at the hands of this beautiful woman will be an extraordinary one.'

Ysa snarled convincingly, showing her perfect white teeth, and gave a sudden crack of the whip that made everyone jump out of their skin. There was a ripple of uneasy laughter. Ysa prowled to the front of the stage and, selecting an Asian man sitting nearby, prodded him in the chest with the handle of her whip. Everyone laughed except for her random 'victim', who blushed to the roots of his dark hair.

Next on stage was a pair of identical twins, introduced as Mo and Flo. Apparently they always worked together. They were small and neat, with high, firm little breasts and nicely-shaped bottoms.

'Imagine what two can do!' the madame coaxed. 'Mo will offer you her sweet little pussy to nibble while Flo lets you penetrate her, or vice versa! Both girls enjoy anal sex as well. Although they always work in tandem, the girls do have some individual talents: Mo is particularly adept at fellatio, while Flo is able to pass water at will, if that is your preference. Just whisper your heart's desire to one of our hostesses and she will be pleased to book you in for our twins.'

The two girls cuddled and caressed each other for a few minutes, looking archly at the audience from time to time, then skipped off stage to be followed by a sultry redhead called Lea. Her gorgeous mane of dark red hair looked wonderful with her creamy skin and shy emerald eyes, and Darrel was definitely interested – until he heard what she had to offer.

'Lea's preference is for dominant men,' the madam began. 'You macho types who regard women as the weaker sex, here's your chance to enjoy a totally submissive woman. She will do whatever you demand, within reason. Light punishment is definitely on Lea's agenda. She also appreciates being bound and gagged. If total control over your partner is what you crave, Lea will satisfy you completely.'

Darrel watched as she held her hands behind her back and sank to the stage, writhing on the ground and gazing with longing at another man in the audience. He played to the gallery, snarling at her so that she gave a shudder of terrified pleasure. Darrel found the display somewhat tacky and felt uneasy about it. The idea of dominating women in that play-acting manner didn't turn him on, but he wouldn't have minded giving that girl a good seeing-to all the same. Aware that he had yet to make his choice, his finger hovered over the button for a few seconds until he decided it was probably best to leave her for someone who would appreciate her talents more fully.

'What do you think of the show so far, Mr Star?' came Choi's voice, tinged with irony.

'Very nice. Very nice indeed.'

'Don't forget, you must make your choice. Choose the girl who most pleases you. That way everyone will be satisfied!'

Just as Darrel was mentally reviewing the candidates, another girl stepped onto the stage. Something about her made him sit up and take notice although, at first glance, she seemed rather insignificant compared to the others. She was an Asiatic, small with delicate features and dainty breasts, and her eyes were nervous as her gaze flicked around the room. Was this her first time? Darrel noticed that one of her breasts was noticeably larger than the other, which meant they must be a hundred per cent natural. No neoplasty surgeon worth his salt would ever let a woman end up lop-sided. Somehow, that endeared her to him and he leaned forward in his seat, eager to hear what the madame had to say about her.

'Gentlemen, meet the lovely Oralie. As her name suggests, "oral" is her speciality but she will also oblige you in many other ways. She is expert in ten different kinds of massage. She is accomplished in the art of yoga and can make love in more positions than you can possibly imagine, stimulating parts of your body that other women cannot reach. She is also able to detect your every desire through her special sixth sense, a wonderful gift of her genes. If total satisfaction is what you require, Oralie should be your choice.'

Darrel managed to press the button this time, despite the fact that his mind was working overtime. That bit about her genes sounded uncomfortably familiar. He raised his brows at Choi, who answered with a knowing smile. Was it possible that Oralie was a 'genie' too – or the oriental equivalent?

A hostess came over to him, smiling, notebook in hand. 'You require the services of Oralie, Sir?'

'Yes, please.'

She tapped the keys of her notebook and reeled off the tariff ending on an interrogative note. 'Massage, three credits per style each lasting five minutes?'

'Yes, I'll take two, please.'

The hostess entered his choice, then went on, 'Hand relief, mouth relief or full intercourse?'

'Can I have mouth leading on to full?'

'Certainly, Sir. That will be ten credits.'

He saw the credit signs lighting up in her eyes as she went on, 'How many positions would you like her to perform in, Sir? Up to a maximum of twelve.'

'Shall we say . . . five?'

'Very well. Will that be all, Sir?'

Her steely eyes seemed to challenge him. Darrel said, 'No, I'd like to perform cunnilingus on her too.'

With a regretful smile the hostess shook her head. 'I'm sorry, Sir. With Oralie that is not permitted. Perhaps with some other girl, before or after . . . ?'

'No, I'm interested only in Oralie. Why won't she let me lick her pussy?'

'I cannot say, Sir. My apologies.'

He shrugged, turning to Choi. 'They do things differently here. Back home, a client can get to do more or less what he or she wants.'

Choi nodded. 'Here they tend to specialize. There are advantages, the girls get to be expert in a few fields rather than just good all-rounders. I think you'll be well satisfied with Oralie. She's one of our newest girls, but she's turning out to be very promising.'

Somehow the way he spoke about her made Darrel angry. He knew how it felt to be treated as a commodity, to have his own personal needs ignored and to lose his self-respect. He'd been in that position for so long that it had become ingrained and only now – thanks to Franca and her friends – did any alternative way of viewing himself seem possible.

The hostess read off from her small screen: 'That will be twenty-six credits, plus tax makes thirty and another five for staff gratuities. Thirty-five credits in all, Sir. Shall I debit your account?'

He nodded, and she tapped away obviously pleased to have clocked up such a large bill. Darrel watched her, suddenly realizing that she and all the other hostesses were older than the courtesans. Was this how the system worked: after you lost the bloom of youth you were moved on to become a hostess? By the same process, did you get to be a madame in middle age?

His reverie was interrupted by Choi getting to his feet. 'I shall leave you now, Mr Star, if you don't mind. After your happy hour is over please return here where we shall meet again.'

He bowed and offered his hand. Darrel got up and, once Choi had gone, looked towards the stage again. A plump blonde girl was showing off her assets with a winsome smile, but she did nothing at all for him. He'd definitely made the right choice.

'There is only one gentleman ahead of you,' the hostess remarked as she closed her notebook with a plastic click. 'When it is time for you to see Oralie I shall inform you. Meanwhile I suggest that you review her details on your screen by pressing this button. Would you care for another cocktail?'

While she went to fetch his drink Darrel pressed the button she'd indicated and the face of Oralie smiled out at him from the screen. He put in the ear piece and her voice cooed at him, 'Hullo, my name's Oralie, I am twenty years old and my vital statistics are ninety, sixty, ninety-two. I came to join the girls at the Orchid Palace six months ago, and I love my work.'

The screen flipped to a sequence showing Oralie in her bath, soaping her small breasts with a coy smile. 'You'd like me to do this to you? There are many other things I could do for you, honoured client. I love to excite men, it turns me on. When I see your cock become big and hard I like it a lot, and become so wet that it is easy for you to enter me.' She rose from the foam, and parted her shaven labia with her fingers. 'You do want to enter me, don't you?'

The promo both fascinated and repelled Darrel. It was so artificial, the words spoken like those of the madame in a sing-song fashion as if being read from a cue or relayed through headphones. It was demeaning to the girl, yet he couldn't see how else it could be done given that she was addressing an unseen, unknown man.

She got out of the bath and went on to contort herself into various positions, displaying her erogenous zones with a complete lack of self-consciousness. Her lithe body twisted and turned like a rubber doll but the effect was oddly distancing, like watching a display of gymnastics, and Darrel found it hard to imagine how her acrobatics might enhance his sexual pleasure.

Oralie tried to explain. 'I like to find the maximum contact between my body and yours. That way we may both derive maximum pleasure from the experience. Believe me, you have not had a full sexual experience until you have made love in the manner of kissing birds, or following the way of the wildcat.'

She casually picked up a banana from a bowl of fruit, placed incongruously on the antique bathroom cabinet, and began to peel it with a suggestive smile. 'Of course,' she murmured, 'I may need to whet your appetite a little, before we start.'

Oralie began to perform convincing fellatio on the fruit, her little red tongue darting up and down the banana and licking around the top. She put the whole thing into her mouth until it almost disappeared, then pulled it out again, intact. Darrel felt his balls grow heavy with lust and a tingling heat began to flow down his fully erect shaft making the ultra-sensitive tip throb urgently. 'God, how much longer must I wait?' he groaned, looking at the clock on the screen.

'Here you are, Sir.'

The cool voice of the hostess as she handed him a frosted blue glass jerked his attention away from the screen for a few seconds.

'Thanks. Any idea how much longer I'll have to wait?'

She wagged a reproving finger at him, playfully. 'Each must wait his turn, Sir! But not to worry. The man who comes second always gets the best deal. The girl is well warmed up but has had no time to become fatigued. You are the fortunate one.'

Darrel sipped his drink, watching Oralie suck at the

banana with increasing fervour. The thought that she was probably doing something similar to a real, live man at that very moment was vaguely disturbing. He wanted to know what had brought her to the Orchid Palace, what her life had been like before. What would she think if he just sat her down and asked her questions for an hour?

He couldn't do that, of course, not least because it would let down both his host and his friends back home. Home. Darrel found the concept meant nothing to him any more, if it ever had. Going from the hostel into the Plaza had meant travelling from one impersonal institution to another, with no respite in between. Only in Franca's flat, or in that rundown hovel in the middle of nowhere, had he begun to get a feeling of what 'home' might signify.

The lovely Oralie had been nothing but a blur for the past few minutes and Darrel didn't like that. He rewound the promo to the point where she 'ate' the banana and then watched with closer attention. He was looking for clues, clues as to the real identity of this woman who fascinated him more than anyone else – except, perhaps, Annis.

She was showing him her bare bottom now, letting it jut out provocatively. Her slender fingers parted her cheeks and showed him the tawny rose of her tight little anus. 'Some men prefer to take me here,' she smiled, over her shoulder. 'They like the tightness, the naughtiness of it. Or maybe you just want my pussy. See how ready I am for you, always ready, always willing.'

Oralie spread her thighs wide and made her entrance open of its own accord, the rosy petals of her sex dabbled with love-dew. Darrel failed to suppress a groan. His erection was straining inside his clothes now, making him most uncomfortable. She seemed to be looking straight at him with those exquisite black velvet eyes of hers, challenging him, amused by his torment. God, how much longer would she make him wait?

The promo was drawing to its close. Oralie was dressed demurely in a silken gown, her black hair reaching to her waist in rippling, glossy waves. She sat cross-legged, brushing it, her tiny, pretty feet bare. He wanted to kiss each of her little toes. Would she allow such intimacies? Darrel felt an overwhelming desire to please her, even though he knew it was her job to please *him*. Was this some relic of his Plaza conditioning, or was it a genuine and spontaneous desire? Perhaps he would spend the rest of his life not knowing how many of his impulses were natural and how many induced by whatever circuitry still buzzed around inside his skull. The thought depressed him, but just as he was finishing his drink he saw his hostess making her way across the room with a broad smile.

'Are you ready, Sir? It is almost time for your appointment with Oralie. But first I must ask you to come with me for your medical check.'

'Medical check?' Darrel stared at her in alarm. 'No one said anything about that!'

'Just routine, Sir. We like to keep our girls in a good state of health. If you have any minor physical problem it can usually be corrected instantly by our expert staff. If you have finished your drink please follow me.'

Chapter Eleven

Oralie was waiting for him in a small antechamber off a corridor. She wore a pretty silk kimono in scarlet, white and turquoise which made her look china-doll-like, her eyes huge in the porcelain skin of her face. Her dark hair was pinned up but small tendrils wafted about the margins of her face. Darrel felt his heart take a dive towards his stomach. There was something so delicate, so vulnerable about her.

'Greetings, honoured sir!' she murmured, bowing low enough for him to see her breasts swing loose in the V-neck of her garment.

'I shall leave you to enjoy each other,' the hostess smiled.

Darrel scarcely heard, or noticed her departure. His eyes were riveted to the enchanting vision before him. She held out a pale hand and beckoned with fluttering, bird-like fingers, her small, peachy-pale lips smiling coyly at him.

They moved into an adjacent room, where lanterns swung producing dim light and the air was redolent of rose and jasmine. There was a large, open couch and a low table set for tea with cushions around it. Erotic prints hung on the walls. A bamboo screen in the corner concealed the bath and shower area.

Oralie's expressive hand gestured towards the cushions. 'Will you take some ginseng tea, good for virility? Or a cocktail, perhaps?'

'Tea would be fine.'

He sat cross-legged on the tasselled cushion while she poured steaming, fragrant tea into his cup. Again he saw the swell of her breasts as she leant forward and had to quash an urge to put his hand in and plunder them. Although he was sure she would have taken it in her stride, he had no wish to appear uncouth. Somehow it mattered to Darrel what she thought of him. She knelt behind him while he sipped his tea, her fingers gently working his neck muscles.

'So tense!' she murmured. 'But soon you will start to relax and then to enjoy yourself. Is this your first time at Orchid Palace?'

Darrel considered. 'It's my first time . . . anywhere like this.'

It was true. Although he worked – *used* to work, he corrected himself mentally – in a similar establishment he had never visited any other.

'Then you are nervous, yes? Don't worry, everything that happens here is good. And you don't need to do anything you don't want.'

Her sly fingers were undoing his clothes, slipping them off his shoulders. Soon she had him naked, an incipient erection already visible at the base of his stomach. Her cool palms slid easily over his back, her thumbs pressing more firmly from time to time. He guessed that she was stimulating his acu-nodes. Whatever she was doing seemed to be working. He could feel the tension oozing out of him like melted butter.

Then her hands left him. 'I think you might be more comfortable over here.'

Darrel rose awkwardly and faced her. The kimono was open now, revealing a long frontal strip of her naked body. His eyes took in the shallow curve of her cleavage, the perfect knot of her navel and the thick bush of dark pubic curls, clipped and shaved into a trim triangle. He saw how slim her thighs were, how petite her feet, and the way all her parts harmonized into a pleasing whole. The thermostat of his libido was soon pointing firmly skyward.

'Would you like to bathe or shower?' she asked. 'Bath comes with massage, shower with oral relief.'

Darrel wanted both, but that would have sounded greedy. He had to keep reminding himself that he was paying her to do a job and the contract had already been made. It shouldn't have been difficult for him to grasp that when he'd been in her position so many times himself, but try as he might he couldn't quite see her as a mercenary prostitute. Of course the whole set-up was carefully engineered to avoid giving that impression.

'Bath, I think. I did order oral relief, though, didn't I?

She giggled at the anxiety in his tone. 'Of course you did, Sir. Don't worry, that will come later. You will get a massage in the bath. Nice and relaxing.'

'Do you have to call me Sir? Can't I tell you my name? I know yours.'

Oralie sighed. 'I'm sorry, Sir. Rules of the house.'

'I could whisper it. No one would know.'

She giggled again, and he discovered that he loved making her laugh. Her eyes shone like some small furry animal's when she did, and she showed her even white teeth and red, active tongue. The thought of her using it on his dick made him shiver with delicious anticipation.

'Better not, Sir. I shall run your bath now. Would you like to choose your scented oil?'

Behind the screen was a chest filled with various floral and herbal essences. While Darrel sniffed at the pretty glass bottles Oralie ran his bath, swirling her hand around in the water to feel the temperature. Glancing at her through the steam Darrel could see the damp silk of her kimono clinging to the cleft between her buttocks: his prick lurched in response. She certainly knew how to get a man going!

When the room was filled with the scent of Persian Orchid, a sensual bouquet of floral and woody aromas, Oralie helped him into the green, limpid water of his bath. There was a specially-shaped perch at one end where she could sit, straddling his shoulders, while she performed the massage. Darrel was delighted to see that she had slipped off her kimono and was sitting there in the nude, her pink pussy lips clearly visible between her spread thighs. But he had to face the other way.

'This isn't fair!' he groaned. 'You're making me lie with my back to you!'

Again came that brittle laugh, like silver against glass but with a throaty, wicked undertone. Darrel adored it!

'You will have plenty time to look at me later,' she assured him. 'Now settle back and let me massage. Soon all your cares will float into water, and then we let them disappear down plug hole.'

This time it was Darrel's turn to laugh. She had a delightful sense of humour too! Did the woman have any vices? It was hard to imagine it.

Soon he had given himself up completely to her capable hands. She worked with rhythmic sureness, first covering his back and shoulders with deep pressure of her fingers and thumbs that broke down the sinewy knots, and then finishing off with a lighter, more sensual touch. When he was lying back contentedly she moved around to the side of the bath and started on his hand. Darrel made the mistake of opening his eyes and then couldn't close them again. He gazed at her beautifully pert breasts, with the dusky rose of her nipples soft and flaccid in the heat, and felt a desperate desire to tweak them into firm points.

'Close your eyes, please, Sir,' she commanded him at last. 'You will be more relaxed.'

With a groan, Darrel did as he was told but the vision of her delicate breasts continued to dance before his eyes, making total relaxation an impossibility. She worked her way up his arm and then took his other hand, giving it some firm stimulation before she moved on to his chest. He was surprised how strong she seemed, her fingers sure and probing. When her fingertips touched his nipples, however, they used a more gentle touch and soon he felt an urgent, tingling response in his groin.

His prick reared out of the water, fully erect, and Darrel longed for her to touch it. But although she continued to massage his stomach under water she ignored his genital area completely and moved to his thighs, smoothing them with long, firm strokes. By the time Oralie reached his feet he was feeling more relaxed again, and she spent a good while rubbing his soles with her thumbs until his whole body seemed to be vibrating at a higher frequency.

'Time for you to lie on the mat,' she said softly, ruining

his fantasy of pulling her into the bath with him.

She made him lie face down, so she could massage his back. Darrel groaned as the air was pummelled out of his lungs, but his groans changed to sighs of delight when her powerful hands began to knead his buttocks. His cock thrust into the soft matting as he imagined her clutching him while he shafted her over and over, and his balls felt hot and heavy. When her touch grew lighter, flicking delicately around his arse-crack and slipping low to tickle his balls, he moaned aloud.

Oralie let him turn over. Now he could see that she was completely naked, her hair tumbling down her back like a shiny black waterfall, and his prick rose to salute her. She smiled and gave it a brief fondle, much as one might pat an amusing puppy, then started on another kind of massage. This time her touch was soft and sensual. Using her palms, fingertips and knuckles she made a rapid tour of his body that Darrel found extremely exciting. Then, at last, when she had him roused and quivering from head to toe, she bent her lips to his body.

'Ooh!' he shuddered, feeling her wet lips against the sensitive flesh of his inner thigh. Her tongue flicked all the way up, avoided his balls then travelled down the other thigh to his knee. By now Darrel was in a state of exquisite torture, his prick straining fit to burst.

The tantalizing lips crept close to his cock and then her sneaky fingers began to caress his balls, scratching delicately with her nails all over the surface of his scrotum. While Darrel was squirming in anticipation he could feel Oralie's body pressed lightly against his legs, the creamy smooth skin of her breasts and stomach warm and inviting. He reached down to feel the silken curtain of her hair, which felt surprisingly heavy as it slipped between his fingers.

Darrel clenched a swathe of her hair tightly as her lips began to move towards the base of his shaft with agonizing slowness. Her nose was brushing his pubic hair. Then she put out her tongue and placed it flat against his cock. The heat surged up into his groin and lower belly, filling him with a rich, throbbing sweetness. The feeling intensified as she began to lick his cock like an ice-stick, savouring it. She sucked on his glans as if she wanted to taste his cream.

But just when Darrel was sure he was going to come Oralie changed her tack and began to mouth his balls, pushing her tongue right into the sac to separate them. She took one completely into her mouth and began rolling it around with her tongue, giving it a thorough tasting. Then she did the same with the other one. All the time her hands were caressing his inner thighs, driving him towards meltdown. He seized handfuls of her long hair and let the cool strands run through his fingers, like strings of worry beads, easing his tension.

Then she returned to his cock, this time with more serious intent. Her deceptively small mouth managed to take in almost the whole length of him, his glans penetrating her throat. Oralie licked around his shaft and across the bulbous head with rapid precision, at the same time moving her mouth up and down his erection. The combined effect was electrifying. Darrel groaned as he felt his climax approaching, sure this time he would be going all the way.

Yet even as he thought he'd reached the point of no return Oralie suddenly changed pace and kept him in suspense, right on the edge. Now she was fellating him with the flat of her tongue in sensual slow motion, delivering measured portions of pleasure that were just enough to keep him hovering in ecstasy, but not enough to tip him over into the cataclysm of release. Darrel released the long silk strands of her hair, letting them caress his stomach and thighs.

The wicked little tongue began flicking across the eye of his glans with rapid precision, tasting the fluid that was now oozing out. The fingers of one hand were round the base of his prick, keeping firm hold while she savoured him at the tip. With the other hand she was caressing his balls, squeezing the sac gently, shifting them around. Suddenly she let him plunge all the way into the furnace of her mouth, his glans ramming down her throat. He was ready to spurt into her, to send his spunk winging down her red lane, but she craftily ejected him just in time and went back to the tantalizing licking of his glans. There was more to lick now, white beads of juice that came in a steady flow from his stalk like milky sap.

Then she did something unbelievable. Turning her back on him she flung the dark curtain of her hair in his face and sat astride his body, letting the end of his cock lodge in the wet groove of her sex. There was no question of him going right in, not at that angle, but the way she used her muscles to stroke his glans with her labia was incredible. Like the wet valves of some mollusc they opened and closed on him, stroking him with their soft profiles. Darrel was desperate to get inside her, but just as the frustration was becoming unbearable she turned round again and let him thrust straight into her mouth.

This time she let him have his head, sliding over soft tongue and pushing against hard walls until his balls convulsed and the unstoppable spasms began. Hot jets of ecstasy spurted from him into her throat and she never flinched, taking it all in one long, continuous swallow. Darrel could feel his nervous system buzzing and exploding like a circuit overloading, and it took a long time for his scrotum to empty itself and his penis to become flaccid again.

He lay immobile while she gently sponged him down and emptied the bath. His entire body felt cleansed of its inner impurities. Oralie settled beside him like a cat, basking in his body heat, and he buried his hand in her wonderful hair again, relishing its still-cool feel.

'That was fantastic!' he whispered, kissing the warm satin of her cheek.

'Good,' she replied, happily. Her fingers strayed to his chest hairs, which she stroked absently. 'I try always to please.'

'And I bet you always succeed!'

'Of course. Satisfaction guaranteed!'

The words made him shudder, breaking his mood. All the angst connected with his last days at the Plaza came back to haunt him. Darrel took a deep breath then said, 'Is that what you promise the clients here?'

Her laughter had a jagged edge to it. 'Oh yes, Sir!'

The way she kept calling him 'Sir' jarred on him. It didn't help to ease the nagging suspicion at the back of his mind, either. 'Tell me how you came to work here.'

Her ebony eyes slid away. 'Oh, I just drifted into it. Like most girls.'

'You're new, aren't you? Where were you before?'

'I lived in a village, just outside Geosan. But you don't want to know about me. I have boring life before I come here. Now everything is wonderful!'

It came out too pat. Behind the blank screen of her eyes he could see something else mirrored, something that looked disturbingly like fear.

'And when you came here, did they give you a medical?'

She nodded, vigorously. 'Oh yes, Sir, of course! All girls here are healthy and clean.'

'Do you remember what happened? What they did to you?'

'No, Sir, I remember nothing.'

He believed her. If they'd put her under she *would* remember nothing. He wanted to question her further but she forestalled him by putting her lips to his and insinuating her tongue inside his mouth, making his cock stir a little. He touched her breasts, feeling the smooth curve beneath his fingers, pinching gently at the flat nipple until it ripened into a button. She made a little mewing noise and he reached for her buttock, smoothing his palm over the firm skin.

It didn't take long for his erection to get going again. Darrel was gratified to find that he could get it up twice running. After his unfortunate experiences at the Plaza he'd half expected problems in that department but it was all going like a dream. For an instant he remembered that this was supposed to be some kind of experiment, that he was being monitored, but he pushed the thought to the back of his mind, not wanting it to intrude on his pleasure.

When he tried to get his fingers into her pussy, however, she backed away.

'Please, not now,' she murmured, redirecting his fingers to her breast. But he had the distinct impression that she also meant 'not ever.' He remembered what the hostess had said about her, that she didn't permit cunnilingus, and his sense that there was some mystery about her sexuality deepened.

Darrel was soon distracted by the realization that she was going down on him again. Twice in one session – had he ordered this double treat? But as soon as his prick was rearing boldly again she stopped and straddled him, making Darrel realize that the intimate kiss she had bestowed upon him had been merely functional, to get him ready to penetrate her. His heart soared in his chest as the moment arrived and he sighed with relief as she inched her way down his shaft with her tight little quim.

It *was* tight too, the most virginal he'd experienced since those naughty girls in Fernlea. How on earth had she managed it? He just had time to wonder if she practised some esoteric yogic exercises to keep her cunt in trim when the sheer voluptuousness of the experience overwhelmed him, and his mind drifted into that delightful limbo where rational thought was impossible and a dark and primal sensuality took over.

She was milking him slowly now, squeezing his shaft in such a way as to send ripples of electric warmth tingling through his body. He reached up and caressed her small, round breasts, finding their delicate shape and texture irresistible. But when one of his hands moved down to her bush she gently removed it, and he contented himself with stroking her spread buttocks instead.

'You like my bottom?' she whispered, her voice an aphrodisiac in itself.

'Oh, yes!' he groaned.

'Then perhaps you like to take me from behind?'

Before he could respond her lithe body had wriggled out from under him, twisted around and got up on all fours. She looked cheekily over her shoulder at him, waggling her buttocks in a blatant come-on. He needed no second bidding, but was up and in there at once, sliding under her smooth, round buns and into the hairy chasm of her cunt. His hands pinched at her fleshy backside and she seemed to like it, squealing in delight and giggling in that sexy way of hers.

But when she began to move her hips Darrel was plunged into a maelstrom of pacy, complex rhythms that he found incredibly exciting. The girl really knew how to move, her pelvis shaking and rolling while she performed a second dance internally, her pussy walls pulsating up and down his cock. He leaned forward and grabbed her swaying breasts, pulling at them as they bounced around and provoking a long 'Aaah!' of satisfaction.

'You're enjoying this too, aren't you?' he murmured, confident of her reply.

'Of course. You're so big and hard, Sir. I always enjoy it when I'm with a real man.'

Despite his suspicion that she said that to all the guys, Darrel was pleased. Her cunt was beautifully wet inside, and he knew from experience that a woman didn't get that lubricated unless she was getting off on it. The thought that he might bring her to orgasm excited him greatly. He didn't want her to fake it, though.

They were getting up a steaming rhythm now, her buttocks weaving back and forth in a sinuous horizontal dance that was giving his cock a real treat. His hands were allowed to rove down her thighs or stroke her bum cheeks. She even let his fingers creep slyly into the dark cleft of her arse. But if he strayed towards her vulva she clammed up on him and he took the hint, retreating at once.

Just when he thought he was heading for a climax, Oralie changed position again. She sank back into his lap and let him have closer contact with the upper part of her body while she continued to wriggle with his cock inside her. Darrel kissed the back of her neck while caressing her breasts with enthusiasm, and she seemed to enjoy it. He loved being able to run his hands all over her front, from the neat triangle up over her rounded little belly to her breasts, and down again. And all the time his prick was being expertly massaged, sending out hot waves of energy to feed his muscles, inspiring him to thrust and wriggle with her.

Then, just as he was really getting into his stride, Oralie got off his lap and knelt for a second or two before turning round to face him. This time she lay on her back and invited him in, but as soon as he had plunged into her again she raised her right leg up on his right shoulder and they ended up in a half-twisted posture that proved to be rather exciting. Darrel felt as if he was wading right into her, his rigid prick slicing between her thighs and delving deep between the wet, slippery folds of her sex.

Now he could see her pretty, aroused breasts and the sight of her flushed, rapt face urged him to greater efforts. He gazed down into the black inkwells of her eyes and thought he saw secret messages there, messages that were meant for him if only he could decode them. It lent an uncanny perspective to the experience, but he had no time to wonder about her since his own body was befuddling him, the feverish rhythms of their congress addling his brain.

Soon Oralie lost her identity and her context, was reduced to some faceless female archetype as the express train of his libido carried him towards his climax. He was scarcely aware of the woman bringing down her legs and holding him tightly between her vice-like thighs. All he knew was that the sensations had somehow heightened and the final push towards orgasm had begun. He gasped as the first sharp paroxysms took him by surprise, ripping through his belly like an electric shock. A steady stream of spunk poured from him, amazingly copious considering that he'd already shot one load, accompanied by more gut-wrenching spasms that took him swiftly to that dark extremity where pain and pleasure mingled. When the spasms softened they were sweetly voluptuous, bathing his veins in honeyed fire.

Darrel sank back utterly exhausted and felt cool lips on his cheek. To have Oralie cuddling up to him was a profound relief. At some level he'd been afraid that once her work was done she would abandon him, but she had the sense to realize that a truly satisfying sexual experience never ended with orgasm. He needed this last little time with her, to be reassured by her continued presence and to know that, despite the commercial nature of their relationship, she had some superficial affection from him.

Because he wanted more from her. The realization hit him right between the eyes as he lay there inert, letting her soothe his brow with her fingers. His hunger for her had not been satiated, although it had hardly been for want of trying on her part. No, he had no complaint against her as a whore. But he wanted her as a woman, however impossible that seemed. He wanted the luxury of having access to her mind and heart, as well as her body. He needed her conversation, her company.

'Tell me about your village,' he began, because he had to begin somewhere.

'Oh, it is small. I live in the orphanage because my mother and father are dead.'

'Orphanage?' Darrel couldn't keep the surprise out of his voice. And something else.

'Yes.' She was unperturbed. 'I stay there until I am seventeen, then I come to Geosan. The nice people took me with them, a man and a woman.'

He felt the hairs on the back of his neck bristle and prickles descended his spine. This was just too familiar, too predictable. Were they up to the same tricks here, so far from home? If so, what did that make Choi? Whose side was he really on? Was Darrel being set up? The implications were alarming. But he didn't want to alarm Oralie.

'You were glad to come here, then?'

'Oh yes! There was no other work for me here in Geosan. If I had not come to Orchid Palace I should be selling myself on the streets, for little money and much danger.'

If only you knew! Darrel groaned mentally. The danger she was in might not be obvious, but it was just as great as that which the illicit street-walkers faced, if not greater. They might face physical hardship and peril, but she was in danger of losing her very soul!

'Do you ever get time off?' he asked.

'Oh yes!'

'I mean time when you can go out of here, say, to a restaurant?'

Her eyes widened. 'Why should I want that? Everything I desire is here.'

He shrugged. 'I don't know – just for a change.'

'I am happy here.'

'I'm sure you are, but ... well, suppose I wanted to take you out for a meal. To thank you for giving me such a nice time. Would you be able to go with me?'

That scared-animal look crept back into her eyes. 'I ... I don't know.'

'Well, I'm asking you: will you come out with me? Just for a few hours. I'm alone here in town tonight, and it would be good to have some company.' He made it sound like she'd be doing him a favour. Gritting his teeth he added, 'I'll pay you well, of course.'

She nodded, understanding him now that he had framed his invitation in terms of her work. 'You would have to ask Madame Kee.'

'Is that the lady who introduces the girls in the cocktail lounge?'

'Yes. She in charge here.'

He gave Oralie a broad smile. 'Very well, that's what I shall do. But if she won't let me take you fair and square I'll have to kidnap you!'

She squealed her delight, giggling madly, but Darrel's smile was empty. He was telling himself, soberly, that he might have to do just that.

After taking a shower Darrel put on his clothes and prepared to leave. His heart fell when he remembered he was supposed to meet Choi in the lounge, that this whole set-up had been designed merely to test out the circuitry around his brain. For a while he had believed himself to be free of all that, acting as nature intended. But now reality was forcing itself upon him, making him doubt whether his new plan – to get Oralie away from the place for a few hours at least – would work.

When the time came to actually say goodbye to the girl, however, Darrel had a horrible feeling he would never see her again. Impulsively he took her in his arms. Her slight body felt fragile in his embrace, the bones of her small frame delicate as a bird's. Yet he knew her to be both strong and agile. He swept her dark hair away from her face and kissed her pale, rounded brow. 'Thank you, Oralie. You don't know what you've done for me. I want to repay you . . .'

'Don't worry, Sir,' she smiled up at him. 'Satisfaction guaranteed, remember?'

Anger seized him, and he could bear it no longer. He would make that fucking madame give her to him or take her by force! Alongside his determination came an even more frightening realization: he didn't intend to just take her out to dinner, either!

Choi was waiting for him in the lounge, sipping from a glass of virulent-looking green stuff. He beamed and patted the seat beside him when he saw Darrel approach. 'Ah, welcome back! What will you drink, Mr Star?'

Darrel balked at the name, not recognizing himself. When he did, he hoped his surprise hadn't been detected. 'Oh, anything,' he replied, airily. 'Something to quench my thirst.'

Choi grinned, knowingly. 'Then I suggest a fortified spa water, to replenish vital body salts.' He beckoned a hostess and gave the order, then sat back with a satisfied smile. 'Well, now,' he continued, in a low voice, 'from our point of view it has all gone very satisfactorily. And from the way you responded . . .'

'You don't know how the hell I responded!' Darrel snapped, suddenly incensed.

Although Choi's brows were slightly raised he maintained his ironic smile. 'Pardon me, Mr Star, but we do know – precisely. If you are in any doubt I could let you see charts that . . .'

'To hell with your charts! I'm talking about intangibles here, things that can't be measured.'

' "Measurement began our might." I have always remembered that line from some old poet. It struck me so forcefully. You could describe man's whole progress in terms of his ability to measure – the world, the universe, himself.'

'I still say there are things that can't be measured. But I'm too tired to talk philosophy, Mr Choi. Is there somewhere I could take a nap?'

'Of course. We have a room for you upstairs. If you would like to retire now I shall arrange for an early morning call. Your shuttle ticket will be in reception.'

'Shuttle ticket?'

Choi's expression became that of an indulgent uncle. 'Have you forgotten that you will soon be bound for Malaku? Surely not!'

'Oh. Yes, of course.'

'Then I shall take my leave of you.' Both men rose and Choi proffered his hand. 'It has been a pleasure knowing you, Mr Star.'

'Is that all, then?'

Choi bowed, slightly, but did not deign to reply. Instead he walked slowly away, clicking his fingers at a hostess who came hurrying to his side. As he moved to the door he was obviously issuing orders. Darrel wondered whether they had anything to do with him or whether he had already been dismissed from Choi's mind, like yesterday's news.

The lounge was almost deserted now and there was no sign of Madame Kee. Darrel beckoned one of the remaining three hostesses. She came over with a fixed smile on her face.

'Yes, Sir?'

'I wonder if it might be possible to speak to Madame Kee?'

He was unprepared for the look of sudden alarm that distorted the woman's features. She composed herself at once, but her fingers fidgeted with the tray she was carrying. 'I am sorry, Sir. This is her rest hour.'

'Then when will she be available?'

'She does not usually see clients herself, Sir.'

'Nevertheless I should like to see her, just for a few moments. Is there someone else I have to see first?'

'Mr Choi, Sir . . .'

'Someone . . . *else*?'

Darrel felt in his pocket for a credit note and pulled one out. As he placed it on the tray he saw that it was a twenty-five. Far too large, but it couldn't be helped. The girl's eyes widened with a mixture of greed and terror. 'Oh no, Sir, I couldn't possibly . . .'

'Does she have an assistant, a secretary?'

'Yes. Her office is just off the main entrance hall. But . . .'

'Thank you.'

Darrel was up and across the room before she could think of any more objections. He had suddenly become a man with a mission, and he found he liked the feeling. It beat impotent rage any day.

Chapter Twelve

By the time Darrel got to see Miss Lan, Madame Kee's personal assistant, he'd made up his mind. If they didn't let him take Oralie out officially he'd do it by stealth and, if he had anything to do with it, she wouldn't be coming back in a hurry, if at all. Quite why he felt like that he had no idea. He wasn't fool enough to imagine that he could persuade a prostitute to fall in love with him. He knew too much about it from the other side, knew how the genies despised those pathetic women who got 'crushes' on them. But something about the girl had evoked his chivalrous instincts and he felt he had to warn her about the set-up she'd got mixed up in. After that, it was up to her.

At first Miss Lan was all sweetness and light, evidently having been taught that the customer is always right. When he made his request, however, her clear green eyes muddied a little. 'Sorry, Sir, it is not permitted for clients to see any girl outside Orchid Palace.'

'My credit rating is good, very good.'

'It is not a question of credit, Sir. House rule. Very strict.'

'Is there no way round this? All I want is to take the girl out for a meal. It's my one night in Geosan and I feel like having a good time, but I can't enjoy myself on my own. Just a little dinner, maybe some dancing, then I'll have her back before the clock strikes midnight. What harm is there in that?'

'Sorry, Sir.' Her voice was firm. 'I can give you the number of an escort agency.'

He brushed aside her suggestion impatiently. 'Can I speak to Madame Kee?'

'She is not to be disturbed.'

'Later, then?'

The pretty pink lips tightened. 'No, Sir, there would be no point. She would tell you the same as I. House rule, Sir.'

It was clear he was up against a brick wall. Darrel turned on his heel and left the office, fuming. He would have to resort to subterfuge, but his task was daunting. He had no knowledge of the layout of the building and no idea where Oralie would be. Was she entertaining another client in her room? He doubted whether he could even find that again. The place seemed to have several floors, each with identical corridors and doors.

As he stood in the hall wondering what to do next a crowd of men suddenly swept through the entrance, laughing and chatting. It was obviously the next wave of clients, and Darrel tagged onto the end of the crowd trying to look as if he belonged. A smiling hostess led them through into the lounge and they began to disperse to the various tables.

'Mind if I join you?' he asked the couple nearest him. They looked like Americans, taller and broader than the Asians, one with a bushy beard. They regarded him askance for a few seconds so Darrel improvised, 'I was supposed to meet a friend here but he hasn't turned up, and I feel a bit of a fool on my own.'

To his relief they took pity on him. The taller of the two men smiled and held out his hand, 'Hi, I'm Taj and this is Bev. Are you noo in town too?'

'Not exactly.'

'Say, you bin to this joint before?' Darrel nodded. 'Great! You can show us the ropes. Can we sit anywhere?'

Soon Darrel had become their appointed guide. Neither of the men seemed any too bright, and they needed prompting every step of the way. He had to summon the hostess, describe what the various cocktails would do for them, explain the credit payment system. Then, when the display of wares began, he was asked if he could recommend any of the girls personally.

'It's all a matter of taste. What are you guys into?'

'I'm a tit-job man, maself,' Bev said, without hesitation. 'Nothin' I like better than to have ma poker squeezed between a pair of big fat bellows. And when it comes ter playin' hokey-pokey I'm a back-door kinda guy, if you catch ma drift.'

'Take a look at Kuru. Unless you dislike blacks . . .'

The man grinned wide, showing gappy teeth. 'Love 'em! They generally know how to use their ass!'

'Just press "Select" on the screen and press again when you see her name,' Darrel advised him. 'She'll be parading in the flesh soon.'

As he started listening to Taj's preferences half his mind was on his own agenda. Once he had the man searching for details of Mo and Flo he beckoned one of the hostesses over. 'I've made my choice already. Can I book her straight away?'

'Certainly, Sir. Who is it you wish to see?'

'Oralie.'

'I'm sorry, Sir, but Oralie is not available right now. Perhaps one of the other . . .'

Darrel rose with a snarl, barely in control of himself. He was furious that he'd gone through that charade for nothing. Muttering to the two Americans that he 'had to go to the john' he raced from the room and found himself in the entrance hall again.

Like a rat in a maze he had no idea which direction to scurry in. When the girl at the desk began to notice him he sauntered through the nearest door, trying to look like he was on official business. The long corridor had closed doors either side, but girlish chatter could be heard coming from a room at the far end. He headed straight for it.

When Darrel opened the door and showed his face there were screams of dismay and he held up his hand, trying to placate the half-dozen young women who were lounging around in a state of undress.

'How dare you!' one of them said, rising to her feet. 'This is private. Go away!'

'I'm looking for someone. Please help me.'

The dark-haired girl came to the door, tried to push him back. Darrel spoke quickly. 'Her name is Oralie. I have to see her. Please tell me where she is.'

But the girl shook her head firmly. 'No! You must go or . . .'

The door at the far end opened and the desk girl appeared with a security man. 'There he is!' she called, pointing. 'That's the man!'

Darrel panicked, his eyes darting round. He raced to the opposite end of the corridor and through a door which took him onto an iron staircase. He leapt up the steps two at a time, then found himself on the next floor. Although he was in a corridor identical to that below, he was pleased to find that every door had a girl's name on. All he had to do was find the door to Oralie's room . . .

He found it just as his pursuers appeared and managed to slip through it without them seeing him. Realizing that they probably had no idea who he was after he reckoned he had a few seconds' grace. A quick glance round the room revealed that these were, indeed, her private quarters. He was touched to see a collection of furry stuffed animals on her pillow. There were only three places to hide, however: in the wardrobe, under the bed or in the shower. He chose the latter.

Stripping off his clothes he bundled them into the laundry basket in the corner, then switched on the shower. He had to bend his knees to avoid being seen over the top of the partition. By the time someone tried the door handle he was splashing around, praying that the smoked glass partition was not too transparent.

'Oh – sorry, Oralie!' a woman's voice called, followed by the sound of the door shutting. Darrel punched the air with his fists in a triumphant gesture. His ruse had worked! Now all he had to do was lie low and wait for the room's rightful occupant to return.

It was strange being in there alone. Darrel heard the hue and cry going on outside for a few minutes but eventually it died down and he felt safe again. He browsed Oralie's screen, discovering that she was taking an 'Improve your English' course, had been visiting a Virtual Zoo and playing Mah Jong against the computer, level three. He enjoyed rummaging in her underwear drawer, finding some pretty scraps of silk and lace that he imagined her filling out very satisfactorily. He read the cards that three of the other girls had given her on her birthday, two weeks ago. And after a while he stopped feeling like an intruder and felt more like her lover, waiting for her by appointment.

When someone finally came, Darrel almost jumped out of his skin with fright. Fearing it might not be Oralie, he crouched down behind the bed but as the door slid open he saw that it was indeed her. His relief was so great that he leapt up at once, making her scream in fright.

Quickly he clapped his hand over her mouth. 'Please, Oralie, don't make a sound,' he begged. 'I mean no harm. I just want to talk to you.'

Her frightened eyes softened a fraction. When he released her, she whispered, 'Sir, they are looking everywhere for you!'

'I know. But I couldn't leave this place without warning you.'

'Warning me?' Oralie stiffened in his arms and took a step backwards. Suddenly Darrel realized that he must abandon his first plan to take her out to dinner. He'd hoped to soften the blow that way, but now time was short and they were both in danger. He seized her hands and drew her over to her bed, quashing the strong urge in him to vent his passion with a kiss.

'Will you hear me out?' he asked her, anxiously.

'Yes, but . . .'

'Then just sit quietly. First I must tell you about myself. I come from a place similar to the Orchid Palace and, like you, I am a *genie*.'

Her puzzled stare told him the term was not used there.

218

'When you first came to work here, did they tell you that you were specially suited to perform sex acts?'

She smiled. 'Oh yes! They trained me in massage and yoga. They told me I had special gifts. They wanted to find out how my mind and body worked together . . .'

'What did they do?'

'I don't know. Experiments . . .'

'Ah! Tell me, when you are making love does your scalp get hot and tingle?'

She stared at him, mesmerized by his suppressed excitement. 'Yes, but . . .'

'And do you feel as if you are inside your client's skin, as if you know their desires exactly?'

She nodded, then asked, 'But doesn't everyone?'

'No! This is because they have wired up your brain. You are being controlled by them, your reactions observed. They are using you still, experimenting on you.'

Her sweet face grew incredulous. 'Why should they do that?'

A sudden thought struck him. 'They'd like to do it to everyone. Make everyone function better. Yes, that's how they'd think of it! They'd like to turn us all into computer-controlled slaves. It would be cheaper than mass-producing robots.'

Oralie giggled. 'That's ridiculous!'

'Is it? I don't know. But I do know that I was sent here as part of an experiment. A different kind, by a group that's trying to resist the controllers. At least, I think that's what they're doing.'

All certainty was slipping away from him as he tried to explain. It sounded preposterous even to his ears. He couldn't blame her for disbelieving him. Yet he sensed that she was in some kind of danger and he needed to give her one chance of escape that she might take if she pleased.

'They have a safe place,' he began. 'An island, far away. That's where I'm going if I ever get out of here, and I would be very happy if you came with me.'

'Oh no, I cannot!'

'I know you have a good life here, or think you do. But there is a price to pay, a terrible price. Please believe me! If you stay you will lose your freedom to be who you are. Trust me, I have been through it all myself. I lost my sexual identity when they'd finished with me at the Plaza. They put wires round my brain, began controlling my body. It was only when I was de-conditioned by drugs that I realized how different sex could be. And I believe I discovered what love could be, too.'

'Love!' she murmured, scornfully. 'I would rather have a full belly!'

'You say that now, because you have been conditioned. But there is another world, Oralie. A world of rapture, of devotion of another human being. It's the world the old poets used to sing of, before the authorities knew how to tamper with men's minds.'

A sense of futility was overwhelming him. How could she understand something she'd never experienced? To her, he was just another client – a crazy one. What hope did he have of persuading her to leave her comfortable nest and go fly with him?

But she was intrigued, he could tell. Her questioning eyes stared deep into his. 'I found an old book once. It was about a man and woman. They felt things for each other, as if they were the only two people in the world. It was strange, and as I was young I laughed at it. But that story has haunted me ever since. I wonder how people can feel such things.'

'You could find out,' Darrel said eagerly. 'There are ways of changing your mind back to how it used to be. That's what happened to me. It's a wonderful adventure, Oralie, but it takes courage. If you come with me . . .'

She shrank from him at once. 'I dare not!'

'I understand. It's hard to take a leap in the dark, especially to trust people you've never met before. Perhaps it was wrong of me to approach you like this.'

She touched his hand lightly, making the hairs on his neck bristle. 'Not wrong, no. I knew you were different when I first saw you. There is something about your eyes. The eyes of the other men are blank and dull, but yours are . . . alive! They do not just take in what they see, they give something back. I have never seen this before.'

'That's because I've been awakened, Oralie. And I long for you to experience what I have felt. I want to take you out of this prison to somewhere you can be free . . .'

'But how can we go?' she whispered, fearfully.

Darrel frowned. 'I don't know. We can't use the shuttle, that's for sure. They'd be looking out for both of us. But I'm sure there's a way to get to Malaku, once we're out of here. It's a risk, but are you willing to come with me?'

A look of terror passed over her face again, and Darrel flinched. The thought that he might be the instrument of her downfall was daunting. What if his plan failed and they were both captured? Would they be turned into lab rats for the controllers to do as they liked with? The prospect was horrible.

Even as he hesitated, she seized his hand again. Her

eyes were bright, her smile dazzling. 'Yes!' she murmured. 'I will come with you, dear Sir!'

'My name is Darrel,' he said, hugging her. It was good to confirm his own identity to her at last. 'And I will take care of you, I promise. I would die to protect you, Oralie. I swear it!'

As he said it he knew, with a flash of cold dread, that it was the truth.

Once she had decided to go with him, Oralie took over. 'There is only one safe way out of here,' she told him. 'Through the laundry room. But you will have to wear my clothes. No man ever goes there.' Quickly she rummaged through her wardrobe and held up a kimono and black wig. 'These are for you. Hurry, put them on.'

Darrel did his best to get into the skimpy garment. It was stretched too tight over his chest, but Oralie ripped down the hem so at least it fell to his ankles. He went barefoot but put his own shoes and clothes in a pillowcase which he slung over his shoulder like a laundry bag.

When he put on the wig Oralie giggled. 'You look like an old peasant washerwoman!'

'And I feel like a wango!' Darrel grinned, using the derogatory term for a female impersonator. He minced and posed, making her laugh all the more until he shut her up. 'Hush, Oralie. We have to be careful. Are you ready?'

She took one last look around her room, picked up a couple of trinkets for souvenirs, then nodded solemnly. 'Yes. Follow me. If we are lucky they will think we are maids. There are many of them, they work in shifts and always come and go.'

The pair walked gingerly down the corridor towards the lift leading down to the basement. Darrel kept his head down but his heart was in his mouth when they passed a maid wheeling a trolley of dirty bed linen. Oralie murmured a greeting and, to his relief, an automatic response was made.

The basement was full of activity, noise and steam that made it seem easier to pass unnoticed. Darrel, still head down, followed Oralie's tiny, tripping feet until they came to the back door which was made of heavy steel. Here they paused, confronted by a combi-lock but, luckily, no Iridiscan.

Oralie turned to a hefty middle-aged worker who was sorting linen bags and asked casually, 'Hey, what's the combi? I forgot.'

The woman's face showed a glimmer of suspicion, but Oralie said at once, 'I lost my inhaler and I got to get some air for five minutes. This cleaning fluid plays hell with my lungs.'

The older woman nodded in sympathy. 'My friend died through working here. You take care now. Seven, three, eight, four, nine, five.'

'Thanks.'

Oralie punched the numbers into the pad and the door slid open. Darrel held his breath, sure that a challenge would come at the last minute, but they slipped through into the open air without any problem. It seemed just too easy. He followed Oralie round the side of the building until they found themselves in a busy street with traffic rushing in all directions but very few pedestrians. Then he suddenly realized he didn't have a clue where to go next!

'Let's go to the shuttle port,' he said, trying to sound decisive. He didn't want Oralie thinking she'd got mixed up with an impulsive fool, even if it was the truth. There was no way they could get to Malaku by regular shuttle, but he didn't want her to know that. Still, the port seemed as good a place to start as any.

They took a *compusha* to Myokoi, where the main shuttle port was situated. Darrel felt edgy inside the two-passenger vehicle and insisted on sitting with his back to the computerized engine, so he could see if they were being followed. By the time they reached the large dome which housed the shuttle terminal he was convinced they were safe. Relieved, he changed into his own clothes under cover of the *compusha* cabin.

Still, it was no time for complacency. As they disembarked Darrel surveyed the area, wondering where to go and what to do. Entry into the dome would be most unwise, but there were several touts hanging around outside. Warily he moved into the forecourt with Oralie in tow, and was soon accosted by one of them.

'Shuttle pass, sir?' the wily-eyed Asian offered, in an impeccable Western accent. 'I can get you and your lady friend anywhere on earth.' He gave a wink. 'All bona fide passes, naturally.'

'No, nothing official,' Darrel said. He kept his voice low and his eyes on the horizon, adding, 'We can't take the shuttle but we must reach Malaku. Can you help?'

'Well, it just so happens I can, sir. Why don't we take a little walk? I'm sure you'd find it to your advantage.'

Darrel knew he had to trust him. If the man was spying for the controllers, too bad. But he seemed genuine enough, with a manner that suggested he was just as

224

scared of being reported to the authorities himself.

The three of them wandered off into a 'garden' consisting mainly of rock and gravel. While Oralie sat on a timber bench keeping a surreptitious lookout, the two men chatted in the opposite corner. The man's breath stank of a peculiar Geosan delicacy based on rotten fish and Darrel, obliged to stay near to hear his low voice, tried to take as few breaths as possible.

'There is another way, but it will cost you. I can put you in touch with someone who runs a pirate airline service.'

'Airline?' Darrel stared at the man incredulously.

'I know, it sounds impossible. But it's true. People will pay a great deal for the thrill of riding in an old-style airplane. Plus there's the extra excitement of doing something illegal.'

'But how on earth do they get away with it? I thought the airlanes were totally controlled. Why can't they track him down?'

'Can't say!' But the man had an air of knowing something he was not prepared to divulge. Not before credit had changed hands, anyway.

'Does he fly to Malaku?'

'He flies anywhere you want him to – at a price. In the old days they called them private charter planes.'

'That's fantastic!'

'Okay, let's talk business. I won't keep you in suspense any longer. It'll cost you five. If you can't afford it just forget we ever met.'

'Five hundred?'

The man sneered. 'Thousand!'

Darrel's face fell. It was about all he had. The man

shrugged, turned to go. Darrel pulled him back. 'Wait! I might be able to manage it. But how would you – he – want the credit?'

'It's complicated. You transfer it to a named account, then it's passed on through another two before it gets to its final destination.'

'Okay. Tell me what to do.'

'Nothing, for the moment. I have to arrange things. Meet me here tomorrow at nine with your account number. If it's possible we'll put the wheels into motion then.'

'But where are we supposed to stay tonight?'

'You got nowhere?'

'No.'

'There's a doss down by the bridge. No place to take a lady, though.'

'Tell me where.'

Darrel listened to the directions, then beckoned to Oralie. They took their leave of the fixer and made for the river bank where there was a walkway. In the distance was the bridge with the abandoned hut nearby. Darrel regarded the prospect of a night in there with horror, but there seemed to be no alternative.

But when they reached it he was surprised how readily Oralie accepted the situation. The single room was filthy, with excrement and litter everywhere.

'Reminds me of my old home!' she grinned, her delightfully snub nose wrinkling. 'We used to share it with the pigs and hens.'

She set to work ridding the place of rubbish and spreading on the concrete floor the kimono and pillowcase, which she filled with the wig. 'There!' she smiled. 'Now we have some kind of bed.'

'Not the sort you're used to. Nor me, for that matter.'

'No, but perhaps I can make you forget about your surroundings for a while.'

She stripped off her silk blouse with unselfconscious ease and Darrel saw that she was wearing no underwear. Her small, full breasts looked perfect in the dim light, their slight difference in size scarcely detectable. She smiled at him and his cock stirred with unexpected delight. Darrel was amazed that he could feel so horny when both danger and disgust were assailing him. Yet the spell that Oralie wove was absolute. She had him in thrall.

Nimble fingers soon stripped off his garments and then her hot mouth was encircling his rapidly-growing erection, the flesh of his glans and shaft melding with her lips and tongue. Darrel moaned her name aloud as what felt like several millivolts of electric heaven flooded through his electrodes. She was going to blow his mind, as well as his prick!

But then she let him go, her hands caressing his balls as she moved up his body. Their lips met in a long, hungry kiss and he squeezed her taut breasts, feeling the nipples harden between his fingers. He longed to thrust inside her, deep and forceful, to feel the soft contours of her cunt again and let them cushion his hard cock while he rode her to blissful oblivion.

'Oralie!' he murmured. 'Let me fuck you!'

'Wait one minute.'

She wriggled out of her remaining clothes, pressing her sleek thighs against his then guiding his penis between them. His glans tasted her love-juice, let the sweet fluid bathe its head before she opened wide to him and he slid straight inside.

'Too hard on floor!' she whispered. 'Let's stand up.'

So he had her against the wall of the hut, her legs clinging monkey-like around his waist while she held onto his shoulders. No matter how hard he slammed into her she remained firm against him, her tight little butt pushing forward as her pelvis tilted to accommodate him more deeply. In the faint light he could see that she was smiling.

The noise of his long coming must have drowned out the sound of another's coming because, without warning, a flashlight shone in through the door. Darrel froze like a rabbit caught in headlights. He turned his head away from the light and felt Oralie doing likewise.

A gruff voice suddenly exploded in the darkness behind the light. 'What the fuck have we here? A fucking couple of fucking tramps, fucking! Hey, San! Come looksee!'

There was a guffaw as the second man joined him. 'Fucking tramps! Shall we set fire to 'em, eh? Pour gas over 'em and set 'em alight?'

Darrel felt his dick go limp and his heart turned to stone. He sensed Oralie's terror too. She was trembling so hard her teeth were chattering.

But then the first man said, in a tone of disgust, 'Nah! Poor fuckers. Let 'em fuck while they can. Prob'ly half dead already. Girl looks half starved. Maybe she got Aids. Anyway, I'm not going into that stinking hole.'

'The doss stinks pretty bad too!'

'Okay, joker. You owe me a cocktail.'

Their voices began to fade as the riposte came, 'Wouldn't have minded getting my cock into that tail. Still, you're probably right about her havin' fuckin' Aids.'

When their talk had faded into the night Oralie lowered

her feet to the floor then sank onto their makeshift bed. She put her hands over her face and Darrel knew she was weeping. 'Horrible men!' she sobbed. 'I thought we would die!'

'But we didn't!' Darrel reminded her, grimly. 'Still, we can't stay here. They might come back, especially if they get high. They might even bring more bastards back with them. We must leave, at once.'

Wearily they gathered up their things and dressed. Darrel had no idea which direction they should go in but he decided to follow the track that led beneath the bridge. Beyond there were few lights and he guessed it was more or less open country. They would be safer there.

The pair of them walked for half an hour then came across an open-sided barn. Oralie said they should spend the night there. 'It reminds me of home, also. We had such a barn near us. On warm nights I used to sleep in the hay with my friends.'

Much as Darrel would have liked to swap childhood reminiscences with her, now was not the time. Footsore and utterly weary they made up their bed on a pile of discarded sacking and this time their embraces led to nothing more than a deep and uninterrupted sleep.

Waking with the dawn, Darrel saw Oralie lying there beside him and was overcome with tender longing. He began to make love to her while she still slept, and a smile crept over her face so he knew when she awoke but she kept her eyes closed, pretending to sleep.

He shuffled down and found her labia open, showing their soft inner lining. First Darrel felt her moist smoothness with his fingertip, letting it go right into her opening which made a small sucking noise. Then he kissed her pale belly and continued to travel on down past her curly bush to the prominent tip of her clitoris. He wanted to give her pleasure, to make her come as she'd never come before. His tongue moved lovingly over her thighs, eliciting soft moans and sighs, but when it began to move towards her vulva her cries increased in volume and became protests.

Not wanting to upset her, Darrel moved his mouth up to her belly. While his mouth worked busily around the undersides of her breasts, watching her pink nipples grow erect of their own accord, he felt his cock swell and knew he would soon have to plunge into her. She was sighing voluptuously now, and he could smell the musky secretions of her pussy. He flattered himself that no other man had ever pleasured her so much before, simply because they had been clients and she had been working. Now, far from the obligations of the Orchid Palace, she was free to respond or not as she wished.

And she certainly wished to respond – oh yes, indeed!

Darrel planted his thighs firmly astride her and teased her labia apart with his glans. As she grew more excited he moved into her, just an inch or so, and felt her vaginal muscles clench the end of his cock. She was adept at using them. With rapid, butterfly-like movements her vulva fluttered against his shaft, caressing him. It took all his self-control to prevent him from lunging straight into her but he knew that he wanted to do things differently, to prolong the sweet agony until neither of them could bear the tormenting pleasure any longer.

Her cunt was throbbing wildly now. Hot and tender, it was responding by swelling up to twice its size and Darrel hoped it would soon explode into orgasm. His own cock was almost there too, despite the fact that he was only an inch or so inside her. Maybe it was time to move in. He delved a little further and felt himself being summarily sucked in, pulled down towards her womb by a force that seemed stronger than gravity. Her muscles undulated along his shaft like miniature suction pads, making it very difficult for him to remain detached. A dark maelstrom of raw feeling was claiming him, pulling him down.

It was Oralie's tiny, birdlike cries of encouragement, together with her powerfully pulsating quim, that finally triggered him. He came in a long gush of pure ecstasy and then collapsed beside her, totally spent.

It was only when Darrel felt her covering his cheeks and forehead with tiny kisses that he opened his eyes and remembered where he was. Immediately afterwards he scrambled to his feet, pulling her up too. 'We must go! That man will be expecting us. If we're not there at nine we'll lose our chance to get out of here.'

Oralie's frightened eyes told him she shared his panic. That meant she was as keen as Darrel was to get to Malaku. For better or worse she had thrown in her lot with him, and that made him feel both good and bad.

Chapter Thirteen

As the shaky old crate heaved itself up off the overgrown runway and, creaking and wobbling, took to the skies, Darrel heaved a sigh that was half relief, half incredulity. When he and Oralie had been ushered onto the ancient airplane just before dawn it had seemed incredible that the thing could actually fly. But after all the suspense of the past twenty hours it was exhilarating to be airborne at last.

Of course they'd been warned of the danger. Round their necks they wore inflatable life-jackets just in case they plummeted into the ocean, but Darrel was under no illusions. If the thing did fall apart their chance of survival was probably nil. He turned to look at Oralie. She was sitting beside him with her eyes closed and a blissful smile on her face. Darrel took her small hand and squeezed it. She opened her eyes sleepily and smiled at him.

'Okay?' he asked, solicitously. There would be no attendants on this trip but they'd stocked up on food and drink which was now stowed in bags beneath their seats.

'Mm,' she nodded, her eyes gleaming. 'Such an adventure, Darrel.'

'Why don't you look out of the window? Say goodbye to Geosan!'

He leaned across, feeling her soft warm body yield to

his, and a surge of desire took him by surprise. Peering through the small porthole they could see the amazing city spread out below, its overall design apparent from the air.

'Beautiful!' he murmured.

Oralie lifted her face towards his. 'A beautiful prison!'

Unable to resist her any longer Darrel pressed his mouth to hers and tasted the sweetness of her saliva. His hand moved over the curve of her breast, squeezing gently. She briefly caressed the bulge in his groin, but it was difficult to do more in that confined space. The flight to Malaku was estimated to take ten hours. Darrel didn't know how he could wait that long.

The other passengers were a motley crew: nine shifty-looking men and three tarty women. He wondered, idly, why they were travelling to Malaku and how they could afford the fare. Was the place some kind of haven for criminals and renegades? If it was, what did he care? He and Oralie were now social outcasts, like the rest of them.

For a while, reflecting on the full significance of what he had done appalled him. He'd come out as a rebel, and dragged Oralie into it too. If the controllers ever got their hands on him again they would show no mercy. Teaming up with Jay and the others had seemed a good idea at the time, but now he wasn't so sure. What fate awaited him on Malaku? Suppose it was all a trap, and there would be a grim reception committee for him and Oralie. The thought sent icy tremors through him and he delved beneath his seat to find one of the cocktails he'd bought.

'Here, Oralie, want to share a Happymaker?' he offered, unscrewing the top of the bottle. 'I reckon we could both do with one.'

As the flight proceeded, and lightning failed to strike, everyone on board began to loosen up. A man with deeply-tanned skin and bushy black hair and eyebrows came swaying up the aisle and paused at the empty seat beside Darrel. 'Mind if I sit here a few minutes?'

'Be my guest!' Darrel grinned, glad of the company since Oralie seemed too fatigued to do much more than doze.

The man offered him a drink from a silver flask. 'Want some Go-Go?'

'What's that?'

'Malakuan native plonk. Better get used to this gut-rot if you plan to stay.'

Darrel swigged it in one long gulp, feeling the stuff burn its way down to his stomach where it lodged like a warm furnace, circulating heat around his body. 'Wow!'

'Are you?' the man asked. 'Planning to stay, I mean?'

'Don't know yet. This is all a bit of a leap into the dark, if you know what I mean.'

'I know exactly what you mean.' The man held out a huge hairy hand. 'My name's Wal.'

Darrel saw no point in concealing his identity from him. He was fairly certain that the guy was as much of a fugitive as he was. Wal's dirty grey eyes surveyed him thoughtfully. 'You got some contact on Malaku? Somewhere to stay?'

'Not exactly. I had a seat on the shuttle but events took a different turn.'

Wal gave a roar of a laugh. 'Events have a habit of doing that, don't they? Let me guess – you picked up the little lady on the way and there's a jealous husband involved. Am I right?'

'Only about the first part. I met Oralie in the Orchid Palace, in Geosan.'

'Ah!' Wal nodded. 'They don't give up their genies easy, man. They put a lot of investment into them. You could be in big trouble.'

'I know.'

'Look, if you want to lie low in Malaku for a couple of days just let me know. I got a beach villa I hire out, but it's vacant right now. Perfect place for an old-fashioned honeymoon.'

'That's very generous of you.'

'I never pass up the chance of doing someone a good turn.' He paused, then his smile grew wicked. 'You never know when you might need to call in the favour.'

Although he was obviously a bit of a rascal Darrel liked the man. And it would be very handy to have a base while he sussed out the lie of the land. Despite his slight misgivings about the strings attached, he decided to accept Wal's offer.

They were left alone for the rest of the flight. Darrel liked having Oralie's head on his shoulder as he stared out at the blank sky. He dozed too, but spent his waking hours going over and over the events of the past month or so, trying to convince himself that it had all really happened. Darrel the genie, who had lived out his cosy routine at the Plezure Palace for well over a decade, now seemed like a stranger. The old Darrel might as well be dead.

But the new one will survive, he told himself through gritted teeth as, with much shuddering and rattling, the plane began to descend, weaving in and out of light cloud. Oralie woke terrified and clung to him, feeling sick.

Darrel didn't feel too good himself as the antique craft lurched and swooped its way down towards the emerald-and-gold island that could just be glimpsed, surrounded by a turquoise ocean.

'Look!' he said, trying to distract her. 'Isn't it wonderful? No comparison with Geosan there. And we already have someplace to stay.'

'We do?'

Her eyes grew huge and wondrous, despite her fear. Darrel laughed. 'Yes, courtesy of a fellow passenger. Don't worry, Oralie. Everything will be fine.'

They eventually touched down on a potholed runway alongside a beach of yellow sand that looked completely undisturbed by human hand – or foot. Peering through the window they could see fringed palm trees and luxuriant undergrowth. A dirt track ran in amongst the trees. Oralie gave a wide, little-girl smile and hunched her shoulders excitedly.

There were no formalities to be gone through, only a small hut at the side of the runway where a few people were waiting to welcome the passengers and crew. Darrel and Oralie got out into blazing sunshine, their skin glowing in the all-embracing heat. While they crossed the patchy tarmac with their bags in their hands Wal caught up with them.

'If you want I could drive you straight to my villa,' he told them. 'My buggy's over there.'

He pointed to where a small collection of vehicles was parked. Darrel stared at him in surprise. 'You do this trip often?'

'Every few months or so. Come on. We have to hurry.'

There seemed no point in distrusting the man. Dumped

237

in the middle of nowhere on an island he knew nothing about, and where he knew nobody, gave Darrel few options. As he and Oralie swung into the open-topped rust-bucket Darrel thought they were fortunate to have met up with Wal.

As they bumped along the crude, rutted track Wal asked all the questions. He soon found out where they came from and then asked how they had found out about Malaku. Darrel didn't know what to say, so he hedged. 'A friend told me I'd be safe here.'

Wal laughed. 'Safe? Ha! Depends who you want to be safe from.'

Darrel decided to take a chance. 'From the controllers, of course.'

'Ah!' Wal gave him a sidelong grin. 'In that case, I may be able to help you both. A bit over-wired, are we?'

'You could say that.'

'Then you've come to the right place. Listen, spend tonight at my place and I'll pick you up in the morning. Take you where you need to go, okay?'

'This is very kind of you.'

'I told you, pure self-interest. Here we go, nearly there.'

He swerved off the main track into what looked like thick undergrowth but Darrel soon realized there was some kind of path beneath their wheels. He put his arm around Oralie, letting his fingers touch her bare shoulder. Her skin felt like warm velvet. They came out suddenly onto a strip of beach where there was a single ramshackle building with a veranda.

'This is it!' Wal said, churning up the sand as he applied the brakes. 'Paradise on Earth!'

It certainly looked like it. The beach stretched in a

horseshoe around a small bay, with pale blue foam-flecked water lapping at one edge while the great swathe of lush greenery occupied the other. Between the two was Wal's 'villa', a small outpost of civilization in all that beautiful wilderness.

Oralie gasped. 'It's so lovely here!'

'Yes, and completely secluded,' Wal told her. He pointed out towards the ocean. 'There are reefs out there, far too dangerous for any boat to cross. Here in the bay it's safe to swim. And no one knows how to get here by land except me. There's a well for fresh water, and plenty of fruit. You'll find the freezer and store-cupboard well stocked.'

Wal kept the engine revving as they got out. Realizing he meant to drive straight off, Darrel asked, 'What time will you call in the morning?'

The man laughed, a touch scornfully. 'We don't go by the clock here, old son.' He pointed to the sky. 'I'll come when the sun gets high. Be ready.'

When the rhythmic chug of the engine finally faded away, Darrel and Oralie faced each other. Her expression was one of timid expectancy, but behind it he sensed a kind of elation, the same as he was feeling. It was weird being there alone, but there was a glorious sense of freedom too. Darrel held out his hand to her and they trudged over the smooth sand, trailing their bags after them.

The villa looked worse from the outside. It was casually furnished but had been left in good order by the last occupants. There were bamboo rocking-chairs on the balcony and, inside, one living room, one small kitchen, and a bathroom with a chemical toilet and makeshift shower. The bedroom, like the rest of the place, was very old-fashioned with a double divan and embroidered coverlet.

Oralie lay down on the bed and gave a feline stretch. 'Oh, this feels good!'

At once Darrel felt his cock harden and lust swept through him like a tropical storm. But it was not purely selfish. He wanted to see Oralie abandon herself to him completely, to climax over and over so that her little cunt was overflowing with luscious juices and her body became satiated with its own pleasure. It was a novelty to want to do it just for her sake, without any reference to what he was being paid for his 'services'. He'd never felt quite like it before, and he was filled with an exhilarating sense of altruism.

'I want you to feel good,' he murmured, taking off her shoes and untying the sash at her waist. 'I want you to feel very good indeed!'

'Mm!' she murmured, rolling over so that he could remove her clothes more easily. Soon her pert young breasts were fully visible, the nipples firming into small pink cones of their own accord. She giggled as his mouth enclosed first one then the other, nipping at them with his lips until they grew even more rigid and the flesh beneath was shaped into two perfectly solid globes.

'You like that?' he smiled up at her. 'I want you to tell me what you like so that I can give you maximum pleasure.'

He was disconcerted to see a small frown appear between her delicate brows. '*I* give pleasure to *you*,' she said, uncertainly.

He laughed. 'No question! But this time I want you to lie back and enjoy it, without thinking about me at all. That's what would give *me* most pleasure right now.'

He felt sad that he had to spell it out. Oralie was still conditioned as a genie, mentally and physically, trained only to service others. He sensed her uneasiness at being asked to wallow in sensuality herself. But he would make it his goal to get her completely relaxed. Soon she would be enjoying climax after climax and he'd get his own satisfaction from that. He smiled ironically, thinking that just a few weeks ago the concept would have been alien to him, too.

She continued to look doubtful but Darrel began to caress her lovingly, his lips travelling from her breasts up the side of her neck until they met hers. Their kiss was deep and passionate, tongues meeting in slow, wet union before he withdrew and licked along her open lips. He felt her shudder as she responded to the tickling softness of his approach. Softly, softly was the style, he decided. Although his own erection was bursting to be inside her it gave him great satisfaction to hold back, concentrating exclusively on her responses.

Again Darrel's lips teased her nipples into prominence and he felt her shudder as the currents of her desire stirred, deep within. His hands moved down her incredibly slim waist and over her bony hips in one long, silky-smooth passage until he reached her thighs. Gently he pushed them apart, overcoming her slight resistance, and then his mouth moved down towards the furry muff over her delta.

'No, not that!'

Her protest had the equivalent effect of a cold shower.

Darrel felt his erection abruptly subside. He lifted his head, looking straight into her anxious face. 'Why on earth not?' Then he recalled what the hostess had told him, about how she never allowed cunnilingus. 'Don't you want me to kiss your sweet pussy?'

Her scared-rabbit eyes pleaded with him. 'No! Please, leave me alone down there.'

Darrel took her in his arms, burying his face in her hair that was full of wind-blown sand. 'Why not?' he murmured. 'Tell me, Oralie. Why do you fear it so?'

'It gives me no pleasure,' she said, stonily. 'And sometimes it gives me pain.'

'I can't believe that!'

'It is true.'

Sudden dread shook him. 'God, what have they done to you? Oralie, at least let me examine you.'

'No! It is best that we avoid it.' Her tone became falsely bright. 'You may penetrate me if you wish. Or I shall perform fellatio. You like that?'

Darrel groaned. 'Can't you understand, my sweet? It's you I want to pleasure. The way every woman may be pleasured. I want to bring you to orgasm with my fingers, my tongue. Just for you.'

She stared at him, puzzled. 'Orgasm?'

'Yes, of course. The summit of sexual gratification, you know.'

She shook her head. 'Only men have climax. Not women.'

He couldn't help laughing, but behind his laughter there was incredulity. 'Of course, women too! Don't tell me you've never experienced it, Oralie! That would be too ironic.'

Her stubborn mouth insisted, 'For women it is not possible.'

'Who told you that? Who's been filling your head with such lies?' Dark suspicion struck him. 'The controllers, no doubt. But how could they stop you – implants?' His mood grew increasingly angry. 'What have they done to you, Oralie? You must let me find out!'

He moved down the bed again and parted her thighs despite her protests. The pink lips of her sex pouted moistly at him but he pulled them open without a qualm and surveyed the configurations of her vulva with minute attention. The red inner lips, with their dark, secret opening, were as normal. But when he parted them to find her clitoris the truth about her condition was obvious. There, surgically inserted into the tender skin of her love-nub, was a shiny silver button that he recognized as a type of electrode. It could be remote controlled, just like the skull cap he knew she was also wearing. And he had no doubt that it had been used to prevent her having orgasms.

'At least they've not removed her clit altogether,' he muttered. But a dull anger was coursing through him as he realized how they had taken advantage of the girl's innocence. For reasons of their own they preferred her to experience only the mildest form of sensory arousal. And while that thing was piercing her clitoris she was still under their control, still prevented from fulfilling her birthright as a human female.

Darrel didn't know quite how to break it to her, but it had to be done. She had to know the full extent of the control those bastards had exercised over her. They were barbarians, no better than those ancient *seigneurs* who locked up their wives in chastity belts while they were away on campaigns. No better than those primitive tribesmen who so cruelly infibulated and castrated their womenfolk.

Tenderly he stroked her, kissed her cheek, tried to win her confidence. He was feeling a strange mixture of emotions and as a result felt raw and vulnerable inside.

'Look, Oralie, I think you should know what the controllers have done to you,' he began. 'Not content with wiring up your brain, they've apparently disabled your sex too. I don't know why they should want you to be unable to experience full sexual satisfaction, but . . .'

'Oh, but I like sex!' she smiled. 'It makes me feel all warm and comfortable. And when a man . . .' she paused, giggled, then went on, 'I mean, when *you* climax inside me I feel so very happy and well satisfied. Do not worry about me, Darrel. Just take your pleasure and . . .'

'But you don't understand. It's *your* pleasure I want!' he said, fiercely. 'I want you to come for me, Oralie. I want to feel your whole body vibrating with bliss as you reach climax after climax.'

But she only shrank from him, her eyes huge black holes in her pale face. 'Please, don't touch me . . . there. It hurts!'

Darrel's tone softened. 'I don't want to hurt you, sweet girl. Quite the reverse. If it upsets you we shall avoid further contact tonight. But I promise you, as soon as we can find someone to reverse this abomination we shall.'

Oralie sighed. 'Can't you accept me as I am, Darrel? Am I so displeasing to you?'

He despaired of getting her to understand. Tenderly he kissed her mouth, then her cheeks and closed eyelids.

He held her close, stroking her soft skin all the while, and then his lips were on her breasts. But his cock, that had been rearing so self-confidently a few minutes ago, was now flaccid and shrunken. Disappointed, he resigned himself to the prospect of a bathe in the ocean followed by a breakfast of fresh fruit and whole grain.

To see Oralie blossom in the unfamiliar surroundings of a Malaku beach was delightful, despite the shadow that discovering her induced frigidity had cast. The pair frolicked in the shallows, where brightly-coloured fish could be observed. Darrel and Oralie splashed each other with the warm water and then ran up the beach to dry off under the palm trees. Darrel brought food out to her on a tray and they picnicked on the beach. Then she leaned back on her arms and raised her face to the bright sunlight.

'Oh, this is delightful!' she exclaimed. 'I can't remember being so happy before. How about you, Darrel?'

He knew he wouldn't be completely happy until they had shared the best that men and women could share, but it seemed churlish to mention that now. So he just smiled and nodded, pretending all was well. But inside he was seething still, and determined to find some way of deconditioning his new lady-love.

Yes, he reflected ruefully, that was what she had become to him. The memory of Franca had paled by comparison, even though she was not sexually impaired. Darrel could never have the same tender, protective feelings for her as he already had for Oralie. The Asian girl had found her way into his hearts as no one else, not even Annis, had done.

They frolicked like innocent children for the rest of the

245

morning and at noon they retired to the veranda for their midday meal. Afterwards Oralie came and perched on his knee, looking out towards the sun's reflection on the ocean. 'It's so hot,' she smiled, stretching luxuriously, her mouth opening in a yawn.

'Time for a siesta, I think. Shall we bring some bedding outside and lie where we can hear the sea?'

She smiled, delighted with the idea, so they made a nest for themselves in the sand within the shadow of the palm trees and lay down in each other's arms. Feeling her sun-warmed flesh against his own was very sensual, and it didn't take long for Darrel to get a hard-on. He decided to let her pleasure him, as she was used to doing. For the time being that seemed the easiest course, especially since he'd grown exceedingly randy all morning, watching her lithe young body skipping in and out of the water and then lying in provocative poses on the warm sand. He hadn't lost his desire to initiate Oralie into the mysteries of the orgasm but, realistically, he knew that would have to wait.

The girl needed no encouragement. She obviously felt relaxed in the tropical heat, ready to explore the erotic possibilities of their new environment as far as she was able. Darrel put aside his sadness and anger on her behalf, giving himself up to her tender caresses as she mouthed his nipples and played with his balls. Revelling in the new sense of freedom, he stroked down the long roller-coaster of her back and buttocks, relishing the smooth feel of her hot flesh beneath his hand.

She was soon fellating him, her mouth working eagerly around his glans and down his shaft, bringing his erection into full bloom. Darrel felt the stirrings within grow more urgent as he reached up and pinched the soft buds of her breasts into prominence. His desire to plunge into her was unstoppable now. Playfully he turned her over and let his glans lodge in her entrance. 'Is that good?' he whispered.

'Mm!' she answered, but her tone was wary and it occurred to Darrel that he might be hurting her. He let his cock penetrate her an inch or so. 'Is that better?'

She nodded, her eyes moving adoringly over his face, and he sank into the hot, liquid heart of her. It was hard to believe that he couldn't make her come when her quim got so deliciously wet and inviting. Had they tinkered with her secretions too, making them flow copiously in response to penetration? Darrel made an effort to dismiss the dark emotions that were beginning to swamp his enjoyment and began to thrust vigorously.

'Ah, that's better! Yes, yes! Ride me till you reach your destination, lover!'

The words sounded false. Ignoring them, Darrel closed his eyes and concentrated on the powerful sensations that were winging through his nervous system, taking him on an inexorable drive towards the ultimate gratification. But soon he was opening his eyes in startled amazement. He felt his buttocks being thrashed by some mildly stinging whip with many fronds!

Darrel soon realized what the little minx was up to. She'd reached out and picked up one of the many palm fronds that were littering their part of the beach, using it as an instrument of correction. Seeing his awareness of the situation, she giggled up at him. 'Naughty boy!' she joked. 'I punish you, you feel better. Yes?'

'Yes. I like it!'

She slapped him harder with the foliage until his bum felt deliciously warm and tingling. Darrel resumed his thrusting, spurred on to copulate at greater speed by the rhythmic thrashing he was receiving. He sensed that Oralie's own buttocks were being driven further into the cushioning sand beneath the thin sheet, and his delight increased. On the margin of his consciousness he could hear the sea lapping against the shore while a light breeze wafted warm air around them. It was idyllic. Revelling in their perfect freedom and harmony with nature, Darrel felt as if all the trappings of twenty-first century civilization had been stripped from him and he was pagan in spirit once more. At the first uprush of energy, the precursor of his climax, he let out a paean of joy. His voice echoed round the small bay, making the birds screech in fright, and as he came the pouring of his seed was a libation to both Eros and Pan.

After a long rest he looked up to see Oralie kneeling at his side, smiling down at him as she prepared to massage his body with warm oil. 'I found it in the bathroom,' she told him. 'It stops sunburn.'

'Fine, but I need a wash down first.' Darrel looked towards the blue, seductive ocean. He grabbed her hand, letting her pull him to his feet, then began to pull her. 'Come on!'

Laughing, they raced down the shore and belly-flopped into the warm water. It was blissful to be diving naked beneath the surface, feeling the currents caress and invade every surface and crevice of your body. Darrel seized Oralie around the waist and drew her to him, their flesh slippery in contact. He kissed her and felt the easy yielding of her body. They performed acrobatics beneath the waves, swirling and turning in a dozen different yogic positions to make an erotic underwater ballet.

It wasn't long before Darrel was hard again. He pulled Oralie's legs around his waist and speared into her, laughing when she gasped with surprise. Legs planted firmly on the sandy floor, he took advantage of their weightlessness to explore new angles, new possibilities, and soon his cock seemed to be in free fall, floating in the warm lagoon of her body. He closed his eyes, feeling the sun on his face as he stood, waist-deep, in the water. Oralie bent back, her torso floating on the surface, and he splashed her breasts until the nipples looked like pink molluscs stuck onto the solid rocks of her breasts.

His ascent to orgasm was sudden but, at the crucial moment, Darrel felt a strong urge to pull out of her and let his seed flow into the ocean like fish sperm. The silken water held his penis in suspension as it pumped with abandon, making him feel as if his whole body was bathed in liquid bliss, inside and out. The experience was exquisite, but afterwards he felt guilty for his selfish indulgence. So much for his wanting to pleasure Oralie!

She didn't seem to mind. Towing him in to the shore, she proceeded first to dry and then to massage his body with the protective sun oil. Darrel gave himself up to sensuality again, and when she succeeded in stimulating him for a third time he gladly let her ride on top of him. Their spell in the water had made her even more limber, and he marvelled at the way her pelvis moved with rapid grace, her inner muscles working to extract the maximum response from her lithe performance.

He came quickly and violently, gushing into her with prolonged force while clutching at the firm globes of her buttocks. Afterwards he saw that his nails had made half-moons in her flesh and he realized that not being able to feel her coming was making him frustrated. Was that all part of his conditioning? It would take a long time before he could think of love-making as mutual pleasuring. It disturbed him to think he was still inclined to think in terms of satisfying the female, as if Oralie was just another client. And the fact that, at some level, she still felt like that about him was doubly annoying. Here, in this island paradise, they were superficially free. But the black technology of the controllers still held sway in both their psyches, linking body and soul in a diabolical travesty of human relations. Could either of them ever truly break free of their physiological and psychological bonds to discover what 'love' might really mean?

The answer lay somewhere on this island, Darrel was sure. If they could get themselves sorted out physically maybe they could relearn their emotional responses and free themselves from their conditioning. If not, there was little point in them having made their escape.

Despite the hedonistic enjoyment of the afternoon, Darrel spent the evening sunk in gloomy thought. He sat on the veranda pretending to read one of the old-fashioned novels that had been left in the villa for the entertainment of the visitors, but it was just a ploy to avoid talking to Oralie. He didn't want to infect her with his pessimism. Gazing out into a glorious sunset he knew his spirit should feel uplifted, but the only effect was to remind him that he could not stay in this idyllic setting for long.

Tomorrow he would meet Wal again and be taken to see other refugees from so-called civilization. He had no idea what kind of society they had managed to build up here, far from the influence of the controllers. It could be heaven, or it could be hell. And how advanced could their technology be in this wilderness? The thought of Oralie having to submit to primitive surgery in some dirty hut or back-street lab was filling him with increasing horror.

Chapter Fourteen

Wal turned up mid-morning, looking hung over, and drove them off at breakneck speed through the verdant jungle. When Darrel asked where they were going he was answered with a grunt and a long pause followed by an incomprehensible name, so he didn't try asking again. The undergrowth began to peter out and give way to crudely farmed strips of land, then a kind of shanty town appeared. By that time, Wal had become a shade more coherent.

'This is the main township,' he explained. 'Mostly refugees, with a hard core of residents in the better houses.'

They drove past shacks that were fabricated from anything under the sun, then found themselves driving along semi-paved streets, where houses of faded elegance lurked behind high walls topped with barbed wire.

'The natives fear the refugees,' Wal said. 'And the refugees distrust the natives, so each group tends to keep to themselves. Only a few of us pass easily between them.'

'Where are we going?' Darrel asked again, with more purpose this time.

'To meet a man called Sven. He's one of the main fixers round here. He knows everybody – and their price. He can get you anything you want.'

'Sounds a useful chap to know,' Darrel commented, wryly.

'He is, believe me.'

There was an edge to his voice, and Darrel wondered why. They entered a shady back street and parked near a bar, where voices could be heard and occasional laughter. Wal led the way inside, pushing through a bead curtain, and at once an extraordinary sight met their eyes. The biggest man Darrel had ever seen was leaning on the bar with his back to the door. He was almost seven feet tall and looked about three feet broad, with huge biceps and legs like tree-trunks. When he turned to answer Wal's greeting his face was a grotesque mask; his brows resembled black caterpillars speckled with white, and he had a flattened nose and broad, thick lips. Thick brown hair hung to his shoulders in greasy coils and black eyes regarded them with faint suspicion.

But the biggest surprise of all was his voice. Instead of the booming tones which Darrel expected to come out of that great mouth he spoke in a quiet, polite whisper.

'Wal! Good to see you again!'

He threw his bearlike arms around Wal, making him look weedy by contrast, although he was by no means a small man. Grimacing slightly, Wal said, 'I've brought a couple of friends, newcomers to Malaku. I think they need your help. Darrel and Oralie, from Geosan.'

The giant shook Darrel's hand gently and then lifted Oralie's to his lips. 'Charmed to meet you, sister!'

'They both need a surgical rehab,' Wal explained, in a low voice. 'What's the score?'

'How creditworthy are they?'

'Not very. Spent all theirs getting here, I gather. But they might have other assets.'

Darrel felt uneasy at having Wal negotiate for them. It felt strange hearing himself referred to as if he weren't there, but he was afraid to interfere.

Sven looked thoughtful. 'Have they got contacts?'

'Don't know.' Wal turned to Darrel. 'How d'you get to this place? Who told you about it?'

There seemed nothing to lose in mentioning names now. And everything to gain. 'Well, I used to work at the Plezure Plaza in New London.'

The giant's black eyes lit up. 'Then you know Jabez?'

'Jabez!' It was a name he'd never thought to hear again. 'Sure I know him! But how on earth . . ?'

'And Brother Jay?'

Darrel felt his heart leap for joy. 'That's right, him too. And Franca, and Annis.'

'But Annis is here, on Malaku. Didn't you know?'

The news struck Darrel right between the eyes. 'No,' he faltered. 'I had no idea. When did she arrive?'

'Couple of days ago. You want to meet her?'

He hesitated, wondering how Oralie would take it. She didn't know that Annis was in love with another woman. Was she prone to jealousy? It seemed unlikely, but he didn't want to risk upsetting her. Then he felt her nudge his elbow.

'Of course we'd like to see her,' Oralie declared. He loved her all the more for that.

'First things first,' Wal reminded them, sourly. 'Sven, can you get us to a skull cracker right away?' He noticed Darrel's puzzled face and explained, 'Slang for rehab surgeon.'

'I don't find the term in the least reassuring,' he said, dryly.

Sven grinned. 'Don't worry, I take you to the best. You have a little cocktail, you won't feel a thing. Wake up a new man.'

'And Oralie?'

'There's a woman specializes in female emancipation. She can go with you, later.'

'Great! But what about paying for all this?'

The grin of the friendly giant widened. 'Don't worry. You'll pay!'

Despite his misgivings Darrel decided to trust the man. He had no other realistic alternative, and if Wal had sold him down the river then at least he and Oralie had got one day and one night of near-honeymoon bliss out of it. Aware of an increasingly stoical streak in himself that was inclined to accept each new twist and turn of fate with equanimity, Darrel placed a guiding hand on Oralie's slim waist and followed the two men to the door of the bar.

As they drove through the chaotic streets in Wal's vehicle Darrel was deep in thought. The presence of Annis on the island had now become a complication, and he was full of curiosity. Had she come alone, or with others from the New London group? He was hungry for news of them. Since he and Oralie had left Geosan he'd felt very isolated, not just from the decadent community of the Plaza, but from the group that had engineered his getaway too. It would be good to get back into contact with them soon.

They got out in front of a pair of high black gates set in a pristine white wall. Sven went through an elaborate set of security procedures and then the gate swung open. Darrel was surprised to find himself entering not the sordid back street hut he had been envisaging but a modern-looking clinic. Inside the chrome-and-glass entrance were smooth-floored corridors down which women in nurse-like uniforms glided on softly-padded feet.

The fact that it was just the sort of place the controllers might have run filled him with momentary dread. But when they reached the office of the rehab surgeon Darrel was instantly reassured. On the walls were two screens showing scenes from both New London and Geosan. A third simply bore the motto: 'Freedom is all in the Mind'. Behind a curved desk sat a charming man of Asian stock, whose warm brown eyes were smiling at them even before his lips followed suit. The man rose and wrapped his arms part way around the giant's chest.

'Sven, old friend! I see you have brought me some new friends this time. Good!'

After the introductions had been made, the surgeon being introduced simply as 'Doc', they all sat in recliners while the procedure was outlined.

'I shall examine you first to determine your needs,' Doc said to Darrel. 'We don't have the most sophisticated equipment here, as you can imagine, but we manage pretty well with what we have got. And our results have been generally satisfactory.'

'Is it dangerous?'

Doc grinned. 'You don't beat about the bush, do you? There is some risk involved, yes. Brain surgery is always delicate, and I expect to find that some of the trodes have been wired right into your visual cortex.'

257

'You mean I might go *blind*?'

'It's not happened to anyone I've operated on yet . . .'

'But it could. Right?'

The surgeon shrugged. 'As I said, there's always an element of risk. You could call it the price of true freedom. Stay as you are, and you will always be wondering about your responses, how real is your perception of the world. And you will carry the obscene work of the controllers in your head to your grave. Some say they are capable of a remarkable degree of remote control . . .'

'Hey, you've convinced me! When do we start, Doc?'

The man gave a wry smile. 'First we must ascertain what you can do for me, young man. I gather you're not credit-rich.'

Darrel shrugged. 'This trip cleaned me out.'

'The usual story. But credit is only indirectly useful here on Malaku. If you were prepared to take part in some experiments before I operated on you, that would be very helpful to me.'

Darrel groaned. 'What kind of experiments?'

'I'm currently researching into sensory deprivation. Prior to the operation your sensory apparatus would spend several hours in a state of limbic disorientation.'

'What does that mean?'

'Cut off from sensory stimuli you will experience a kind of madness, a waking nightmare. Random memories and random emotions will be generated, many quite inappropriate. You will also fantasize and experience both true and pseudo-hallucinations. I shall attempt to not only monitor the imaging in your brainwaves but to record it, using an ultra-sensitive scanner in a magnetically shielded environment. The readout will be put onto a chip and inserted in someone else's brain for playback.'

Through all the psychobabble a daunting picture was being communicated to Darrel. 'You mean, you'll be recording some of my impressions then transmitting them to someone else?'

'Hopefully, yes. Work in this field was prohibited world-wide at the start of the millennium but we have reason to believe it continues covertly, amongst the controllers. We have to catch up with their technology if we're to have a hope of beating them at their own game.'

'I see.' Darrel looked at Oralie. Her face was puzzled, slightly wary. He wondered whether she might have to undergo a similar set of experiments in order to get her implant removed. He hoped not. But if he went ahead it might give her the courage to face whatever she had to undergo.

He smiled, suddenly making up his mind. 'You've got yourself a deal, Doc.'

'Good!' the surgeon said. Both he and Wal were beaming at him, though Oralie still looked apprehensive.

'What about Oralie?' Darrel asked at last. 'Will you operate on her too?'

Doc shook his head. 'Not my province, I'm afraid. We have a lady surgeon who deals with clitoral implants but she won't be here for . . . let me see . . .' He consulted his screen. A diary flashed for a few seconds. 'Three days. I can get an appointment fixed up now, though.'

'If you would. What about payment?'

'That's between you and the surgeon.'

Darrel nodded. He was thinking that if he had to undergo more experiments to pay for Oralie's op he would do so. Except he might not be so keen once this first ordeal was over. 'When do we start?'

'Now, if you like. I have some slack in my schedule. A nurse will take you through to the prep suite where you'll spend the rest of today. Your companions may stay, if you wish. I shall begin the experiment first thing tomorrow. It will last for six hours but you will have no conception of time. At the end of the experimental period, provided you are physically fit, I shall proceed to the operation.'

'I see.' Darrel was silent for a few seconds, wondering if he was making a big mistake in putting himself in this man's hands. But something about Doc made him trust the man and, after all, to free himself from the controllers' influence was the main reason he had come to Malaku. 'Very well,' he said at last. 'I'm ready.'

'I can't stay, I'm afraid,' Wal said at once. 'But I can assure you that you are in safe hands. Good luck! When it's all over you're welcome to convalesce in my villa. Just ask Doc to give me a call.'

He left just as the nurse was entering. She smiled pleasantly at Darrel, exchanged a few words with Doc then led the way down the corridor to a small room containing a bamboo bed, chair and primitive washbasin. 'Take off your clothes and put on this,' she told him, handing him a thin cotton gown. 'Then lie down, please.'

Oralie helped him undress. When he was in bed the nurse returned. 'Medication,' she said, handing him a phial of pink liquid. 'Then I must shave your head.'

Darrel hadn't bargained for that, but of course it made sense. He recalled how short his hair had been after the controllers had first implanted him. There had been long, thin scarlines in his skull that had soon disappeared when his hair had grown again. Now, though, there was something very enjoyable about having rather an attractive young woman first snip and then clip his hair until it was short enough to be shaved. Oralie sat watching, her face aglow with anticipation, and when the operation was finished and his bald skull was revealed she gave a broad grin.

'Your head, it's like a Sechzuan quilt!'

Darrel gazed into the mirrors that the nurse placed in front and behind his head. The yellow parchment of his skull was criss-crossed with a grid of thin red lines. 'I see what you mean!'

'That is usual for one who has been controlled,' the nurse said, matter-of-factly. 'It's nothing to worry about. When the wires have been taken out and your hair has grown you will be as normal again.'

Normal! Did anyone really know what that meant any more? After the nurse had gone he felt sleepy and lay down, looking out through the small window at the lush vegetation beyond. Everything had seemed unreal since he found out about what had been done to him. Yet when he looked back on how his life had been before that momentous revelation, his years at the Plezure Plaza seemed like a vacuous dream. Was he about to discover a 'real' reality at last?

For a few minutes he drifted in and out of consciousness, chatting idly to Oralie almost without knowing what he was saying. Gradually his periods of vague incoherence increased and the room grew blurred. His vision blanked out and returned hazily several times, then he remembered nothing of where he was or what he was doing there. A period of dreamless sleep intervened, and when he returned to awareness he was in a twilight world of shadows and fleeting images.

Suddenly it was as if a light had been switched on in the dark attic of his mind. There were some strange crackling noises, accompanied by dizziness, then he realized that his whole body felt constricted. He tried to move his hands and feet but they were securely bound, every muscle held in rigid confinement. His breathing was shallow and seemed to be regulated by some external control. His eyelids were taped down, his mouth bunged up. A terrible panic seized him and, somewhere in his throat, a scream was stifled at birth.

The panic was short-lived. A sudden flood of vivid images overwhelmed him, driving all thoughts of his physical discomfort out of his mind. Darrel was in the park he used to visit as a child. There were huge, exotic blooms everywhere and the air was filled with a heavy scent of mixed spices and floral essences, a cross between an old-fashioned kitchen on baking day and a florist's shop. The associations brought with them memories: of sitting under an old-fashioned pine table rubbing his erection through short trousers, and of a buxom assistant in a yellow low-necked top coming towards him with an armful of roses, their bobbing heads caressing her cleavage.

The weird thing was, he was sure they weren't his own personal memories. Darrel guessed he had somehow tapped into the racial subconscious and the images that surfaced were those from other lives, other times. But they were extraordinarily real. His imagination went with the nubile florist, who was smiling lasciviously at him as she advanced. Her skin was tanned to a honey brown and when she bent forward to place the bouquet on a chair he could see the deep swell of her breasts and felt his cock harden.

The girl extracted a single pink rose and stood up, right in front of him. The scent of the flowers was rich in his nostrils, mixed with musky feminine body odours. His balls felt heavy inside their tight casing and the sweat started to pour off him but, having nowhere to go, he began to steam in his own liquid. It was very unpleasant at first but as the scenario continued he became engrossed again and the feeling of having warm, liquid skin became quite pleasant.

With a small sigh, the florist caressed her chest with the rose petals, letting the flower drift down between her ample breasts. With the other hand she slipped off her shoulder straps until her whole cleavage was exposed and Darrel realised she was not wearing any undergarments. The yellow top was held on only by her erect nipples, which were acting as clothes hooks. She laughed at him, and took his hand. He felt the coolness of her fingers and let her lead him forward into a dark corner of the shop where there was a whole heap of fragrant rose petals.

Still trilling with laughter, she pulled him down beside her. Amidst the rough and tumble her top became dislodged, exposing one huge, ripe nipple. The dull fire in his lower belly surged into full heat as he grabbed her tit and thrust the nipple into his mouth where he began sucking vigorously.

Flashes of the other scene kept intervening as he played with her smooth globes. He extracted his little-boy's willy from his trousers and began to play with himself beneath the table while looking up the skirt of the woman who was rolling pastry on top. He saw stocking tops and suspenders, a white pouch edged with lace through which dark, wiry hairs were visible, and his junior erection increased to adult size.

The well-endowed girl was suddenly naked in her bed of roses, and Darrel's lips were fastening on the rosebud of her sex. He could feel the cool petals caressing him, moving over his back and buttocks while he tasted her. The scent of cinnamon reached him, and he was vaguely aware of the table above him and his cock responding to the furtive friction. Then, just as Darrel felt himself to be nearing a climax, the whole fantasy changed beyond recognition.

He was on his back, passive and restrained, with two women standing over him. He recognized them as the players in his previous fantasies, but now the sexy florist was dressed in figure-hugging black vinyl through which only the ripe buds of her nipples appeared in naked, pink arousal. Her blonde hair was scraped back severely and she wore a mask that reduced her eyes to small slits, although her luscious lips were still visible, painted exactly the same shade as her nipples.

The other woman was a matronly type, wearing a bibbed apron and long, black dress. She had elbow-length rubber gloves that glistened with some kind of lubricant. Darrel felt his guts churn at the sight, finding it ominous.

The blonde beauty began to play with his erection, smoothing it rhythmically between her long, cool fingers until it stood up like a pylon. She was murmuring all the time to the other woman, who was replying in grunts. At first Darrel couldn't make out what they were saying. Their voices were muffled, as if coming from under water. Then he realized that the interchange was being played over and over, like a tape loop. He listened with more attention and eventually distinguished the words.

'I'll make him nice and big so he's nice and loose,' the blonde girl was saying. 'When he's good and open, it's your turn.'

'Dirty boy!' the matron muttered. 'I'll teach him! Wash his arse out with soap!'

The exchange echoed over and over, making Darrel feel more and more uneasy. Far from loosening up he could feel his sphincter tightening protectively as his rod grew more rigid. Suddenly the blonde woman flicked a switch and the table he was lying on flipped over so that he was face down. There was a mechanical hum and he felt a section of the table to which he was strapped open up, revealing his behind.

With clenched buttocks, Darrel stared down at the carpet beneath him. It was a complicated pattern of flowers and spirals that appeared to move with his gaze. Despite his fearful state he began to recognize images of frolicking creatures in the carpet: voluptuous nymphs, exotic winged fairies and satyr-like men with huge penises. The panorama extended to fill his field of vision and the figures began to separate into couples, threesomes, foursomes.

Their tastes were indiscriminate. Darrel saw one satyr thrusting into a willing nymph while another satyr buggered him. Two fairies performed mutual cunnilingus to the evident delight of a lone satyr, who sat masturbating while he watched them. In one corner there was a crowd of the creatures performing cunnilingus or fellatio on each other in a long, erotic daisy chain. His eyes were dazzled by the frantic activity of myriad sexual couplings in one vast orgy.

Then he felt firm hands part his buttocks, opening up his anus, and the dread which had been momentarily eclipsed by the extraordinary visual display returned in force. It was now impossible to prevent the oiled finger from entering him.

The scene before him changed subtly until every figure in the erotic landscape was engaged in sodomy, either actively or passively. Darrel groaned but the noise was smothered deep in his chest. The woman slipped first one, then two slippery fingers into him, working them round and round so that his arse was obliged to become more accommodating. She pushed further up and as he yielded Darrel felt a deep, hot gratification spiral through him from the sensitive nerves of his rectum.

The questing fingers withdrew but still he lay limp and exposed. Before his eyes the strange couples were engaged in more elaborate activities once more. Some nymphs and satyrs were on all fours to receive the rampant organs in their front or back passages. Others were completely submissive, flat on the ground with their butts well plugged. Some had a male or female licking their parts while they were being buggered. Others were sitting in each others' laps to perform their assorted sexual acts.

Darrel felt his anus being stretched once more and something thick and hard was slowly introduced. As it was pushed into him it began to vibrate, stimulating his sensitive inner tissues until he began writhing around in helpless abandon, longing for release. It reached a certain point then stopped, continuing to stimulate him with a slow, relentless rhythm, inducing a frustrating tension.

There was another mechanical noise and he felt the table give way beneath him a little, exposing his genitals. His stiff cock protruded through an opening and his balls hung heavily in space, but his belly and thighs remained secure. This time, when he looked down, the erotic spectacle on the carpet was obscured by the smiling face of the blonde woman. She was kneeling directly below him, naked now except for the mask, and manipulating her long nipples between her fingers.

The generous pink lips parted and made a perfect O. A shudder went through Darrel's loins as he realized – or hoped he did – what she was about to do for him. His prick reared impatiently and she caught it with her right hand while continuing to caress her breasts with her left. She squeezed the base of his prick between her thumb and forefinger, exactly as she'd just been doing to her nipple, and a blob of viscous white liquid appeared in the slit of his glans like a bead of sweat.

She opened her mouth wide and put out her long, pink tongue. Delicately she transferred the white globule onto the tip of her tongue and swallowed it. Then she licked slowly up his shaft while her fingers scratched lightly over the tense surface of his balls. Darrel silently pleaded with her to complete the job as rapidly as possible. His arse was on fire now, and he was burning like hell for the slow massage to develop into more rapid friction both back and front. He didn't care about anything other than his own satisfaction but because, at some level, he knew this was all an illusion, he also knew that this time satisfaction was by no means guaranteed.

The dildo was slowly withdrawn from his anus, making him feel vulnerable and exposed once more. This time something thinner was introduced, something which he recognized as a long tube. Liquid started to gush into his rectum and he felt his bowels loosening while, all the time, the woman kneeling below was licking his tumid shaft with the flat of his tongue and teasing his balls with her tickling fingers.

The release, when it came, was not the kind he'd been expecting. Instead of the comforting rush of an orgasm, both his bowels and his bladder were triggered simultaneously. While his arsehole was experiencing the sensation of evacuating into space, he watched with helpless incredulity as a stream of bright yellow urine flowed down onto the blonde woman's face and splashed onto her breasts. She seemed to be loving it, but before he could tell whether any drops were actually going into her mouth the entire fantasy faded and all his senses were suddenly plunged into dark, silent oblivion.

Darrel remained conscious, however, wondering what would happen next. His genitals which, only moments before had been inflamed and inflated with extreme lust, were now completely lacking in sensation, as was his arse. Before he had time to wonder how he could be so hot one minute and so cold the next his senses were flooded with an onslaught of new impressions.

He seemed to be floating in free fall, surrounded by thin air but with beams of energy darting through him. Where the radiation entered his body the skin burned and prickled for a few seconds, like thousands of electrodes firing at random.

At first it felt disconcerting, even irritating, but after a while Darrel became accustomed to the sensation and it grew quite pleasurable, like being in a warm shower. As soon as he had mentally drawn that analogy the air changed to water and he found himself in an underwater situation with the same weird prickling going on all over his body. Now, though, it was associated with swimming through a vast shoal of fishes. Every time one of the tiny creatures touched his skin he received a mild electric shock. There was a cave up ahead, offering some chance of shelter, and he pushed against the heavy resistance of the water to reach it.

Inside he could see that somehow he was on dry land again and the cave was full of remarkably phallic formations. When he became used to the dim light he could see that there were several naked women in there and it was obvious at once that they were putting the penis-shaped stalagmites to good use. their moans and groans of desire and ecstasy filled his ears like a musical chorus, echoing round the huge cave.

A musky, earthy smell that he recognized as a heady mixture of female sexual secretions, raw minerals and fungi filled his nostrils. His body was still half-immersed in wetness but it was a thick, muddy substance and his genitals were being sensually caressed by the stuff as he moved through it. Wallowing in the warm slime, Darrel tried to wade through to the rocky area where the women were pleasuring themselves.

The girl nearest him was evidently on the verge of coming. As she twisted and turned, her pussy impaled

on the tall, thick limestone prick, she was stroking her
pert small breasts and pulling at the aroused nipples, her
face a mask of erotic self-indulgence. Darrel felt an urge
to thrust his cock into her ecstatic, open mouth and join
in her dalliance, but the more he strove to reach her the
more the thick mud held him back, swirling around his
groin and thighs.

As his lust grew more and more inflamed, the cloying
stuff began to heat up. Soon Darrel felt as if he was
wading through fire. He looked down and found it was
literally true: he was immersed in a river of molten lava
that was sweeping him forward, towards the now completely stranded women who were continuing to writhe
and moan in their private bliss, oblivious of all except
their own arousal.

The stone stems on which they were perched reared
up like blackened stakes out of a lake that was glowing
dull red. Steam filled the air and sparks flew up onto the
bare rock where they were arrayed. Darrel watched
one of them reach a climax, her head thrown back in
voluptuous abandon and her rounded breasts and belly
shuddering as the spasms shook through her overheated
system. The sight made his body convulse with fevered
lust and he knew that his own orgasm was imminent.

When it finally arrived the explosion racked through
him like a volcano. At the same time a ghostly voice
informed him, 'You have been through the four magical
initiations of air, water, earth and fire! Soon you will be
empowered to take full command of yourself and fulfil
your birthright!'

The echoing words faded with the last spasms and
then Darrel sank into mindlessness again. After a while

fitful dreams disturbed his sleep, random images that were purely visual with no coherent logic to them, and that were forgotten as soon as they were perceived. A period of disturbing hallucination followed where all his senses were assailed at once. While ever-changing patterns of zig-zags, spirals, and checkerboards danced before his inner eye he smelt a rapid succession of odours that he could scarcely identify before they changed again: burning rubber, ripe peaches, manure, aniseed, lilac. To add to his confusion he could feel hairy roughness one second, squelchy gloop the next, and all the while he was tasting flavours that followed the scents in a weird sensory time-lapse: while he smelt manure he tasted peaches, and so on. Through it all the crackling buzz of the white noise continued unabated and almost unnoticed beneath the rest of the stimuli.

The disturbing synaesthesia continued until Darrel's senses were in utter confusion and he could scarcely tell what he was seeing, smelling, feeling, hearing or tasting. Just when the jumble was becoming unbearable total blackness fell upon him again and he gave himself up thankfully to the void of unconsciousness, where his sleep was absolute and scarcely distinguishable from total extinction.

Chapter Fifteen

Darrel was slowly regaining consciousness. He could hear the sound of muffled voices, smell the faint odour of disinfectant and something floral, feel the weight of a soft cocoon around his naked body. But he could see nothing, nothing at all.

He jerked himself into a sitting position and the fabric fell away from his chest, exposing him to warm air. His hands went up to his eyes and he felt the pads over them, secured by tape. Although he longed to tear them off and discover the state of his eyesight he restrained himself, calling out to whoever might be within earshot: 'Hallo! Is anybody there?'

A voice-activated alarm rang, followed by hurrying footsteps. He heard someone come into the room and recognized the nurse's voice as she said, 'Ah, good! You're awake. I'll just fetch the Doc.'

'Please!' Darrel waved his hand in the air, longing for the reassurance of human contact. 'Please tell me, are my eyes all right?'

Warm fingers curled around his hand. 'I should think so. You have to keep the pads on for a while. I'll fetch the Doc. He'll be able to tell you more.'

The wait seemed endless. Eventually Darrel heard, not a man's voice, but that of Oralie. 'Oh Darrel, I'm so glad you are back with us!'

He felt her lips brush his cheek, but they did little to still his inner panic. 'Is the Doc there?' he asked, hoarsely.

'Right here!' came the Doc's voice, jovial, confident. 'I'm glad to tell you that everything went smoothly. I don't know how much you can remember, but . . .'

'My eyes, Doc! Am I going to be able to see?'

'There was no damage to the optic nerve.'

'Can't you take these damn shades off? I want to see!'

'Not yet. You'll have to wait a while longer until we're sure the healing process . . .'

'How much longer?'

'A few hours. Why don't you rest now? Oralie can stay with you.'

Darrel heard the Doc and nurse leave the room, sensed he was alone with Oralie. Only to her was he prepared to admit the extent of his fear. 'I'm afraid of going blind. What if I can't see when they take the pads off?'

'You'll be all right.' Her voice was soothing. 'Look, why don't you let me give you a relaxing massage. Then you'll feel better.'

He nodded, letting her pull off the lightweight bedding and loose shift until his whole body lay naked on the bed. Since there was nothing else to be done he uttered a deep sigh then gave himself up to Oralie's practised hands.

As the massage progressed Darrel became aware that he was feeling things differently. It was very hard to quantify, but his skin felt more sensitive than before, as if some sense-deadening top layer had been removed. It was most extraordinary, and he tried to explain it to Oralie but the nearest he could come to it was that it must be like some kind of rebirth.

'It's like when you're in pain, you can't imagine what it's like to be free of it. Now I can't remember how I felt before.'

Oralie giggled, and he realized it was not just his sense of touch that was enhanced. 'You sound different, too. Clear as a bell. Did I have some blockage in my ears before?'

'I don't know.'

She was smoothing her fingers up his thighs. His leg muscles vibrated with pent-up force and his balls started to tingle. The tips of her fingers brushed his pubic hair and ripples of electricity spread through his groin. Darrel luxuriated in the new responsiveness of his flesh, feeling as though he'd only been half alive up to now.

'What about you, Oralie?' he asked, remembering that she was to be operated on too. 'Have you met this woman surgeon yet?'

'No. They wanted to make sure you were well first.'

He lapsed into silence, enjoying the soft, rhythmic feel of her caressing hands as they swept over his belly in a spiral motion. She was massaging his guts, working with his etheric body, easing the emptiness within. The good energy was flowing through him without any hindrance, bringing him fully back to life after the strange limbo he'd been experiencing.

Now he could remember his dreams, vaguely. They had been erotic, fantastic, but this was better. If he could choose between the fevered over-stimulation of his imagination and this quiet, healing contact he would take this every time. Oralie's fingers moved up to his face, tracing his brows and pressing gently on the light-obscuring pads. He saw bright flashing stars, but was that a good sign? Did even blind men see stars when their eye-balls were stimulated? He had no idea, and the anxiety returned.

'Ssh!' she sensed his agitation and kissed his mouth. 'It's going to be all right, Darrel. The Doc said so, and I trust him. He is a good man – like you.'

'Don't make me out to be any kind of hero!' he said, gruffly.

She giggled softly, and her hands moved down to his cock. Enclosing it within her palms she said, 'I wonder if you are ready for this? Doc didn't say we shouldn't.'

Darrel groaned as he felt her mouth encircle the soft head. His glans began to swell, pushing out from the shaft that was also thickening. The exquisite delicacy of her lips made him gasp with longing and he began to pray that no nurse would appear to interrupt them.

Reading his thoughts Oralie said, 'I'll just move some-thing against the door. If someone tries to come in we will have some warning.'

He heard her push the wheeled trolley across the floor. The wet imprint of her lips on his glans felt cool until she returned and kissed the spot again. Her fingers moved more boldly up and down his shaft, bringing it swiftly to full erection, and then she let the whole of his glans enter her open mouth. Her tongue worked into the groove, licking out the sticky residue.

Darrel was filled with a languid peace. The old urgency that usually took over at this point, propelling him towards a climax, was replaced by a deliciously lazy sensuality. Although Oralie was concentrating on his genitals he could feel the sensations spreading throughout his flesh, like radio waves from a transmitter.

Every nerve in his body was being subtly stimulated, bringing him into a state of extreme arousal that was nevertheless relaxed and calm.

'I like this,' he murmured. 'You're making me feel all soft and floaty.'

But, even as he said it, Darrel felt a subtle change taking place. He recognized the approach of his climax, but this time it was sneaking up on him instead of announcing its arrival with a blast of trumpets. Slowly his cock was preparing to discharge itself, the quivering glans stretched to capacity. Everything seemed to be in slow motion. Even the first spasm of his orgasm was a long-drawn-out vibration that seemed to travel up to his ears and down to his toes before finally gathering force. His come spewed out in slow, thick bursts of prolonged bliss that gradually turned his cock into a melting heap of warm jelly.

A guttural groan issued from somewhere in his belly as the last drops of his semen were squeezed out and the ecstasy faded. His body still felt more alive than ever before. Where Oralie was touching him her fingertips were like warm pearls.

'You liked that?' she asked, silkily.

'Mm. What do you think?'

'I think you like very much!' she giggled, kissing him. He seized her and pinned her to his chest, feeling her breasts squirming playfully out of reach of his grasping hands. He caught them in their thin covering and pinched the burgeoning nipples, making her give a soft 'Oh!'

'I can't wait to make love to you properly,' he whispered.

'Not good now. Someone may come.'

'The question is, will it be you, me, or both of us?'

It took a few seconds for his meaning to sink in. When it did he delighted in the hilarious surprise of her laughter. But their merriment must have reached the ears of the nurse because they heard her soft shuffle along the corridor, just a few seconds too late. The door jammed against the trolley that Oralie had placed in front of it.

'What is this?' called the nurse. 'What are you doing?'

Oralie giggled, leapt off the bed and went to let her in. 'Sorry. It rolled there.'

'Really!' Darrel heard the suspicion in the woman's voice and grinned. She said to Oralie, 'I think you had better leave now, don't you?'

'Can I come back later?'

'If you promise to behave yourself.'

'Of course she will,' Darrel broke in. 'She's always as good as gold. Aren't you, love?'

The last word lingered long on his lips and echoed in his head, making him wonder if that was what he was truly feeling. He thought he might well be in love, like people used to feel. It was as good a label as any for the way he was feeling about Oralie right now.

'Here, take your medication.'

The nurse held a small container to his lips. He recognized the smell of the pink medicine and knew that he would not remain awake for long. But now he was happy to drink himself into oblivion.

When Darrel awoke for the second time the room was dark but the pads had been removed from his eyes. He lay there for some time, afraid to summon the nurse. Was he really able to make out dim shapes in the room, or was it simply wishful thinking? He didn't want to discover that he had, indeed, been made blind by the operation. On the other hand, he felt he had to know. Eventually he reached out for the buzzer that he knew was in the wall behind the bed and eventually the nurse came into the room.

She didn't switch on the light but, in her hand, she held a small torch. The beam was circular, illuminating a round patch of space, and through it Darrel could clearly make out the woman's white uniform and dark legs. He let out a loud sigh of relief.

'I can see!' he exclaimed. 'Thank God, I can see!'

The nurse came to his bedside, shining the light onto his bed where the intricate geometric pattern of the quilt was displayed in every detail. Darrel stared at it, mesmerized, a joyful relief coursing through his body like wine.

She said, 'I told you everything would be all right.'

'Will you put the room light on?'

'I'm sorry, I'm under orders to restrict your field of vision. Mustn't overstrain your eyesight. But tomorrow, when you wake up, you'll be able to see everything by daylight.'

'What will happen tomorrow?'

'Doc will come and examine you. If he's satisfied with your condition preparations will be made for you to accompany your friend to the female surgeon.'

Darrel experienced a surge of joy. The sooner both he and Oralie were fixed the sooner they could resume their honeymoon romance in Wal's beachside villa. The prospect made his dick stir and reach half-cock, which particularly delighted him. Nothing amiss in that department either, then!

The nurse picked up a phial from the bedside trolley and poured him a measure of the familiar pink medication. Darrel drank it down then settled back, knowing sleep would soon come again.

This time it was deep and dreamless, and he was awoken by a bright light streaming directly into his eyes. He sat up blinking, and when he opened his eyes all he could see was a golden radiance obscuring everything. When his eyes got used to the dazzle he realized that the sun was streaming in through the window and soon he could see everything illuminated in sharp detail.

For several minutes he gazed in rapture around the small room. It wasn't as if he didn't remember the place from before. But now he was seeing it almost literally through new eyes. Far from the blindness he'd feared his sight had been restored to a crystal clarity that, unbeknown to him, he had long been missing. What he'd once thought of as normal vision now seemed dull and indistinct compared to this.

The door of the room slid open and there was Oralie smiling at him, every nuance of her features striking him anew. He noticed how smooth and translucent her skin was, how delicately arched her brows, how pretty were the sultry dark eyes with their soft-fringed lashes. And her mouth! It curved exquisitely and was a gentle coral pink, the full lips plump and voluptuous with their film of dew.

'Darrel!' she said, coming towards him with outstretched arms. 'Can you see me?'

'I see you!' he said, giving a deep, throaty laugh. 'And you look wonderful! I can't wait to see the rest of you, in the flesh!'

'You might not have to wait long. The Doc is coming and, if he agrees, we may meet the lady surgeon today. She will examine me, to see what can be done.'

Darrel took her in his arms and lightly kissed her forehead. She smelt of lilies or lotus, something exotic, and when she was close to him he could see the tiny pores in her skin and the smattering of downy hairs above her upper lip, aspects he would never have been able to focus on before. His lips met hers in a more passionate kiss, but as their tongues were duelling boldly within her sweet mouth there came the sound of the door opening once again. They broke apart just as the Doc entered.

'Ah, I see you are feeling yourself again – and Oralie, too!' he joked. 'But if you wouldn't mind lying down again, Darrel, for me to examine you. We must observe the proprieties.'

Obediently, gratefully, Darrel sank back onto the bed and let the Doc peer and probe at him until he was satisfied.

'Oh yes, I think you'll do!' he said at last. 'We'll give you a scan this afternoon, but meanwhile you may take Oralie to see her surgeon. I'm sure you'd like to see her together, wouldn't you?'

Darrel was allowed to shower and change into his own clothes. Oralie helped with the shower, although he was quite capable of managing by himself. He found her slippery little hands very arousing, but there was no time to take it any further. Their appointment was in ten minutes.

It was obvious that Oralie was filled with trepidation as they approached the surgeon's office. Darrel squeezed her hand, made reassuring noises. His operation had been a spectacular success, so why shouldn't hers be? But she seemed to take a more superstitious approach, as if two successful outcomes were more than they had any right to hope for.

When they entered the office and saw the woman sitting at her screen, Darrel gave a sudden gasp of recognition. 'Zee! What on earth are you doing here?'

Zee rose, smiling ironically, as he stared at her in astonishment. 'Hullo again, Dee. How are you? I heard you were having a rehab. How do you feel?'

But Darrel would not be side-stepped. 'I don't understand – why are you here on Malaku? I heard about Annis, but – you as well?'

'We work together, and pass freely between Malaku and New London. My job there is only a cover. This is my real work.'

'What?' The truth was only now starting to sink in. 'You mean *you're* the surgeon who's going to operate on Oralie?'

'If she wants me to, yes.'

'But how? I mean, how long have you . . . ?'

It dawned on him that she might well have been the surgeon who had operated on Annis, changing her features so spectacularly. Was that why the two women had fallen in love?

Zee smiled. 'Don't worry, I'm quite experienced. This will be my eighty-ninth such operation. We know quite a lot about the technology of the controllers by now, and it's no longer so much of a challenge to undo their handiwork. But I need to examine Oralie first, of course.'

Darrel fell silent, dumbfounded. Deciding that he'd

better just let her get on with it and take a back seat himself, he crossed his arms over his chest and waited while Oralie answered a whole list of questions. She could tell that the pair were warming to each other. A cosy woman-to-woman atmosphere was developing between them that made Darrel feel left out. When the time came for Oralie to be examined he felt decidedly awkward, and asked if he should leave.

'Not unless you want to,' Zee said, surprised.

He shook his head and looked quizzically at Oralie. She giggled. 'It's not as if you haven't seen me naked before!'

But when she stripped off and stood waiting for Zee to prepare the couch Darrel felt as if he was viewing her for the first time. His more acute eyesight was regarding her nude body with keen interest, noting the creamy texture of the skin on her breasts, the slow puckering of her nipple as it came into contact with the air, the delicate knot of flesh in her navel, the black lattice of hair that guarded her pubic mound. His eyes were feasting on her, taking in every curve and hollow of her body, and it was a richly sensuous experience that delighted him profoundly.

She lay down on the high couch and, at Zee's instruction, spread her thighs wide open. The surgeon beckoned him over. 'See the implant in her clitoris? That's been preventing her from achieving orgasm.'

'I know,' he replied, dully.

'It's a favourite ploy of the Geosan controllers, who like to keep their women genies ignorant about their own sexual potential. That way they are considered to be more free to concentrate on their clients' satisfaction. It's a complete nonsense, of course.'

'Can you remove it easily?'

'Remove it, yes. Easily, I don't know. They're getting cunning, using implodes – that's electrodes that join up physically with nerve-endings, plugging in directly to the central nervous system.'

'You mean, it could all go horribly wrong?'

Zee nodded once, brusquely. 'But, as I said, we've not had a serious failure yet. One or two operations haven't been quite as successful as we'd hoped, but we did regain fifty-per-cent sensation, and that's not bad.'

Oralie looked scared. She asked Zee, 'How long will it be before I'm . . . normal again.'

'Just a couple of days. You'll be a bit sore afterwards, though. We'll keep you in here for a week. By then the pair of you should be up and running.'

She gave Darrel a wistful look as if she envied him his first taste of Oralie's regenerated pussy. He smiled back at her, with forced confidence. It was difficult to equate this confident professional with the woman who had cavorted uninhibitedly with him and Annis, back at the Plaza. 'When will you do the op?'

'Later today. Annis will be helping out.'

'Great! Will I see her?'

'You could see her now. Room 17, just down the corridor. Why don't you pay her a visit while the nurse gives Oralie her pre-op?'

Darrel nodded, then went to take Oralie's hand. 'It's going to be fine,' he whispered. 'I trust everyone here. Look what they did for me! I feel like a new man.'

'You look wonderful!' She reached up and placed her hand on his shaven neck, pulling him down to her. Their lips and tongues mingled briefly, then she let him go. For a few long seconds he gazed into her eyes, hoping that what he felt for her was easily readable in his own.

He heard Zee slip out and her place was taken by the nurse, with her little phial of pink gloop. Darrel felt in the way and slipped out too, while Oralie was taking her medicine. He didn't want to say goodbye or good luck.

His step quickened as he reached Room 17. The scanner gave him instant admission and as soon as he entered the small office Annis was out of her seat and coming towards him, arms outspread.

'Dee! I heard you were here, but I've been so busy. How are you? Have they operated on you yet?'

'Yes. I think it's okay for you to call me by my real name here, by the way. I'm Darrel.'

They spent a hectic five minutes catching up on news. It seemed that Annis, like Zee, commuted regularly between New London and Malaku. She had news of Franca, Jay and the others. 'I shall tell them all about you when I go back,' she promised.

The implication was that Darrel would not be returning too. Not that he wanted to, but how could he still be of service to them, stuck on Malaku? He asked her, and her eyes grew suddenly sad. 'You have already been of great use to us. But you are too high-profile at the Plaza to continue there. The only way would be to undergo extensive neoplasty.'

Darrel was shocked. The idea of totally changing his appearance through plastic surgery, as Annis had done, was daunting. Much as he admired the bravery and dedication of the others he felt he could not go that far. Not now he had Oralie.

She seemed to read his thoughts. 'Doc said you had a

lady friend. Did you meet her in Geosan?'

'Yes. She's having surgery today.'

'I know, I'm helping Zee. Which reminds me, I have to finish this work so I'm ready when she calls. Please excuse me, Darrel. We shall meet again soon, in more relaxed circumstances.'

She gave him one of her rare gorgeous smiles that put glowing lamps into her dark, lustrous eyes.

The next few days were difficult ones. Darrel was thrown into a depression once the euphoria of regaining the full power of his senses had faded. Doc told him it was normal, and he was given drugs to put him on an even keel, but he hated the emotional limbo they put him in. Life seemed grey and dull for the first time since leaving New London, and there was the added suspense of not knowing whether Oralie would be all right.

As far as Zee was concerned everything had gone well, but they would not know the outcome until she was healed, and her clitoris was stimulated for the first time. 'I expect you would like to be there then, wouldn't you?' Zee said, smiling.

Darrel was shocked. 'But of course! I mean, won't it be me who . . . ?'

He had nurtured dreams of making love to his woman and making her come for the first time. Those dreams had sustained him through the dark nights following his own operation. Now, looking at the bland, knowing expression on the lesbian surgeon's face, he knew it was not to be. A dull anger hit him in the pit of the stomach.

Seeing his upset, she spoke gently to him. 'I'm sorry, Darrel, but we can't risk having the delicate tissues damaged by rough handling. I know you would try to be careful, but it takes another woman to understand exactly how it feels.'

'You mean *you* . . .'

She nodded, her pale blue eyes impassive as if it was just part of the job. But Darrel knew she would get off on it, the bitch!

No, that was ungrateful. He wouldn't begrudge the surgeon her *droit de seigneuse*. She was entitled to know if she'd done a good job. But he was bitterly disappointed, all the same.

Whenever he saw Oralie she looked pale and drawn, but insisted that she was feeling well. He spent long hours at her bedside, reading to her, watching the screen and talking. Zee was afraid of infection, so Darrel had to wear surgical gloves. It was all very clinical and off-putting. When Oralie had to pee it was an ordeal, and she gripped his gloved hand tightly as the urine flowed down the sterile catheter.

Then, one morning, he arrived to find the catheter had been removed. Oralie was exulting after being able to urinate in the usual way.

'It felt fine!' she assured him. 'And Zee says I can be tested tomorrow evening. She will come with Annis, and you may be there too.'

'I'm not sure I want to,' he grumbled, afraid he would feel horribly left out.

'But *I* want you there,' Oralie insisted, softly. So he knew he must be.

The occasion took on the characteristics of a deflowering ritual. It was taking place in the 'Guest Suite' and when Darrel arrived the room was filled with the tall, pale Malaku lilies and pink roses which, Annis announced proudly, had been brought in cryogenic packaging from New London and thawed for the occasion. Oralie wore a pretty old-fashioned white lace gown, her dark hair had been newly washed and her skin was clean and gleaming. If ever a woman looked virginal, Darrel thought, it was her.

'Welcome!' Zee smiled. She was wearing a silk shift that skimmed her small breasts and well-formed buttocks, making it obvious that she was wearing no underwear. Recalling their erotic play, Darrel felt his cock stir even though he knew she felt no real desire for him. Without the status conferred by her surgeon's overalls she looked young and fresh, her short blonde hair and androgynous features giving her the appearance of a beautiful youth.

Annis led Darrel to a chair by the bedside. 'Is this all I can do, sit and watch?' he asked, petulantly.

She smiled sympathetically, her glossy brown hair falling like a curtain between them as she smoothed the bedcover. 'I'm sure Oralie will want you to participate, won't you, dear?'

Oralie came up and put her arms around him, letting him nuzzle in the lace and perfume of her bosom. He felt his erection swell beneath his loose-fitting pants. 'Of course! You may kiss and cuddle me, sweetheart. All you like.'

Darrel sighed, only slightly mollified. What he really wanted was some satisfaction for his throbbing dick. But he mustn't be selfish. This was Oralie's party, and he doubted whether he would get more than a small slice of the cake but he wouldn't begrudge her.

Zee handed her a cocktail, a pale turquoise one that Darrel guessed was a mild sedative and aphrodisiac combined. Then the two women led Oralie ceremoniously towards the large bed and she lay back, sighing in voluptuous anticipation.

'You can help us undress her,' Annis invited.

Darrel untied the bow at her neck and the gown fell open, revealing her rounded breasts. The nipples were still flaccid, rosy whorls on the unblemished pale mounds. He brushed his hand across them and they stirred into life. While Annis pulled the gown down over her flat stomach he pinched her nipples softly, warming to the task. They were soon firming, darkening into tawny pink cones.

'We shall massage her first,' Annis murmured. 'To relax her.'

Zee went over to a shelf where some antique-style bottles were displayed. 'What do you think?' she asked. 'The "Sensual Oriental" or the "Libido Rapido"?'

'Oh the first, definitely. We don't want to rush things on a first date!'

Oralie giggled, and Darrel found himself empathizing with her, forgetting his own growing frustration. He kissed her smooth forehead and stroked back her hair. She smiled up at him, quietly confident.

The two women poured some of the massage oil into the palms of their hands. Darrel wanted to join in, but was reluctant to seem pushy. He watched enviously as the glistening oil was spread all over Oralie's legs and body, giving her skin a high gloss. Then Zee got to work on her small feet while Annis smoothed her thighs and stomach with long, languid movements. 'You can do her breasts now, if you like,' she offered, at long last.

Darrel found her already well-oiled and his palms began stroking the warm slopes of her breasts lovingly. He used a light touch and was amazed at how sensual the feedback was. Both his palms and fingertips were revelling in the silky texture of Oralie's flesh, feeling the firmness of her muscle tone beneath the skin and the tingling of her nerves as she responded to his gentle caresses.

He watched Zee work her way up Oralie's languidly spread thighs while Annis let her fingers describe lower and lower circles on her stomach. Soon the women's hands would meet in that erogenous zone in the middle. Darrel swallowed his feelings of envy, concentrating instead on the shapely firmness of her breasts. She opened her eyes and gazed up at him, the liquid black pupils widening as her arousal increased.

Yet even while Darrel stroked and squeezed her straining breasts, drawing the nipples up between his fingers to elongated peaks, his gaze was absorbed by what was going on below. Zee had let her shift ride up as she worked so that the peachy mounds of her derrière were visible. Annis removed one hand from Oralie's pubic mound and stroked her lover's buttocks with easy familiarity while they continued to pleasure their patient.

Now Zee was lifting up Oralie's compliant thighs, letting them fall open to reveal her sex.

'Beautiful!' Zee breathed, echoed by Annis. 'Your pussy looks really lovely, Oralie. Come and see, Darrel!'

He needed no further invitation. Moving down the bed he stared between the girl's thighs where her labia had unfolded like the petals of a flower. Above the dark entrance to her vagina was the tight bud of her clitoris. While he watched, Zee put more oil on her finger and gently stroked the little button until it stood out proud. There was scarcely any evidence of the surgical operation that had been performed on the organ. Only a small red mark in the pink flesh testified to where the cruel implant had been inserted.

Oralie moaned gently, not in pain but with growing pleasure. Zee smiled, her touch becoming a shade firmer, more rapid. Darrel couldn't bear to just stand there and watch. He returned to caress Oralie's breasts, leaning over her flushed face to plant kisses on her increasingly warm cheeks and forehead. He could see the two women embracing now, rapt in their joint concentration on the swelling, moistening tissues as they responded to Zee's careful fingering. Then he saw Annis slipping her hand beneath Zee's bottom to stroke her secret places while she continued to stimulate Oralie's.

Darrel's cock was rock solid now, needing relief, but the sight of the three women locked in mutual arousal was riveting. Annis turned for a moment and saw his wistful expression. She held out her free hand and drew him close. 'When she comes you could slip one finger inside,' she told him. 'But be careful!'

He grinned, glad to have the chance of some participation. Oralie must be very close to her first orgasm, he thought, seeing her reddened tumid clitoris and the copious flow that streamed from her open cunt. The thought of dabbling in there almost gave him a climax.

Suddenly Oralie's moans reached a crescendo and small, fluttering movements of her abdomen could be seen while her thighs trembled. 'Now!' Annis whispered, stepping back a little to give him access to the wide-open vulva.

Darrel slipped his finger under Zee's and found the slippery wet entrance. He thrust in as far as he could and felt the velvety walls envelop his stiff digit, squeezing hard in rhythmic contractions. She was coming! He bent his head and kissed her naked stomach, sharing her rapture. Her cunt was filled with warm liquid, streaming out over his finger, and he felt his penis leak in sympathy but the longed-for climax evaded him. Zee took her hand away and turned her attention to Annis. The pair of them, turned on by witnessing Oralie's first orgasm, couldn't wait to get at each other and be equally satisfied.

Tempting as it was to watch the lesbian pair at their passionate play, Darrel's thoughts were all for Oralie. He lay down beside her and took her into his arms, kissing her face and stroking her perspiring breasts. 'Was it good, sweetheart?' he murmured.

She opened her bliss-laden eyes and giggled at him, incapable of speech. He laughed and hugged her, glad that everything had gone smoothly, the way Zee and Annis had promised it would. Now that Oralie knew what she was capable of experiencing it could only get better and better for them both.

'Soon we'll be able to make love properly, just the pair of us,' he assured her. 'And when that happens it's going to be even more wonderful for you.'

Oralie was wide awake now, a concerned look on her face. 'It must have been hard for you,' she said, putting her hand down to feel his erection through his trousers. 'See? You're still worked up. Here, let me help you.'

To his delight, she opened up his clothes and took out

his rampant penis. Her expert fingers began to slide up and down his shaft, smearing his own juices over the glans with her thumb. He knew it wouldn't be long before he came, and as soon as she increased the friction he felt the familiar prickling in his balls and the rapid build-up of tension. He had masturbated a couple of times since his operation, but to be the subject of Oralie's tender ministrations was incomparably preferable. His satisfaction was emotional, not just physical, and when the first spasmodic voiding of his scrotum began it was accompanied by the most delicious sensations, subtle feelings of warmth and security that he'd never experienced before.

Soon afterwards, hearing the two lesbians gasp and moan their way through a mutual climax, Darrel felt the last vestiges of his envy and frustration drain away.

Chapter Sixteen

The prospect of staying in Wal's beach villa with Oralie sustained Darrel through the two further nights that they were obliged to remain in the clinic. Doc wanted to make sure they were both fighting fit before discharging them. Oralie was under strict orders to rest, and Darrel found he had a lot of time on his hands. When he met Annis in the grounds they spent an hour sitting together near a fountain, chatting.

He had so many questions that still needed answering. 'How do you manage to get from here back to New London so easily?' he began.

'We use a pirate ship.'

'A what?'

'It's a shuttle run by drug smugglers. They ship cocktails out to the undeveloped world and refugees as well. The craft was hijacked two years ago and the controllers know about it but they can't stop it.'

'Why not?'

'Because the smugglers are too clever for them. They fly at higher altitudes than the normal shuttle and only ever land at night. It's risky, but the pilots know what they're doing. They were all trained to fly fighters. And they never land in the same place twice. That's why they call the ship *Lightning*.'

'So how do you contact them?'

'I don't. They contact me. Through a special high-frequency radio that no one else can pick up. They tell me where to go to catch the shuttle, and arrange transport to get me there, along with whoever else wants to fly.'

'It sounds very professional.'

'It is. But we all have one thing in common: our contempt for the controllers, and our determination that one day their corrupt regime will be overthrown.'

Darrel admired, almost envied, her dedication. If Oralie hadn't come into his life he knew he would have been tempted to join them permanently, whatever the dangers. His thoughts turned to the woman who had first introduced him to the group.

'Franca said she'd see me here on Malaku. Do you know when she's coming?'

Annis shook her head. 'Difficult to say. Franca has a tricky assignment on right now. Besides, she's involved with Jay. But I think they plan to spend some time here together while the heat's on in New London.'

'I met a man called Sven . . .'

Annis laughed. 'Ah yes! We all know Sven!'

'He seemed to know a genie called Jabez, someone I worked with in the Plaza. Is he one of us too?'

'Sort of. He's one of our agents in the alleys – we call them alley cats. He leads a double life, of course, and is always in danger.'

Darrel recalled the man's quiet manner and dark, secretive eyes. It hadn't really surprised him to know that he, too, was mixed up in all this. But it made him feel useless once again. Now that his circuitry had been decoded and the wiring removed from his skull, was he really of no more interest to them? The thought of idling away the rest of his days on Malaku, even with a woman as alluring as Oralie, did not appeal.

'What are you thinking?' Annis demanded.

'Oh, just wondering about the future.'

'Wonder all you like, but don't worry. There will be a place for you here – or somewhere else.' She took his hand and squeezed it. 'Enjoy your time with Oralie. None of us knows how much longer we have. Let the future unfold as it will, in its own good time.'

It seemed sound advice, and Darrel felt superficially comforted, but he couldn't still the restless ache in his soul. The idea of settling down to anything resembling a normal life seemed impossible. He had no idea how he was going to survive on this strange island where everyone seemed to live by their wits.

Wal turned up on the morning that Darrel and Oralie were given a clean bill of health, admitting that he'd been sent for by the Doc. 'He reckoned the pair of you needed a convalescent home, and he knew I'm always ready to oblige.'

The man gave a wry grin, and Darrel began to suspect he was running some kind of scam but he couldn't imagine what. They got into the rickety vehicle and followed the route by which, apprehensive and disorientated, they had arrived at the clinic. It felt very long ago now. This time Darrel felt a whole lot better, conversing brightly with the islander.

'Don't know how I'm going to earn my living round here,' he admitted. 'Any ideas?'

'Well, there's bar work. Then there's working in a bar. And there could be a bit of work behind a bar someplace,'

Wal grinned. 'Seriously, though, I could do with an extra hand on my ranch. And if Oralie can cook, she'll be welcome too. But first you got to get your health and strength back.' He swerved down the almost invisible track that Darrel remembered led to the beach. When they drew up outside the villa the pair of them clambered out eagerly.

Wal called, 'Don't you two go overdoing it, now. You're here to rest, remember?' He winked before adding, 'I'll drop by in a couple of days. Ciao!'

This time, when the noise of his engine died away, Darrel relished the peace and quiet, proof of their solitude. Oralie looked up at him with dark, questing eyes. On impulse he picked her up and carried her bodily into the dwelling, loving the way her slight body nestled into his. He set her down carefully and drew down the blinds, making the place into a dark, warm haven, then went to open his small case.

'Malaku champagne!' he said, producing the bottle that the Doc had given them to celebrate the restoration of their bodies. 'It should be served chilled, but what the hell!'

He let the sweet, fizzy stuff run free, pouring it straight from the bottle into Oralie's wide, giggling mouth. Then he kissed her, tasting her own distinctive flavour beneath that of the alcohol. He took a long swig from the bottle, burping as it went down, then handed her the rest. She began sipping in genteel fashion but he tipped up the bottom of the bottle and it ran down her chin and soaked her chest.

'Oh dear, now look what I've done!' he grinned. 'That top will just have to come off!'

The champagne had soaked right through to her breasts, making her nipples taste sweet. Darrel's tongue spent a long time making sure that every vestige of the sticky drink was removed from them, and by the time he'd finished Oralie's nipples were stiff with longing. She followed him into the bedroom, her small breasts bouncing enthusiastically as she flopped onto the bed, and gave herself up to his wholehearted embrace.

Darrel tore the clothes off her, then off himself, needing the exquisite contact of their bare flesh. Once he had her in his arms, however, caution slowed him down. It wouldn't do to hurt her in any way. Their lovemaking became measured and tender, long, luscious kisses gave way slowly to more passionate advances until he tentatively approached her tender parts with his mouth.

'May I?' he asked, looking up past her dark bush and round, excited breasts to her distant face. She smiled down at him, looking like a woman in love, and nodded. Her fingers caressed his shaven head. She'd already told him she liked the feel of his new-grown hair, that it made her think of a furry animal.

Gently he parted the soft folds of her pussy where her clitoris was already red and demanding. He touched it with the tip of his tongue and she shivered. Looking up again to see what had caused the reaction, whether pleasure or pain, he saw her smiling at him and tasted the little bud again.

'Oh, yes!' she murmured. 'Now you may do it for me as much as you like!'

He took it by easy stages, always ready to back down if she showed the least sign of discomfort, but she seemed to enjoy everything he did. While he licked at her clitoris his fingers probed both her quim and her anus, feeling her open up to him back and front. The more obviously she revelled in his actions – hands moving to stroke her own breasts; breath coming in brief, ecstatic gasps – the more Darrel was encouraged. At last he had his fingers right inside her tight little cunt and he was flicking his tongue rapidly over her love-bud, willing her to come for him. She did so at last, to spectacular effect, and the minute her thrashing arms and restless thighs had subsided into languor Darrel raised himself between her thighs and slowly introduced his penis into her melting cunt.

He was careful not to be too rough with her but it was hard to control his lustful appetite as his cock sank into the slick embrace of her pussy. For a while he rested there, content just to be in that warm, cushioning environment with his lips mouthing her nipple. But soon the urgency of his desire was overwhelming and he began to shaft her more vigorously. To his delight, the minute he increased the friction she began making her little pleasure-noises and soon she was moving with him, their hips and pelvises gliding in sweet synchronicity.

Oralie placed one foot on his shoulder and hoisted herself up into a sitting position. 'Oh, it feels wonderful like this!' she exclaimed. Realizing that she had many new sensations to discover with her newly sensitized clitoris, Darrel knew they could look forward to a great deal of sexual experimentation in future. The very thought of it brought on a climax. With shuddering force the seed shot out of him and he groaned his way through the accompanying throes, feeling the hot fire invade his whole body.

At the same time he was dimly aware of the orgasmic contractions that Oralie's pussy was making as she joined him in ecstasy. They clung to each other and, for a few seconds, Darrel felt his whole body meld with hers into one pulsating organism until the sensations faded and they were left hot and breathless and spent. He slipped out of her and took her clammy, limp body into his arms. After exchanging kisses they both collapsed into quietness, with only the continual slow lapping of the ocean outside to break the silence.

There followed a time of almost primordial bliss, although Darrel realized that it was only his newly-awakened senses that made it seem so. Like carefree children they played on the beach and in the water, although their 'play' very often took on an adult dimension as they succumbed to their erotic impulses over and over again. Neither of them had expected to feel such happiness, but beneath the feeling of freedom and hedonism Darrel was aware of an undercurrent of anxiety. Now that they'd discovered this new universe of sensual indulgence they were both scared that, for some reason or other, they could not remain in it, that the illusion could not last.

Oralie said as much as they sat breakfasting on fruit at dawn next day, facing the endless ocean. 'What will happen to us, Darrel? We cannot stay here forever, like this.'

'Why not?' he teased her. 'Are you bored already?' But she'd voiced his own thoughts.

Oralie frowned. 'I mean, we cannot stay here much longer. Shall we go to Wal's ranch? Is that where we shall live now?'

'I don't know. It may be a good idea for a while, until we can find our feet. But I can't see it becoming our permanent way of life, can you?'

She shrugged, lying back against the sand so that her pert breasts were pointing upwards. Darrel resisted the urge to tweak her nipples, realizing that she needed to talk. Her frown deepened as she said, 'I don't want to go back to sleeping with men for money. But there is nothing else I am trained for. I feel so ignorant, Darrel.'

'Me too, if that's any consolation. But we can learn, Oralie. We're not stupid.'

'When I was a little girl, I wanted to be a dancer,' she said, wistfully.

'Then dance for me now.'

'Oh, no!'

Darrel sat up, putting on a mock-stern tone. 'Yes, I insist! Dance for me, woman, as if your life depended on it!'

Slowly Oralie rose to her feet, giving him an arch smile. Her slim, naked figure looked very attractive against the background of yellow sand, swaying palms and blue ocean. Already, Darrel noted, the sun was lending a golden duskiness to her skin. She struck an attitude, standing on tiptoe and raising her arms above her head so that her breasts were uplifted. Although her dance had begun as a kind of parody, there was a grace and beauty to her figure that promised well.

Darrel sat with his back against a young palm tree, a spectator about to enjoy a show. He watched her pirouette on the brilliant sand, her lithe body constantly twisting and turning through a hundred different positions, showing off her slim but voluptuous figure. She ran to the water's edge and became a nymph, splashing in and out of the water. Then she turned into a siren, luring him on.

When she tired of simply posing she played the fool, pulling faces at him, pelting him with handfuls of the small shells that littered the beach. 'Come and join me!' she begged. 'Let's go for a swim!'

The prospect became irresistible. Darrel got to his feet, already anticipating the delights of plunging into warm, limpid water, but he suddenly heard a loud humming noise overhead. Shading his eyes from the glare of the sun he stared up into the azure sky and made out the shape of some airborne vessel. Oralie saw it too. They stood in fascination as the silver craft crossed the sky directly above them.

Then, to their amazement, something came hurtling out of it. A small silver pod had ejected itself from the mother ship and was racing towards the island, but whether by accident or design was difficult to tell. It reminded Darrel of newsreels he had seen of twentieth-century war, when bombs were dropped from airplanes to devastate whole cities. The memory chilled him to the bone. Transfixed, Darrel was only aware that he was holding his breath when he tried to speak. 'Dear God, what is it?'

Oralie came to his side, clinging to his arm. Instinctively she shared his fear, asking tremulously, 'Is that the shuttle?'

Neither of them had any answers. The mother ship was disappearing over the horizon and there was now no sign of the silver pod. Darrel wondered if it could have been some kind of illusion, brought on by the midday sun.

But then he heard a faint beeping coming from the villa. He recognised the noise at once: it was the emergency signal emitting from the computer. Back at the Plezure Plaza, Darrel had heard it used a few times for fire drill.

'We must go look at the screen!' he said, tersely.

With long strides he returned to the villa, Oralie running anxiously along in his wake. He put his arm around her as he stared at the ominous message that filled the flashing screen: 'Emergency, emergency! Press any key.'

When he did so a longer message scrolled up. It informed them that a 'Control and Search' operation was in progress and they should remain where they were, indoors, until the officers reached them and delivered a 'clearance pass'.

'What does this mean?' Oralie asked, obviously scared. 'Is it to do with what we just saw, that thing falling out of the sky?'

'Probably.' Darrel's tone was grim. He was thinking fast. Although the authorities evidently wanted them to believe they would be safe in their own houses, he realized that was only true for so-called law-abiding islanders. For him and Oralie the very reverse was true. A shudder passed through him as he realized that they stood no chance whatsoever of being cleared. It was far more likely that the pair of them were on the officers' wanted list.

'We have to get out of here!' he said, starting to gather up as many of their personal possessions as he could fit into his small bag. 'I think it's people like us they're looking for.'

'But where on earth can we go?'

'I've no idea, but we obviously mustn't stay here. We'd be sitting targets.'

Oralie looked petrified. He tried to smile at her, but it came out as a grimace. 'Come on, Oralie. Help me. Go into the bedroom and see if there's anything important lying around. We mustn't leave any clues to our presence.'

The worst thing was having no idea at all how much time they had. Malaku was not very large. Wherever that pod had landed it wouldn't take its occupants long to reach any point on the island. If Darrel and Oralie were to find an effective hiding place they must do so as quickly as possible.

Darrel found the drabbest clothes he could and pulled them on, handing Oralie a sludge-green tunic to wear. Then he grabbed her hand and pulled her out onto the veranda where he paused to take stock. The beach looked just as calm as before, gentle waves lapping on the shore. He wondered in which direction to head. The obvious thing was to go away from where they had seen the pod landing, over on the western horizon. He turned right and they made for the cover of the palms. Maybe they could hide out in that thick undergrowth for a while, keeping watch on the beach. Once the search party had found the villa empty they would surely move on to the next target. It should then be safe to return to the house and lie low.

There was a thick tangle of bushes within a few yards of the shoreline and Darrel headed straight for it. He picked some fronds of vegetation and handed them to Oralie. 'Here, cover yourself with this as best you can, to camouflage yourself. Then get in among the bushes.'

'You too?'

Her scared face looked up at him from the mass of green. 'In a minute. I'm just going to see if there's any sign of life out there.'

'Be careful! Please be careful!'

He kissed her distraught face briefly, then pushed her into the tangle of leaves, branches and creepers. Satisfied that if she stayed there, crouched down, she was almost invisible, he began to crawl on hands and knees to where the bright sand could be seen framed by a couple of palm trunks.

Reaching the margin of the undergrowth he paused and looked up, out to what he thought would be a deserted beach. But to his horror there was a figure standing there, just a few yards away. He had already been spotted and was now being regarded with a wry amusement that nevertheless chilled his soul.

It was a woman, dressed in a close-fitting grey uniform with her grey-brown hair tied back severely. She was broad-shouldered and big-bosomed, and there was nothing remotely attractive about her appearance. Her face was coarse-featured and her steely eyes narrowed as Darrel scrambled to his feet. When she barked an order to the man who could now be seen running across the sands her voice broke the tense silence like a crack of thunder. 'Get him!'

Darrel scrambled to his feet, turned tail, then ran along the beach in desperation. His one aim was to divert his pursuers as far away as possible from where Oralie was hiding. From some niche in his memory he recalled a bird called a 'lapwing' that would feign a broken wing in order to lure predators away from its nest. Unfortunately, that bird was now extinct.

The young man pursuing him was fit and strong. He caught up with Darrel in seconds and pulled him to the ground, overpowering him. His arms were pulled behind his back and manacles were put on his wrists, then he was pulled roughly to his feet and marched back along the beach to where the woman was standing, a grim smile on her face.

'You run because you have something to hide,' she stated, baldly. 'But we will find out everything about you. Come, Varg. Bring him back to the villa. We'll soon see if we have caught a prize fish or only a minnow!'

The sun beat down heavily on the exposed nape of his neck as Darrel staggered along, given frequent shoves by the animal called Varg. But all he could think of was Oralie, lurking in her green foxhole. Could she see what was happening? Would she have the good sense to lie low? Probably this obscene parody of a woman believed him to be alone, so Oralie would be safe as long as she kept in hiding.

Darrel stumbled up the villa steps. Varg threw him onto the floor as soon as they were inside and delivered a hefty kick to his thigh. Darrel moaned with pain and shock, but the woman said, 'That's enough for now, Varg. You'll have plenty of time for that later. First we must find out who this swine is.'

She opened the small bag on her belt and took out a portable iriscope. Darrel blinked as Varg pulled back his head and the woman shone the thing into his eye. He cursed himself for not disguising his eyes with the contact lenses when the alarm had sounded. Well, it served him right for being complacent.

With a few long strides the woman reached the screen

and swiped the scope over it. At once Darrel's bio appeared, in full detail. He saw references to Fernlea, the Plezure Plaza, Franca, Zee. His image was stamped with the word 'Insurgent' in red.

The woman looked back at him with a nasty smile, then said to Varg, 'Well, well, it seems we have captured a big fish after all. This will earn us both credit, my boy. But I think we can do better than this, don't you? If we can get the swine to give us some information, the controllers will be even more pleased with us, don't you think?'

'Yes, Mam.'

'We won't call reinforcements straight away. We'll give ourselves time to work on him before we hand him over. Watch, listen and learn, Varg. Now, how do we begin?'

'Physical assessment, Mam?'

'Good.' She was reading the screen all the while she was speaking. Taking in Darrel's details with a practised eye. 'You've not forgotten all they taught you, then. What is your assessment?'

'Health and strength medium, agility medium to good. Weight average for height.'

'Good. Susceptibility to pain?'

'Difficult to assess, Mam.'

'What if I told you the man is a deconditioned genie. What then?'

A slow smile spread over Varg's ugly face. Darrel wanted to hurt him, badly. 'Increased susceptibility, Mam. High sensitivity. Low threshold. Vulnerable to emotional and psychological pressure.'

'Exactly. Our work should be easy. But never be fooled by a man's bio, Varg. The information is only as good as the agent who obtained it. Perhaps we should start to make our own practical assessment.'

'Yes, Mam!'

Varg's piggy eyes gleamed in the dim interior of the villa, making Darrel's guts churn with fear. He was helpless in the hands of these psychopaths. They could do what they liked with him and no one would know, or care.

'Strip him!' the woman said. 'Let's see what manner of man we're dealing with first of all.'

Darrel tensed as the clothes were ripped off him with Varg's knife. The skin of his chest was nicked and began to bleed a little, eliciting a sneering laugh from the bastard. Darrel had a horrible feeling that the man was like a shark: once he smelt blood he would lust for it. The sick feeling in his stomach intensified and he started to tremble.

'He's showing symptoms of fear already,' the woman said in a matter-of-fact tone. 'See how pale he's gone. Let's have a look at his cock.'

To Darrel's horror she knelt down and pulled at his shrunken penis. Her coarse face leered up at him. 'Not much use to anyone like this, are you?' she mocked. 'But I'll bet they paid good money for you back at the Plaza, didn't they? All those disgusting old women with their reconditioned bodies and fat credit. What made you give it all up, eh? Did they send some beautiful girl to seduce you to their cause, was that how they got you?'

Darrel said nothing, but then she gave his penis a vicious twist with one hand and screwed his balls round with the other. He gave a scream of pain. 'Answer me!' she barked. 'My questions are not rhetorical, they require answers! How did those scum get you to join their cause?'

'They . . . they didn't. I . . . found out. I wanted to . . . it was all me . . .'

She nodded at Varg who came over and kicked Darrel abruptly in the ribs, making the air spew out of him in one choking gasp. 'Tell the truth,' the woman said, her voice soft, almost cajoling. 'It will be far better for you to get this over with quickly.'

Through the welter of pain that was flooding his mind Darrel recollected. 'A woman came . . . took me to a place . . .'

'Not good enough, dog! What woman? What place? Varg, apply a little persuasion. Do something that will jog his lazy memory.'

The beast grinned and put his boot on Darrel's back, flattening him abruptly to the ground and making his chin hit the floor with a sickening crunch. The impact made him bite his tongue and his mouth filled with blood.

'That's enough!' the woman snapped. 'We want the bastard to be able to speak, don't we? Wipe his mouth with something. I want to hear him clearly.'

Varg pulled at a cloth covering a small round table. It came away in his hand and the fragile bowl and cup that were standing on it flew to the ground, shattering. He pulled Darrel into a kneeling position and stuffed the wad of cloth between his lips, staunching the flow. When he took it away the woman continued, still in the quiet, reasonable tone that curdled the blood even more effectively than her staccato barks.

'Right. Now, the name of this woman. She will certainly be known to us already, so you will not be giving her any more trouble than she's already in. Her name?'

Desperately, Darrel prevaricated. 'It wasn't her real name. None of them use their own names.'

'No matter. The name you knew her by will do.'

'Fee.' He said. It was what Franca might well have been known by, following the pattern of Dee and Zee.

He'd hoped that would satisfy the bitch, but she waved at the screen saying, 'Check it out, Varg.'

After some time he turned back with a horrible leer. 'No such name recorded, Mam.'

She looked down on Darrel with contempt. 'Well now, that could mean one of three things. Either this really is someone we know nothing about. Or we know about her under a different name. Or this man is lying in a misguided attempt to protect himself and others. How do we find out which is the truth?'

'Apply more pressure, Mam?'

'Precisely. This time it's my prerogative.'

Darrel scarcely saw her take the coiled whip from her belt and only realized that she meant to strike him with it when he saw it snake through the air in front of him, followed by a resounding crack. She then dealt him a stinging blow on the genitals. Only one, but the searing pain lasted a long, long time so that the interrogation that followed was conducted through a bleary haze of excruciating agony. The questions followed in rapid succession, giving Darrel hardly any time to think of a lie. If he hesitated for more than a second the whip snaked towards him again and he quickly continued.

'Her real name?'

'F–Franca.'

'Domicile?'

'S–somewhere on Parkside.'

311

'Safe house?'

'What? Oh . . . oh, please don't! I think . . . near a . . . Mobility Junction, that's it! Halfway between Tabor Sound and Parkway I think it was . . .'

'Never mind. More names. Give me more names.'

'I don't know. I didn't know.'

'NAMES!'

'Well, there was . . . Jay, yes. And . . . a woman beginning with A. I can't remember. And Zee. Yes, A to Zee, that's right.'

'We know about those two. Varg, check out Jay. More names!'

Darrel hesitated. The whip lashed out again, this time landing on his buttocks. 'I don't recall. Please, honestly, I don't remember!'

Humiliating tears stung his eyes. He was so terrified that he really couldn't remember. His mind was numb with fear, and his body a trembling mass of apprehension. The woman nodded at Varg. 'See, he wants to oblige us, but he can't. Very well, we shall try a different tack. Tell us what happened after you left New London. Did you come straight to Malaku, or did you stop somewhere en route?'

Her tone was light, almost conversational now, but Darrel wasn't fooled. He knew that if he wasn't very careful he would betray Oralie, just as he'd betrayed the others. A desperate shame seized him, overshadowing even his fear of what they might do to him. At all costs he must avoid mentioning Oralie. 'I came straight here,' he lied.

There was an ominous pause. The woman's voice was chilling as she said, 'How strange. Then you must have a double. Because someone exactly fitting your description was seen entering the Orchid Palace in Geosan just a couple of weeks ago.'

Had it really been that recent? Darrel paused in his agony of suspense to consider that, during that time, he had begun in limbo, had been to heaven and was now in hell.

'I didn't . . .'

The whip caught him on the side of the cheek, making him scream out. No sooner had she delivered the punishment than she handed the lash to Varg. 'Administer another stroke each time I give you the nod,' she told her henchman. 'I leave it to you which part of his anatomy to target.'

She put her booted foot under his chin and lifted his face up so that he could not avoid meeting her eyes. They were cold and grey as a winter's sky in New London. 'Now, answer me again. Why did you go to Geosan?'

'I was told to go there. I met someone called Choi. It was some kind of experiment they wanted to do on me.'

'What kind?'

'I don't know.'

He sensed that she had nodded to Varg. The interrogation was proceeding to a set pattern and Darrel was picking up the cues. He tensed, awaiting the blow, and felt the whip crack down on his defenceless head which was still tender from the recent surgery.

When he opened his streaming eyes, the woman was smiling at him. 'How very appropriate. I think Varg has answered for you, hasn't he? They wanted to know what was inside your skull, didn't they?'

He opened his mouth, but no words came out. She knelt close to him and pushed up his chin, forcing him to look into her hateful eyes again. 'DIDN'T THEY?'

He nodded, speechless. She pushed him roughly to the floor so that his nose hit it first and began to bleed.

'Varg, the cloth!' she said, in a tone of disgust. She went over to the screen and began scrolling through the bio, concentrating intently on the text.

While her back was turned Varg pushed the handle of the whip between Darrel's buttocks so that it penetrated his arse. At the same time he whispered in his ear, 'Bet you like that, don't you, genie? You fuckin' genies are all the same. Pussy-suckers for credit, but cock-fuckers for fun. How many cocks have come in your crack, pussy-sucker? Fancy mine, do you?'

He gave him a last, vicious poke then pulled out the whip and went to stand at the woman's side. 'Found anything interesting, Mam?' he asked, politely.

Darrel wanted to kill that arrogant little swine even more than her. He looked around the room, desperate for some means of making his escape or doing the pair of them in, preferably both. But with his hands tied, his eyes blurred with tears and his mouth still streaming blood he felt utterly helpless.

The woman turned back to him, her expression contemptuous, and Darrel's stomach churned again. 'I don't think you've been telling us the complete truth,' she said, walking slowly towards him. 'I have a feeling – call it my woman's intuition if you will – that you have been telling us a few lies along the way. Now that's a very foolish thing to do, isn't it Varg?'

'Oh yes,' he grinned happily. '*Very* foolish!'

Darrel was stunned. He honestly didn't know what they were talking about. Frantically he scanned his memory of the last few terrible minutes. 'W–what . . . do you mean?'

'According to your bio, you never went to Geosan. The sighting there has since been recorded as unreliable. According to your bio there is no trace of your movements between New London and Malaku so it is presumed that you were hiding out somewhere until you could find transport. How did you get here? That's what we want your puny little mind to focus on now, don't we, Varg? How in hell did you get from New London to Malaku if you didn't come via Geosan?'

'But I did go to Geosan!'

The whip sneaked out to his cock again, stinging his glans and curling round his balls with equal ferocity before retreating to Varg's side again. Darrel's moans reached a screaming peak as the excruciating after-effects rocketed through him, turning every nerve in his body into a searing hot wire.

'You wanted the truth!' he cried, desperately. 'And I'm telling you the truth! What more do you want?'

'You never went to Geosan!' she repeated, with slow deliberation. 'So how did you get here?'

Will this nightmare never end? Darrel thought. He was damned if he lied, and damned if he didn't. What the hell could he do or say to placate these fiends? He began to spill out a garbled account of what Annis had told him. 'They sent me a message, told me when the ship was ready to go. Told me where to go. I don't remember exactly where, it was dark. Night time. They only fly at night . . .'

315

'They? Who are they? Names, Darrel, we want names!'
'I don't know. There were no names. No . . . aargh!'

The whip inflamed his back and buttocks with searing force. The taste of blood from his mouth and nose was sickening him and he felt the urge to vomit. Was he to die here, in a pool of blood and vomit? Suddenly a wave of self-pity engulfed him, surprising him with its intensity. 'Please!' he pleaded. 'I don't know how to help you any more. I've told you everything I know.'

In his abject state he clung to the legs of the ugly woman who was towering above him. He felt utterly degraded, utterly alone. Looking up, he saw her smiling down at him almost kindly, almost pityingly. Except that there was a cruel look of irony in her eyes that made his heart sink to his feet.

'One day, we shall perfect the art of discovering what people know. We shall plug directly into their brain and suck the information out of it. But until that wonderful day we have to use more crude methods. Especially here, on this godforsaken island. Now, will you answer me correctly, or do I have to give Varg here permission to break your fingers, one by one?'

Darrel gave a shuddering moan and prostrated himself before her, squealing out, 'No, no! I will answer you!' He no longer had any sense of his own identity, his own history. The interrogation was proceeding along lines of its own that seemed to have very little to do with him, or with any memories he might have, let alone with the truth, whatever that was.

She squatted down beside him. 'Now then, I want you to describe, in as much detail as you can, this craft that you came here in.'

'It was night . . . very dark. I remember . . . a ramp we walked down to get to it.'

'A ramp, good. What next?'

'It was an old airship, yes, that's right. Quite an antique vessel, not like a shuttle. And it made a terrible racket.'

'Yes, we know all about their contraptions,' she said, impatiently. 'Who was on board? Describe them. Did you know any of their names?'

'No, not names. But there were a couple of women and the rest were men.'

She took his sore nose between her finger and thumb and tweaked it, pushing his head from side to side. 'Details, idiot! We must have details. Describe them.'

Darrel began to make up descriptions, to say anything, anything he thought would appease his torturers. One woman was fat, one thin. One dark, one fair. He could see his interrogator growing more impatient and embroidered his descriptions with a wart here, a scar there. One man had a limp, another an accent. He fed her anything he thought might stay her wrath and keep the whip by Varg's side.

But she wasn't fooled. After she'd let him ramble on for a couple of minutes, she turned her back on him abruptly saying to her minion, 'He's lying, making it all up. Whip him into shape for me, Varg!'

'NO!' Darrel heard his cry rising to heaven, but there seemed to be no compassionate god to answer him. He felt the stinging bite of the whip on the naked soles of his feet and sobbed out his agony. But just as he was bracing himself for the next strike, and the next, an acrid smell filled his swollen nostrils. He looked up, and saw that his tormentress had noticed it too. She was standing by the screen with a puzzled frown on her face. Smoke began to curl in through the door and windows then, with terrifying suddenness, a great blaze of flame suddenly appeared, sweeping through the open doorway and licking across the wooden floor at terrifying speed.

'Fire!' she exclaimed. 'Quick, Varg, fetch water from the . . .'

To Darrel's amazement a huge figure suddenly appeared amidst the flames. He recognized the mighty Sven and his heart surged with relief. The giant came towards him and, hauling him to his feet, proceeded to bundle him over his shoulder in a fireman's lift. A few strides got them through the door and onto the disintegrating veranda.

The searing heat and choking smoke enveloped them both for a few seconds but then there was just a short dash down the beach to clear air, open skies and freedom. Best of all was the glorious sense of triumph that filled Darrel's tortured soul. Before his evil persecutors had realized what was happening, their captive had disappeared through the wall of flame and been rushed to safety while they were left to the mercy of the holocaust.

Chapter Seventeen

Darrel stood at the water's edge, staring in stupefaction at the blazing villa. As he watched, a couple of screaming, agitated figures appeared in the doorway, surrounded by a halo of flame. They staggered out and moved onto the balcony which promptly collapsed, sending them rolling down the sandy slope until they came to a halt, horribly inert. Even from a distance their bodies looked like chargrilled meat.

But Darrel's attention was soon drawn to the adjoining land where the palms and other vegetation were ablaze, the light breeze fanning the flames into an inferno. He dashed forward with an animal howl. 'No-o-o!' he yelled, half out of his mind. 'Oralie's in there! Oralie!'

'It's no good,' he heard Sven call from behind. 'Come back, you can't go in there. You'll roast to death!'

As the blast of heat hit him from fifty paces away, Darrel knew he was right. The barbecued bodies of his torturers were still smouldering in the sand. Oralie would be in the same state. No one could come out of that conflagration alive. Resisting a suicidal urge to plunge on into that wall of fire and let himself suffer the same fate, Darrel paused to give vent to his torment. His cry rent the air, then he felt Sven's strong, comforting arms envelop him.

'Come on,' the giant said, gruffly. 'Don't stop to think. We got to get out of here. There's a boat waiting for us, along the beach.'

In a daze of pain and misery, Darrel let himself be led along towards the small craft he could see moored to a distant jetty. The tears streamed freely down his bloody cheeks, all thought of his earlier physical torment eclipsed by this, far worse, emotional one. He blamed himself for leaving her there, even though he knew it was futile. If she'd stayed with him she would have been captured by those fiends and tortured too. But then she might, ultimately, have had the chance of escaping with him, too. Round and round went the arguments in his head, accompanied by the most traumatic feelings he'd ever experienced.

At last his weary legs got him to the boat, where he was surprised to see Wal waiting. 'Thank God you're safe!' the man grinned. 'I knew it would be risky, starting that blaze, but I didn't have enough men to storm the place.'

'*You* started the fire?'

Darrel stared at him blankly, but nothing surprised him now. The knowledge that the man had set fire to his own villa in order to save him was touching, all the same. He clambered into the open boat and soon they were halfway out to sea. The two other men sat keeping silent watch while Darrel was sunk in depressed thought. Poignant memories of their last, ecstatic lovemaking, along with Oralie's beautiful dance on the beach, kept returning to haunt him. Neither of them could have known that it would be her last dance, a dance of death.

Wal threw the anchor over the side and the boat

remained in position, bobbing slightly in the waves. 'What are we doing?' Darrel asked.

'Waiting for the hydrosub.'

'The what?'

'You'll see. It won't be long now.'

Neither of the men asked what had happened to him. They must have sensed the depth of his pain, his loss. There would be time later to go into detail, if they insisted, but right now he was grateful for their tact. The silence took over his mind, broken only by the gentle lapping of the waves. It was a noise that could drive you mad, eventually.

At last the distant hum of a craft could be heard and an extraordinary silver cylinder appeared on the horizon. At first Darrel regarded it warily, noting its superficial resemblance to the pod whose arrival had triggered his ultimate nightmare, but as it approached he could see that it was quite different. It seemed to have fins – or were they wings? – and was very streamlined in appearance. The way it skimmed the surface of the water suggested some kind of hyrdofoil. It came to rest a short distance away. Wal started the motor and they began chugging towards it.

The prospect of rescue cheered Darrel a little, despite his depressed state. Leaning over the side of the boat he splashed his face with sea water to get rid of the caked blood and make himself more presentable. The salt made his eyes and nose sting horribly. When they reached the giant craft a porthole slid open and a steel ladder was wound down for them. As Darrel climbed up, a strange but friendly face smiled at him, and welcoming hands came down to pull him aboard.

'You must be Darrel, otherwise known as Dee,' the man said, once he was inside. 'I'm Pino, skipper of this vessel. We'll be picking up Doc and his team along the shore here, then we can make our getaway.' He paused, his blue eyes sympathetic. 'Sorry about your lady friend, by the way. There was nothing anyone could do.'

'I know.' Darrel gulped back his tears and went to join the others in the cabin.

The craft was furnished basically but quite comfortably, and obviously designed to go long distances. Darrel sank into a recliner and drank thirstily from the pitcher of pure water that had come from a Malaku spring. 'Where will we go?' he asked Wal. 'After we've picked up the Doc, I mean?'

'We'll go to another island, one even more remote than Malaku. It's fairly primitive, but easier to hide in. Anyone who doesn't know the territory is bound to get lost. And if the controllers dare to send a search party there the chances are they'll be ambushed within ten minutes of arrival. The natives hate them even more than they do here.'

'What about us?'

Wal laughed. 'Don't worry, just stick with me and you'll be okay! Fortunately, the natives are friendly to the likes of us. Anyone who hates the controllers is a mate of theirs.'

But as they surfed the blue waters, getting closer in to the shore, Darrel felt guilt, remorse and grief assail him again. He felt deeply responsible for Oralie's horrible death. If he'd left her in Geosan she might never have known sexual fulfilment, but at least she would still be alive. And what future was there for him, bereft of her?

She had become his reason for living, and now he was like that open boat they'd left behind them, adrift on an empty ocean with no real purpose or destination.

Through the porthole he could see a small crowd standing on a jetty. He recognised Doc at once and thought he saw Zee too, but he couldn't be sure. He left the comfort of the cabin and went onto the upper deck with the others, to welcome them aboard. The door was sliding open, and through it he could see the waving, smiling throng. Yes, it was Zee. And next to her . . . no, it couldn't be! He blinked, squinting through the bright air. It looked just like her, but that was impossible. His eyes must be playing tricks on him, cruel, wishful-thinking tricks!

Then he heard Wal say, 'There's Oralie. Look, Darrel! She's safe!'

His heart leapt with excited optimism. But his mind was still filled with disbelief. He turned to Pino, anger welling up irrationally. 'But you said she was dead!'

'I never did!'

'You said you were sorry about my lady friend. Didn't you mean her?'

'Not her, Annis. She was your friend too, wasn't she? Annis is dead.'

Horror and a shameful relief gripped him equally as Oralie's features became clear, unmistakable in the bright sunlight. His joy was barely containable yet he must contain it for a few seconds longer. 'Oh God!' he muttered, 'I'm sorry.'

Darrel felt Sven's heavy hand on his shoulder but already his eyes were drinking in the wonderful sight of Oralie's face, and he scarcely heard what the man said.

'Don't grieve for the dead now. There'll be time enough later. Be happy for those who escaped Death's clutches this time around.'

He needed no second bidding. As soon as the ladder was down he thrust out his arms and bent down towards her eager, uplifted face, calling, 'Oralie! Thank God you're safe!'

They let her be first on board. Darrel took her in his arms and held her tight, covering her face with kisses. She looked exhausted, but otherwise fit. He led her into the cabin where they sank into a recliner together. 'What happened to you?' she asked, anxiously. 'When I saw the fire I was so worried! But Doc said I must go with him.' Her face grew distraught. 'We could not stay, it was too dangerous.'

'So Doc rescued you?'

'Yes. He had come to see if we were all right. I managed to stop him on the track and told him you'd been taken into the villa by two bad people. He said . . .' Her voice broke and tears came into her eyes. 'He said if we tried to rescue you we would all be in trouble, so we had to go, to leave you . . .'

'He was quite right.' Darrel reassured her with a hug. 'Look how it's turned out. We're all safe now.'

'All except Annis,' she reminded him, solemnly.

'What happened to her?'

Oralie shuddered. 'It was horrible. We went back to the clinic and found it burning. Most of the staff were hiding in the bushes, but Annis lay on the path. They had slashed her face, her pretty face . . .'

Darrel clenched his fist, a deep anger welling up in him. Someone would have to avenge that poor woman's death. How she had suffered at the hands of the controllers, and yet she still fought bravely against them to the end. His previous shame returned with punishing force. He remembered how abject he'd been under torture, how despicably weak and ready to betray those whom he most admired. No matter that the only two witnesses to his shame were dead. He had survived, and he would carry the disgrace of it with him to his grave.

Feeling as if he didn't deserve to have his Oralie restored to him, Darrel rose and went through to where the others were. He found Zee and held her in a close embrace, silently acknowledging her bereavement. But immediately she went through to speak to Oralie, questioning her kindly about her state of health, and again Darrel felt unworthy to be in the company of these selfless people.

'Darrel, it's good to see you safe and sound,' Doc smiled, clapping him on the shoulder. 'I was afraid you'd perished in the fire, but I knew you would rather I saved Oralie than risked us all dying.'

'You're right, of course. That couple who captured me were fiends, brutes. And there was no way of knowing how many more of them might be out there. But have they raided Malaku before?'

'Once only.' Doc's eyes dimmed. 'I lost my wife that time. But it only made me more determined to carry on my fight against those bastards. That's when I decided to open the clinic. Talking of which, how have you been? Any problems at all? You don't look too good right now, I must say. Did those devils give you a hard time?'

'You could say that,' Darrel grinned, wryly. He didn't want to talk about his ordeal for fear that he might give himself away. 'But your clinic is burnt down, Doc. That must be very hard to bear.'

'Oh, it can be rebuilt. The people are more important than any building. My only regret is that poor Annis had to die, but she was the only casualty. Thank God.'

The hatch was closed, and Pino was telling his crew to decompress the vessel. Then he gave the order to dive. Looking through the nearest porthole, Darrel was amazed to see them go below the surface of the waves and start to descend. 'It's a submarine!' he gasped.

Doc grinned. 'You ain't seen nothin' yet. This is a triphibian vehicle.'

They cruised along through shoals of highly coloured fish, illuminated by the ship's searchlights. Darrel watched the magnificent display with Oralie in the rear cabin, and suddenly he realized that the rest of the people on board had discreetly left them alone. The part of the ship they were in had been designed as a detachable pod, for emergency use only. When he pressed the button to close the door they were in a hermetically sealed compartment with access to everything they could possibly need: latrine, food, water, sleeping accommodation and, of course, each other.

'This is wonderful, another world!' Oralie breathed softly as they reclined on the couch near the porthole, arms around each other. 'Look at that wonderful creature with the big eyes!'

Darrel turned her face towards him and grinned. 'I am looking at her, and she's more wonderful than I ever imagined.'

'Oh, Darrel!' she giggled, and in seconds they were pulling off each others' clothes, eager to forget the trials of the recent past and return to happier times, to renew the love they'd shared so rapturously. They slipped into the shower together, both revelling in the clean freshness of the water that seemed to wash away not just the dirt and bodily excreta but also the stench of their close brush with death.

Darrel kissed her sweet-smelling breasts and took the roused nipples into his mouth. She stroked his shaven head while he mouthed her, giving little cries of approval as her desire for him grew. Her roving hands found his growing erection and nurtured it with gentle strokings. Gradually they emerged from the constricted cubicle onto the greater freedom of the couch, with its luxurious trappings, and their love-play began in earnest.

Darrel was delighted to see that Oralie wanted him as much as he did her, wriggling round until their genitals and mouths were in full, simultaneous contact. He gasped as her expert tongue licked along the ridge below his glans, finding the sensitive frenum. She proceeded to tongue him into a state of tumescent bliss where nothing mattered but the delicious sensations that were filling his consciousness.

Better still, no longer did she flinch when he kissed her pussy. The bold little clitoris presented itself for his attention and he gave as much as it craved, licking and sucking the proud organ until he sensed that a climax was imminent and the temptation to plunge inside the hot, pulsating quim was just too strong. Darrel entered her in one long, swift glide right up to the hilt and she gasped when his glans made contact with the hard nub of her cervix.

'Oh, I love to feel your cock deep inside me!' she

groaned, becoming, in that one blatant admission, the sensual woman she was born to be. Her naive declaration, devoid of any trace of insincerity, filled him with joy and he kissed her fervently, starting to plunge into her over and over with an equally innocent enthusiasm.

Somehow the experience felt like a healing one for Darrel. With every deep thrust into that welcoming pussy he seemed to become more whole, to recover aspects of himself he never knew he had. The love he felt for Oralie was all-consuming, ennobled him. And when he triggered her coming he knew that, this time, they would climax together in a soul-searing crescendo of selfless ecstasy.

They rested awhile, but she was still hungry for him. After much kissing and caressing she presented him with her delectable rump and as Darrel stroked her smooth buttocks he felt his cock hardening once again. Most alluring was her rosy little anus, spread shamelessly open. He licked his finger and began to play around the tightly puckered entrance, feeling it slowly yield. When he introduced a fingertip she gasped her pleasure, and he pushed in further to her forbidden place, enjoying the shiver of pleasure that ran up his spine as he did so.

Kneeling behind her, Darrel nudged between her love-lips with his sturdy organ until he found her other moist orifice. Still gently manipulating her arse with his finger, he pushed his glans through into the welcoming wetness of her quim, delighted when Oralie began to wriggle her bum voluptuously against him. Sensing that she needed greater stimulation he reached round her with his other hand and found her dewy, jutting clitoris. She seemed to melt into sensual heaven as all her most erogenous zones were aroused at once. Her whole vulva became flooded with juices and he knew it wouldn't be long before she gave herself up to a second shattering orgasm.

The thought increased his own lust and he began to drive into her with prick and finger simultaneously, provoking her to buck and twist her lower body in her reckless quest for fulfilment. From time to time his fingers left her throbbing clitoris to pull at her erect nipples, which she evidently loved, and all the while he could feel his own thrusting cock through the thin wall that divided her back and front. It was tremendously exciting, and Darrel knew he couldn't contain himself once the unstoppable acceleration of his libido had begun. He groaned aloud as the hot spunk streamed out of him and feelings of sheer bliss suffused his body.

When the paroxysms began to subside he was aware that Oralie was still coming, her cunt twitching and clutching at his relaxing penis as if reluctant to let it go, and her anus convulsing around his finger. He stroked her breasts, prolonging the sensations, and she moaned louder until she finally collapsed face down with a long sigh and he withdrew from her sated body.

When it was all over he lay with her in his arms, feeling like a child again. It seemed several lifetimes ago, long before he'd been taken to the Plaza, that he had felt like this. Was it when he'd made those adolescent visits to Fernlea? Had Oralie restored to him his lost innocence? He felt so open, vulnerable and clean. It made him question everything: the unreality of his former life, his own identity, his aspirations. In the blinding light of such passion as he now felt all kinds of things seemed trivial, irrelevant. Including, he was relieved to find, the charade that those two bastards had put him through and from which he had been saved in order to go through this new baptism of fire.

'Oralie!' He murmured her name like a prayer.

'Yes, Darrel?'

'What are we going to do with our lives, my love?'

Her look told him she'd been wondering the same thing. 'I only want us to be together. Beyond that, I don't mind.'

'I feel a debt to these people who helped us to know our true selves. And now they've saved our lives and reunited us. We must do something for them, Oralie.'

'I agree. But what? How?'

'Perhaps they are the best judges of how we may help them.'

She nestled back into his embrace again. 'I'm sure you're right.'

Darrel lay there dozing, and as he rested in his hypnogogic state the face of Annis came before him, sad and pale but still beautiful. He had once thought he might be in love with her, he recalled wistfully. But that was before he came to know what love really was. Now he understood that such feelings had to be mutual before they could be dignified with the name of love.

Lulled within the dark ocean, they slept. Hours later Darrel awoke and looked out of the window. His amazement was such that he shook Oralie, waking her up too.

'Look, my love! See where we are!'

She directed her bleary eyes towards the small window. Her jaw dropped with amazement. 'Clouds! We're in the clouds!'

It was true. After skimming the surface of the sea and

then plumbing its depths, this remarkable craft had taken to the skies. Like excited children the pair of them looked out, huddled together, and saw the Earth far below them. At the same time the door slid quietly open and the voice of Doc wished them good morning.

'We're getting ready to land on Arcania,' he informed them. 'You'll find fresh clothes in the closet. I suggest you join the rest of us for breakfast.'

'Arcania?' Darrel frowned.

'Yes. It's described as the "hidden island" because it is so hard to find. It floats, you see, and cannot be charted with any accuracy. And there is a belt of reefs all around it which makes any approach by sea perilous. That is why we are now airborne, since it's easier to spot from the sky.'

'Sounds intriguing,' Darrel smiled.

The mood was light at breakfast. Everyone was looking forward to a time of peace and freedom when they could recharge their batteries before the next confrontation with the enemy. Darrel understood that they played a constant game of cat and mouse with the controllers, that such periods of calm were rare in their hectic, dangerous lives. Yet he knew he must become one of them and share in their lifestyle because he now shared their ideals.

He glanced at Oralie sitting by his side, listening intently to the conversation round the table, and knew he wasn't in this just for himself but for her, too. She believed in him, trusted and honoured him. Unbeknown to her he had been tested to the limit and failed, but he would never again fail her – or any of the group who were now the closest to a family he'd ever known. As the remarkable ship began to descend towards another emerald-and-gold island set in a sea of turquoise Darrel knew, for the first time in his life, that it was good to be alive.